# THE DECEIVERS

By the Same Author

NIGHTRUNNERS OF BENGAL

# THE
# DECEIVERS

A NOVEL BY

## JOHN MASTERS

New York : THE VIKING PRESS : Publishers

*1952*

PUBLISHED BY THE VIKING PRESS IN APRIL 1952

PUBLISHED ON THE SAME DAY IN THE
DOMINION OF CANADA
BY THE MACMILLAN COMPANY OF CANADA LIMITED

A condensation of this book appeared in the
*Ladies' Home Journal*

SET IN LYDIAN AND ELECTRA TYPES
PRINTED IN U.S.A. BY THE VAIL-BALLOU PRESS

CRIGHT 1952 BY JOHN MAST.

TO

JOHN AND ADA MASTERS

FROM

THEIR SON

# THE DECEIVERS

# Chapter 1

"**W**ILT thou, William, have this woman to thy wedded wife, to live together after God's ordinance in the holy estate of Matrimony? Wilt thou love her, comfort her . . ."

The bridegroom shifted his weight from his right foot to his left, rubbed his fingers together, and felt the clammy sweat inside his palms. The high leather stock cut into his neck; he stretched out his chin, eased it round, and tried to remember when he had last worn a stock. About the time he left his regiment—ten, eleven years?—a good long time, anyway.

Mynah birds squabbled raucously in the afternoon heat outside the church. The bridegroom's hands were cold. The best man had forgotten the ring. No, that was a fantasy born of panic. George would not make a mistake like that. George was as likely to forget the scroll which in a few days he would present to Chandra Sen as to forget the ring. Both were impossible. George knew all about weddings. He was always going to them—as the best man.

The bridegroom, William Savage, stared woodenly ahead as his thoughts wandered. He considered for a moment the injustice of God, who gave His creatures such unequal gifts. He had no qualities or assets to compare with George Angelsmith's. George stood over six feet two, and he under five feet ten. The blue broadcloth ran smoothly up George's back; his own old scarlet coat was thin and smelled of neem leaves. The religious light cast a halo about George's tight gold curls: how strong was that light on his own head? He smoothed his hair in a nervous gesture, his hand touching the gray at his temple and continuing down over the lined skin at the side of his face and neck. His hands, and the skill in them—those he was proud of. He dried the palms surreptitiously on his trousers.

An elbow nudged him. He started and muttered, "I will."

1

"Wilt thou, Mary, have this man to thy wedded husband, to live together after God's ordinance in the holy estate of Matrimony? Wilt thou obey him and serve him . . ."

The Reverend Seymour Matthias was showing his years. His scrawny neck stuck out; the crosses on the ends of his stole shivered as he spoke; the stole's silken lightness bowed his shoulders. The church was full of whispers. William Savage began to calculate how many people had come to his wedding. The back of his neck tingled as he imagined them all staring at him. They would be snickering, too, at the idea of Mary Wilson obeying him . . . wondering why she'd said "I will" . . . where he'd found the nerve to ask her to . . .

From the corner of his eye he examined Mary's firm profile, and, beyond her, the square angles of her father's face. Before bringing his daughter to the church Mr. Wilson must have stood in front of a mirror and composed his features in the proper mold. He was a widower, and held the office of Agent to the Governor General of India for the Kaimur and Mahadeo Territories. An expression of stern but not oppressive solemnity would therefore be expected of him at all times. So now his face was stern and solemn, but calm. It was not hypocrisy on his part, for calmness and unbending rigor were the props of his character. He had been angry about the marriage, but he had swallowed his anger. William admired and respected Mr. Wilson.

Beyond him, the cavalry colonel's wife, who liked to regard herself as heaven-sent in place of Mary's dead mother, cried intermittently into a tiny lace handkerchief. Her happy whimpers mingled with the squabbles of the mynah birds. A pencil of sunlight pierced the branches of the tree outside, leaped down through the high white glass, and touched Mary's hair.

"I will."

He looked full at her. Bright blue eyes, bright black hair. Life, and fire, and the touch of sunlight, and no sadness of years. He loved her, if he knew what love was. He wasn't sure of that. He must have been out of his mind when he proposed. And had she accepted only because she was young and foolish? But Mary wasn't a fool. Because she was too recently out from England to know the difference between the men of promise and the others—be-

2

tween the racehorses and the carthorses, between George Angelsmith who was her father's assistant and would become a Commissioner, and William Savage who would not? That couldn't be it; her father had explained all that to her in great detail, and more than once; she had told him so.

He knew that George Angelsmith had wanted to marry her, but he, plodding "Dobbin" Savage, had got her. Her body, at any rate. He clenched his hands suddenly. He was damned well going to win all of her, in time—her heart and her mind.

She had been different every time he met her, and for the past month that had been every day. Young, flighty girl . . . young, lovely girl . . . lovely, distant woman . . . loved . . . loving, wise, shy, bold—she'd bearded her father. He wished his mind worked faster, as fast as his hands on the carpenter's bench, for instance. By the time he caught up with this Mary who said "I will," she would be someone else.

". . . they also may without the Word be won by the conversation of the wives; while they behold your chaste conversation coupled with fear . . ."

Surely this must be near the end?

". . . whose adorning, let it not be that outward adorning of plaiting the hair, and of wearing of gold, or of putting on of apparel . . ."

Old Matthias's voice was a thin trumpet. Surely he didn't want Mary to take off her clothes?

". . . the hidden man of the heart, in that which is not corruptible; even the ornament of a meek and quiet spirit, which is in the sight of God of great price."

The old priest drew a deep, quavering breath, and William bowed his head. He had left his regiment, though he loved it, because he thought he had a meek and quiet spirit. He had hoped to find a place for himself in the civil administration of India. After a fashion he had; but he was not of great price in the sight of Mr. Wilson, or of George Angelsmith, or of anybody, except perhaps the villagers of the Madhya District. They valued him because many storms had beaten over them, and because he did his best for them. English people seemed to tolerate him with a sort of weary good temper. They admired the tables and chairs

3

and carriage wheels he made and laughed as they admired. He raised his head.

". . . For after this manner in the old time the holy women also, who trusted in God, adorned themselves; even as Sarah obeyed Abraham, calling him lord; whose daughters ye are as long as ye do well, and are not afraid with any amazement . . ."

He found himself out on the steps, but his mind was still in the church, echoing the eerie magic of the words. *Afraid with any amazement.* Unwillingly he came back from that unpeopled place. There were people here, scores of them. The young officers of the cavalry were laughing and shouting. They and the smiling women and the shouted congratulations and blessings enclosed him and carried him forward. He was in a tight circle of English faces, English customs, English values, and he could not find happiness or success here. He had tried many ways and failed.

Beyond the wall at the foot of the churchyard and down the hill a still haze of smoke and dust hung over the city of Sagthali. Beyond again, the sun was sinking behind the half-seen, half-sensed hills of the Bhanrer range. Tomorrow he and his bride would be on their way out there, through those hills, to his own people. The cool of the coming night was in the air, and he took a deep breath, pushing out his chest a little.

He could still get into his uniform, but then people always said the stomach began to spread at forty. His chest deflated and his shoulders came forward. Mr. Wilson would lead him aside at the reception and, amid his parting good wishes, remind him of many unsatisfactory matters in the Madhya District: the old Deori revenue records, probably; the fact that he had not prevented the old woman at Garhakota from becoming suttee six months ago. How could he have prevented her? Suttee was not against the law— yet. Wasn't there enough interference with old customs, old religious beliefs? How did Mr. Wilson know God was always on his side?

He smiled dumbly to right and left as he began to walk down to the carriage. He was on the wrong side of Mary. He should be on her right, so that his sword arm was free to defend her. It was not such a strange conceit, on this newly conquered Mahratta frontier. The English circle was tight about him, but it was small and thin, and beyond it the old gods ruled.

He had better do what was correct. Flustered and stammering, he stumbled round his bride. Once in position, he muttered an apology. The men and women about them were smiling, grinning. He recognized the familiar weary good temper.

Mary was not grinning but smiling; one hand rested lightly on the side of the carriage. His feet stopped moving and he stared at her, not hearing the shouts and seeing nothing but her face. A radiance surrounded her It was blue and dark-edged and sparkling. It was not the sun, for the sun had set.

He knew nothing of women. Perhaps all brides looked like this. And even if her radiance was real, he did not know where he could find in himself the quality to make it last. But he must, because he loved her.

The corners of his mouth drooped, and he began his habitual gesture, running his left hand over his hair and down the side of his face and neck. But he had a shako on now, and he heard the tittering again. While he fumbled desperately to put back in its place the armor of stolidity that protected his inmost self, he felt her hand on his and heard her say, "Come on, darling."

A pain swelled in his chest, choking off his breath, so that in the carriage he could say nothing. He wanted to hate them all, who could hurt him so—Mr. Wilson, and George Angelsmith, and the laughing subalterns, and Mary above all, who could hurt above all. But he could not speak and he could not hate. His strong hands rested on his knees. The road ahead would take him, after only a little more delay, only a little more talking and explaining and answering, out of this English place where he was nothing. The road would take him through the thickset hills to Madhya, where his work lay.

5

# Chapter 2

SAGTHALI lay forty miles behind them, and in the freshness
of another afternoon they rode side by side. They had passed the
Bhanrer hills, and the road ahead would bring them to Madhya;
and, if they followed, to every habitation of man in India.

For in India, that year of 1825, the roads were not lines joining
point and point, each road separately identifiable, each beginning
and ending at a pinmark on a map, each absorbing and being
absorbed at named and definite junctions. They were not many
roads, but one. It was a web of fragile thread, irregularly woven
by a hundred generations of travelers. It did not begin anywhere,
but it went to everywhere. In one place, by one tree, this year—
it was. Next year, perhaps—it was not. A traveler might strike a
westward-leading ray and at that point find a single rutted track
and follow it. A mile farther on it might turn south, or north,
or back on itself; or it might break up into ten weary threadlets.
It might disappear among rice paddy and reappear at the edge of
a grass jungle. It might be wide here, narrow there; it might guide
the traveler, in a line straight as the shaft of a spear, for miles
between double avenues of mahua and bijasal; it might take him
to a ruined temple in a forgotten village and desert him there.

Mary knew a little of this, for she had come up from Bombay
to Sagthali, and William told her more, forgetting his shyness
as he spoke. "See, there!" He pointed to one side, where a path
ran in a gorge between six-foot cliffs of tiger grass. "That used
to be the road, twenty, fifty years ago. I expect some obstinate
old farmers still use it. But those two flame-of-the-forest trees, so
close together, wouldn't let a cart between them when they
grew up. Someone turned aside. Now this is the road. The tree
roots here aren't properly beaten down into the earth. The bullock
carts have no springs, you know. They go bump and crash as the

6

carts move along, and you can hear them from a long way off."

A bullock cart was coming, and they drew aside to let it pass. William leaned forward in the saddle to see if he recognized the driver. In this sunny semidrought of late February, as in the full blast of the hot weather, the dust lay thick on the road, dust of the creamy texture of kaolin, which curved back and over under the wheels. A child lying on the cart stared down into the dust, mesmerized by its steady roll, and did not see them where they watched. The child's father salaamed perfunctorily as he passed, and William smiled and waved his arm. The people here were not as a rule an obsequious lot; or perhaps it was only he among their rulers that they treated so offhandedly. He glanced at Mary, but she did not seem to have noticed anything amiss. He smiled at her, and they moved forward together.

She said, "Is this the main road?"

"Yes. Well, there isn't exactly a main road. They're all like this, some wider, some narrower. A track from one jungle village to another might be as wide as this in places. It depends whether the zemindar or patel wants to make an impression. You see, people always choose their own course. If a hundred travelers were to set out separately from Delhi for Madras, perhaps no five of them would follow the same roads. They have to cross the rivers at the fords, of course—that's where a road really becomes 'main.' At the deepest rivers there are ferryboats, usually leaky old barges. In the hills, too, the road has to squeeze through where it can— even through the Bhanrers. Do you remember?"

Yesterday evening they had passed under the ghostly slope of Jarod and come out of the hills. She had asked him about the half-discernible extent of its ruins, and he had told her.

With her he was experiencing a new ability to speak. Even now he was not fluent, but at least he could find the words to express and transmit his feeling for this country and his absorption in his work. The flame-of-the-forest broke out in scarlet splashes along the roadside. Brick-colored dust dulled the surface of the leaves on all the trees; under the dust they held still a remnant of their monsoon richness.

He reined in at the top of a small rise, remembering that the rest of the party would be a mile or more behind. Back there a string of coolies carried the palanquin, which Mary refused to use. Beside it went his butler, Sher Dil, on a donkey; a trudging trio of servants; Mary's tirewoman; two bullock carts loaded with trunks and boxes and new furniture—and George Angelsmith. George had protested many times that he did not want to come with them on this honeymoon journey, but duty was duty, and he had to come as far as Bhadora.

William hunched his shoulders, feeling uncomfortable for the first time today. He muttered, "We're just about there. Better wait for George. He has the scroll."

Down the shallow slope ahead water gleamed among the trees. Mary laid her hand on his bridle, stooped over, and turned her face to his. "Don't mind about it, William. This is—oh, I can't think of the words—peaceful. Look at the smoke among the trees, so blue."

William tried not to mind that Mr. Wilson had deputed George to present the commendatory scroll to Chandra Sen. Perhaps it was a more signal honor for Chandra Sen that a personal representative of the Agent to the Governor General should come specially from Sagthali. Certainly he himself wanted Chandra Sen to have all possible honor. But this was his District; it was he who had cited Chandra Sen for his good work; he would have liked to make the presentation; and George Angelsmith was officially his junior.

He said, "That's Bhadora. It has thirty-six houses—no, thirty-five. One burned down in December. The river's the Seonath. The village was a ruin when we took this area over from the Bhonslas eight years ago. Wars. Civil wars. Dacoits. Pindaris. Every kind of robbery under arms. My predecessor put the place on its feet, with Chandra Sen's help. It's grown even in my time—that's three years."

He turned at the dust-dulled thud of hoofs from behind. George was approaching at a slow trot. They had not seen him since leaving Jabera early in the morning, but he was as immaculate now as he had been then. He lifted his hand in salute as he came up. Mary smiled curtly, and blushed, and turned down her eyes. William saw, jerked his reins, and led the way at a canter down the hill, not turning to look at the others.

8

The village of Bhadora lay on this, the east bank of the Seonath River. The dusty road became a paved street where it passed through between the houses. Generally there would be women and children and old men about at this hour, but today the place was deserted. Down by the river the usual crowd of travelers waited, the usual piles of blackened stones and gray wood-ash littered the grass, the usual chatter and clamor arose. The ferryboat was on the far side, loaded for its return trip. William saw a small crowd over there, not at the ferry site but a good distance farther to the left, upstream. That was not usual, but they were too far away for him to see what they were doing. It did not seem to be anything violent; he made out that some of the people were walking about, some apparently arguing, the majority squatting motionless in irregular groups on the ground, all waiting for something.

He turned back and looked at the ferry site directly opposite. Beyond the approaching barge, he saw Chandra Sen's party at the front edge of the jungle. He half raised his hand to wave a greeting, but lowered it again. It would be poor etiquette for them to notice each other before they met at the appointed place, which was the west bank of the river.

"Is that this fellow—Chandra Sen—who's going to get the scroll?"

George's voice was at his ear. He answered, "Yes. The thin one in white, alone, in front of the others." It always astonished him that the people at headquarters should know so little about the districts. Chandra Sen, Jagirdar, Patel of Padwa and Kahari, was a very important man. He had been a senior revenue official for a time at the Bhonsla's court in Nagpur. As patel of two villages, he owned most of the lands, was the police chief, magistrate, mayor, and tax collector. As jagirdar, he held fifty thousand acres of jungle in feudal tenure and was responsible for the protection of the hamlets enclosed in it.

George's supercilious tone nettled William, and, as much to change the subject as for any other reason, he added, "I wonder what that crowd upstream is doing."

George said, "Your friend Chandra Sen will tell us, I expect, if it's any of our business."

William flushed slightly. It was very easy here to imagine that

9

everything was your business. He turned his eyes away from the mysterious crowd, dismounted, and watched the ferryboat come to land.

As the flat, straight prow touched the bank and the passengers began to scramble off, the waiting Indians surged forward to get on. Goats bleated, cows mooed, children yelled, mothers screamed. The ferryman, a tall old fellow with bloodshot eyes, jumped down onto the grass, while his four big sons rested on their poles and held the boat steady. The old man bawled, "Get back, you daughters of darkness! Do you think the great lord Collector-sahib wishes to smell your stinking carcasses in the same boat with him?"

The crowd halted, muttered, and ebbed patiently back. William cried, "Let them on. Just leave room for us and our three horses." The crowd surged forward once more, grinning and chattering.

"Your worship is a great king," the ferryman said, bowing briefly. "The quality of your honor's magnificence is such as to dazzle the eye." He broke off to kick a young farmer out of the way.

William handed Mary into the boat, and George followed. The grooms, who all day and every day ran unnoticed thirty paces behind the horses, led them up the ramp. William made way for George to stand in the very front of the boat.

On the far bank Chandra Sen moved slowly down toward the river. A jumbled array of servants, coolies, and tenant farmers surrounded a palanquin among the trees. The members of a six-piece band marched into view, formed a rough circle, raised their instruments, and waited.

Mary reached out her hand and twined her fingers in William's. The brown women in the boat stared at her slim back and whispered excitedly to one another, nodding their heads so that their nose ornaments flashed in the sun and their gold necklaces jangled together.

The boat grounded, grated forward under the thrust of the poles, and stopped. Mary made to move forward, but William held her back, while Mr. George Angelsmith, the accredited representative of the Agent to the Governor General of India, stepped down and stood alone on the bank, one foot slightly advanced, his head up and his left hand negligently on his sword hilt. The band struck up a loud cacophony. Chandra Sen bowed from the waist. The serv-

10

ants and farmers bowed. William saluted. From the barge a kid bleated for its mother's milk, a long agonized *maaa-a-a-a-ah!* George Angelsmith touched the peak of his cap and stepped forward.

William and Mary jumped down from the boat. A servant handed garlands of flowers one by one to Chandra Sen, and Chandra Sen lowered them in turn over George's neck, then Mary's, then William's. At last he stepped back and stood with head bowed and hands joined in front of his face. He was tall, thin, and pale, dressed in white and wearing a white turban. A white caste mark was painted on his forehead. His face had a tired charm, and his large eyes were wide open, as if in perpetual mild surprise.

The band made a deafening noise a few feet off. Mary shouted in English, laughing and blushing, "Thank you so much, Mr. Chandra Sen." The patel bowed, took her by the hand, and led her to the palanquin. William saw that George, watching the easy swing of her riding habit, did not seem to notice the goats and children and women easing past him off the barge. Mary stooped and put her head through the curtains of the palanquin to talk to Chandra Sen's wife, and George looked away.

Chandra Sen returned, and William grasped his hand. "I'm glad to see you." Crinkles sprang up round the corners of the patel's eyes. He replied, "And *I* am glad to see your memsahib. It was time you married—past time. It is not rude of me, by your custom, to say she is beautiful? A princess!"

George joined them, and they chatted idly. From the corner of his eye William watched the other ferry passengers group themselves and prepare to face the road. As a score of times before, it struck him that India was always moving, always going somewhere. Between Kashmir and Cape Comorin, how many hundreds of thousands of people daily faced the dangers, known and guessed and unguessed, of the road? In the sixty-year anarchy of the dying Mahratta power, how many had failed to reach the place they were going to? How many still died on the way and were not missed?

Chandra Sen was talking, a little hurriedly, about a court case; telling him the ins and outs of the relationships involved; whose mother had quarreled with whose great-aunt how many years ago; the exact amount paid by one ancestor for false title deeds in the

11

time of the Saugor Pandits, and by another for later, false deeds. William knew Chandra Sen well and thought he seemed to be disturbed about something. As for the court case, it was too involved. George was nodding as though he understood perfectly; he probably did, but William himself could only shake his head unhappily.

In the background Mary straightened up under a shrill volley of congratulations from the voice inside the palanquin. A small brown hand, aglitter with many rings, slipped through the gap in the curtain and gestured violently.

The grooms led up the horses; George swung easily into the saddle; William cupped his hands between his knees, heaved Mary up, and mounted his own horse. The band straggled into place ahead of them, the leader shouted, "Ah!" and with a tumultuous noise the procession started off.

George rode a horse's length ahead of the others, just behind the band. Chandra Sen, the patel, stepped delicately forward with long strides, the dust squirting up and over his open sandals. William and Mary rode behind him. Then came the palanquin, then the patel's servants, then the tenant farmers.

The road led through jungle so thick that the undergrowth threatened to strangle the trees. Flocks of green pigeons whirred up in alarm at the racket; monkeys swung from bough to bough among the recesses of the trees. William glanced at Mary; she rode with her lips slightly parted, and he thought she was looking anywhere but at George's back ahead of her. He did not know what she was thinking about.

She turned suddenly. "Isn't this bizarre?"

"What is?" he said foolishly.

"Oh, this. Bands are for big streets, big parades, not for marching through a jungle with so few of us here, and no spectators."

He considered what she had said. "There's us, dear."

She laughed. "My dear, literal husband, I love you . . . husband . . . husband." She spoke the word louder each time, as if there were magic in it, and so loud that George must have heard even over the tumult of the band.

She went on, shouting to make herself heard, "This Eastern music is fascinating, weird. Do you know if this tune they're playing has a name?"

"Yes. 'Rule, Britannia.' "

She choked, catching her hand to her face and spluttering. William was puzzled. The bandsmen weren't playing very well, but they were doing their best. Perhaps he too wouldn't have recognized the tune if he had not heard bands like this one play it so often. He did not see anything particularly funny about it though.

The road forked, and the bandsmen shuffled to a halt while two servants ran up with Chandra Sen's horse and helped him into the saddle. "Now, sahib," he said to George, "it is fitting that I ride, for I am on my own land."

The side track curved sharply off to the right. After a mile the forest began to thin out, small fields ate into it, then the fields grew together and lonely hovels dotted them, and the trail came into the open. The village of Padwa stood on a little knoll ahead, raised above the level of the September floods. Wild plum, peepul, and tamarind trees surrounded it; the sun shone down on thatch and tile, on the broad brown acres and the green carpets of jungle. William fidgeted in the saddle and knotted his right hand against his thigh. What extra value, or importance, did a parchment scroll place on a man who owned this?

The village did not contain many houses, but they were all in good repair, grouped tidily around Chandra Sen's own house, a large two-storied building of white-painted brick with a tiled red roof. The other houses were made of earth and cow dung and straw. The living quarters of Chandra Sen's house occupied the upper story, which was reached by a flight of wooden steps. The ground level was walled only at the back; cows and carts and piles of straw could be seen among the wooden uprights supporting the upper story. A deep courtyard, stone paved and surrounded by a low dry-stone wall, extended back from the street to the house.

Most of the men of the village were already in the patel's procession. The women stood in the doorways of the houses, their hands or an end of clothing thrown up to cover their faces. A thickset man stood under the patel's steps, holding two gray-coated dogs

13

by the collars. The dogs snarled and strained forward to get at the strange men and horses approaching.

Haphazardly, ceremoniously, with India's unique blend of pomp and squalor, the presentation began. George Angelsmith rummaged in the depths of his saddle holsters and pulled out a white scroll bound with red tape and heavily sealed with scarlet sealing wax. He broke the seals, unrolled the parchment with a flourish, and coughed to clear his throat. The villagers were silent. Chandra Sen had dismounted and now stood alone and dignified, a little stooped, beside his courtyard wall.

George intoned in a sonorous voice, "Know all men by these presents . . ."

At the tail of the throng the band struck up a mournful tune. They could not see what was going on at the front. Men ran back, shouting and gesticulating to them to be quiet. George flushed angrily. Mary giggled and William frowned. The noise died down in unwilling jerks.

George began to read again, his suppressed ill temper giving the banal phrases force and significance. "Know all men by these presents . . . His Excellency William Pitt Amherst, Earl Amherst, Governor General of India . . . Mr. Benjamin Wilson, Agent to the Governor General . . . disturbed state at that time of the territories ceded to the Honourable East India Company by the Rajah of Nagpur . . . Krishna Chandra Sen . . . unfailing influence for good, unflagging endeavors for the betterment of his tenants . . . rising revenue . . . no man more fitted to wield the sword of justice, the staff of discipline . . . Chandra Sen . . . record our high and enduring appreciation . . . Chandra Sen . . . Chandra Sen . . ."

Fitfully throughout the reading a child screamed, terrified of the great horses and the people with the bleached faces.

The village clerk stepped forward when George had finished, received the scroll, and began to read it again, translating into hand-hewn Hindi as he went.

At last it came to an end. The clerk gave the scroll back to George. George gave it to Chandra Sen. Chandra Sen bowed. The English party dismounted from their horses, the villagers ebbed

14

away to their houses. William's bullock carts squeaked down the street. Sher Dil, the butler, dusty and tired, dismounted from his donkey and walked up to ask about the accommodation allotted for the night.

Chandra Sen crossed the courtyard at William's side, apologizing for the poverty of his house and its unsuitability for the reception of European ladies and gentlemen. William absently brushed aside the protestations; he had stayed here before and knew that the patel's words were a matter of form. His mind searched for the source of its present distraction. Something had unsettled him so that he could not attend to the patel, or George, or even Mary. It was not the confusion of the ceremony just ended. That was nothing; in his own court he had to hear cases and give judgments through a similar turmoil. It might be George Angelsmith's attendance on his honeymoon and the palpable tension it aroused in Mary. He frowned and kicked at a pebble. The pebble rolled toward one of the dogs. They were still snarling. He noticed the flat, expressionless face of the man who held them, the thickset man, Bhimoo, the village watchman; a strong, taciturn man.

The black anger was running away in the recesses of his mind, but he saw it and caught it. It was George's veiled insult at the river, about the crowd waiting upstream. Chandra Sen had not mentioned it; therefore it was none of his, William's, business—according to George. George could go to hell.

He said, interrupting Chandra Sen's easy apologies, "Patel-ji, what was that crowd doing upstream from the ferry, on this bank?"

The patel stopped with one hand on the railing of the steps up to his house. He turned slowly to face William. His long face was contained and sad. He paused for a full minute. George came up, and stopped, and raised his eyebrows. William felt Mary's hand come to rest on his arm.

Chandra Sen said, "I was going to speak about it when we were alone." He glanced at George as he spoke, and away again, and in his eyes there was a world of sorrow and distaste. William's heart warmed to him, because he felt that there was an affinity between this man and himself; because the distaste in the large eyes was for the smart, the clever, the brilliant George Angelsmith;

because the sorrow was for him, that he should have brought up this thing, its portent nameless still but taking an evil shape, at a time when George could hear to run back with the tale to Mr. Wilson.

Chandra Sen said, "The wife of Gopal the weaver is going to become suttee tomorrow evening."

# Chapter 3

S UTTEE—a Sanskrit word meaning "a virtuous woman"; hence, along a road of thought fitfully brightened by the Hindu spiritual values, "a woman who burns herself alive on her husband's funeral pyre; the custom which expects her to do so."

Suttee—the next morning William's mind still ran with the word, and the idea, and with the particular example of it now facing him. All his life in India he had tried to feel for suttee the automatic revulsion of his fellow Englishmen and Christians. In part he had succeeded, but always underneath there was a glow of respect and admiration. His slow mind fought with itself. A man died; his wife had loved him, perhaps as Eve loved Adam—"he for God only, she for God in him"; then her spirit, which was a part of his, had no house on earth; she became a husk of flesh, untenanted, blown through by cold winds; only when her body had gone to join her spirit, which was with him, could she live again. Was there any concept more beautiful? But why, then, was not man a part of woman? Why did a man who had loved his wife not go to her in the same way.

Still, the idea was beautiful. When the time came for a woman to become a widow her body might indeed be an ugly husk, scarred and distorted by the hardship of the years. With faith, it was so small a step to climb up into the fire and away from the bending back and the aching joints and the cold hearth. One step up into the flames, then to soar on the rising oil-fed smoke to a place near the brilliant sun, where there was no night and no hunger.

But what if the woman was young, what if there had been no love? He had heard of cases where a man's relatives had a place in the world to maintain, and the strict observance of religious customs was a part of that place. Then sometimes they came in the

17

evening, muffled the young widow's face so that she could not cry out, and carried her soundlessly screaming to the burning ghat. They ran in silent procession with the draped thing, among the trees, and cast it onto the scented flames, and struck up a loud noise of music and wailing.

William tried to understand, tried in the Western fashion to separate the good from the evil, to balance the beauty of sacrifice against the ugliness of waste, which is an essential of all sacrifice. But to these Hindus there was no conflict between God, who is all-powerful, and Satan, who yet flouts and perverts His intentions. Here, creation and destruction were opposite faces of the same medal, equal energies of the same universal spirit. He had to understand it if he could. Men and women who thought and acted in those beliefs were his charge. If he failed to understand, he could work only from a single sweeping generalization: that Indians were fatalistic, brutal, and loveless. That was the depth of untruth, in spite of the many who believed it.

The battle within himself formed only a part of his trouble. He was a servant of the Honourable East India Company, and that huge organization was as torn by indecision as he was. Suttee was the people's custom and religion; only an act of despotic power could abolish it. Yet, could Christians, having power, tolerate willful self-murder?

Talk of abolishing suttee had been going on for years. Nothing had been decided. William and the other officers in civil charge of districts lived in a vise, squeezed between the Hindus, who wanted to be left alone, and the superior British officials, who thought that suttee ought to be put down. A district officer might expect official disapproval if he failed to prevent a public suttee, though he had no power to forbid it. Mr. Wilson's disapproval, for instance, would be genuine and severe; the Garhakota suttee of last year still obsessed his militant Christianity. It was easy to say that Mr. Wilson was a long way off and did not have to deal with the problem face to face, but it was an excuse. William knew that no doubts perturbed his father-in-law. If Mr. Wilson had been the Collector of Madhya, there would have been no suttee in Garhakota then, and there would be none now, whatever the cost.

18

Mary, George Angelsmith, and William sat on low stools in the patel's sunny courtyard. The dogs, chained up, lay silent ten feet off under the house, their noses resting on their paws and their eyes unwinkingly fixed on William's face.

George pulled a heavy gold watch from his fob, glanced at it, and put it back. "I must go, William, and leave you and your bride to connubial bliss. But I'd like to have some word to take back to Mr. Wilson What I can't make out is why the woman's doing it if her husband's not definitely dead. She doesn't know whether he is or not. Seems an awful waste."

"He has been gone for over a year," said Chandra Sen respectfully. He was standing against the wall at William's side. "He went away on a journey and has not come back. Journeys do take a long time—we all know what the road is like—and the woman was not worried until recently. Then she dreamed the same dream three times. In the dream she saw her husband's dead body in a dark place, with a mark on his neck and another woman looking at him. So she knows that he is dead, and she must go to him."

"Is he old? Is she?" Mary asked in halting Hindustani.

"No, memsahib. She is young, your age, no more, and beautiful. I have not seen her recently. Gopal her husband was no older than Savage-sahib, in the prime of life." He looked thoughtfully down at William. "He was very like you, sahib; a broad forehead, short jaw, your height, strongly built. He was rather dark in skin, and not disfigured by smallpox like so many of us. Brown eyes. His hair was blacker, of course—what you could see of it under his turban."

William listened self-consciously. Every morning he looked in the mirror to shave, but he could not have described himself.

"Well, old boy," George said heartily, "what are you going to do? Six hours to lighting up time! As far as I can see, it ought to be easy enough. Just go down there and tell 'em not to."

"You know I have no authority to do that," said William uneasily. "Besides . . ." He did not finish the sentence. Mary was on her feet, walking to the wall, stooping over it to play with a small brown girl in the street. She had gone a little distance away, and left William to fend for himself against George and Mr. Wilson and Chandra Sen and his own indecision.

19

Chandra Sen said earnestly to George, "It is not easy here. Your honor holds office in Sagthali. Here the people are so pleased with the new security, the first there has been in living memory, that they have found time and energy to complain about the things they do not like. Ten years ago they struggled from dawn to dusk, from sowing time to reaping time, just to keep alive, and dodge the freebooters and robbers, and fend off new tax extortions. Do you know the Saugor Pandits made me collect, and pay, twenty-seven different kinds of tax in a good year? Now the people have a little time to think. And no one fills their mouths with gunpowder and explodes it if they make a protest about something. Life has changed under your benevolent government. Much is for the better. But the people want this changed and that left alone. In this matter of suttee they are ready for violence here."

"Are you afraid of a riot, patel-ji?" said George with a small sneer. "What about all your power and influence mentioned in the scroll? Look here, William, my horse is saddled, I've got to go. What shall I tell the Old Man?"

The little naked girl ran off to recount her bravery to her friends. Mary came back and stood to one side, watching the three men, her face expressionless and strong.

George was on his feet. William rose slowly. He didn't know what to say, what to do. George waited, and behind George, Mr. Wilson; on the other side, Chandra Sen, all the people who wanted to live their own lives and die their own deaths; the young wife of Gopal the weaver. He stood in unhappy indecision. He said, "Tell Mr. Wilson—tell Mr. Wilson . . ."

Chandra Sen wanted to help but could not; Mary could help but did not want to. He got out some words at last. "Tell Mr. Wilson I'll see to it."

George hesitated briefly, then shrugged his shoulders. "All right. I'll tell him that. You'll report in due course, won't you?" He turned to Mary with a smile. "Your father takes a keen interest in these things." Then he was on his horse, and in a minute the clop of hoofs faded away down the street.

When he had gone, and the dust had settled, the three in the courtyard were still standing where they had been. William felt a little sick; Kali, the Destroyer-Goddess of the Hindus, was close, pressing down on him, and he did not know whether Kali was lovely or detestable or both, and Mary had deserted him. It was no problem of hers; but she knew, and had known from the time of their first glances, that he needed her. He turned away to go up into the house and be alone. He would have to make his decision by himself, as in the past, before Mary with the bright eyes stood so firm and strong against his uncertainties.

Her voice was soft in his ear. "You know what you want to do, William, don't you, really? You don't need me. You couldn't make a mistake if you trusted yourself. But I'm always here."

It was her voice, gentle-toned, hard-based, of the days when they were discovering each other. Her face had softened and was quite unlike the combative provocation of her attitude while George had been here. A thin gold chain hung round her neck; the little oak cross on it was hidden in her bosom.

He said humbly, "I'm not sure, darling, really I'm not."

"Don't let her die, William."

Yes, he could take the thought and the decision from there. Now that the words had been spoken he knew he could follow no other course. But how—without letting other people die, perhaps, inflamed to riot by their anger? He did not know just how strained things were, down there in Kahari. In George's presence Chandra Sen had been uncommunicative.

William said, "Patel-ji, how do the people feel about this case?"

Chandra Sen's long thin fingers twisted about as he groped for the words to translate the unquiet of his people. "It is a—a test. Without the physical presence of the dead man's corpse they— we"—he lifted his large eyes, not apologetically—"we cannot feel that our religion is being deliberately insulted. But this rests on the woman alone, as we feel it always does and always should. She might not have dreamed her dream. There is no earthly power that could make her tell of it if she did not want to. So it is she, by herself, who cries out from her spirit to join her husband. There is no law written anywhere that she should not be allowed to. The people are determined that she shall do as her spirit wishes."

While George had been here, his very presence, so clearly dedicated to departmental advancement, had deflected William's think-

ing into the same channels. He had thought, What will Mr. Wilson do if the wife of Gopal the weaver becomes suttee? How much deeper will this affair load the scale already weighted against me by adverse appeal rulings, mismanaged settlements, long-delayed civil causes? He was not a very good paper official, and he knew it.

But the problem for him, if he was to be himself, was much simpler, and much harder: "Do not let her die."

Chandra Sen said, "Sahib, we can save her."

"Of course we can." He was not afraid of the people. They might kill him, foolishly, but he was not afraid. "There'll be a riot though."

"No. There is another way." Chandra Sen paused a long time, and when he spoke he picked his words. "If she saw her husband alive, or thought she did, her dreams would be false. She would not become suttee. She would not be allowed to. Her relatives, and Gopal's, who now insist that she must be allowed to, would then insist that she must not."

William nodded slowly. "Yes, that's true."

Mary stared at Chandra Sen with a sudden hard, concentrated look. Then she examined William carefully, her eyes narrowed.

William said again, "That's true. But we can't decide her dreams for her. She won't be going to sleep again, anyway, if she is going to burn herself tonight."

"Not in a dream, sahib. You look like Gopal the weaver. With a little care, I do not think you could be told apart in the best light. In the dusk, never."

William felt for the stool and sat down. It was a strange notion. Mr. Wilson would not approve. He pulled himself up short. He had just decided, or Mary had decided for him, that no important personal problem could be resolved by measuring it against the wishes of Mr. Wilson.

Chandra Sen went on, "I have suitable clothes in the house. No one need know but you and I and your memsahib, and the woman of my house perhaps. We can make the stain."

"I will be seen leaving here. Someone in the village will run after me and later tell them it was me, and not Gopal."

"It can be avoided. I will send you in a covered cart as far as the edge of the jungle. Leave here one hour before dusk. When you

22

reach the jungle, get out and go on foot round the back of Kahari to the burning place down by the river. There will be a few people there. Stand back and call out. Say you have killed a man, or done a robbery—anything—and you will return to her when it is safe to do so. Gopal's voice was hoarse and easy to imitate. We can practice."

William walked unhappily across the compound and back. His Hindi was good enough; he spoke three of the languages of India, all well. The sun was high, the time past noon. It was getting hot. He had a lot to do.

He said, "Isn't it cruel to deceive her? Gopal must be dead."

Chandra Sen shrugged. William saw it was unfair to ask him for arguments when he believed that the woman should be let alone and had made his suggestion only to help William.

He glanced at Mary. She knew what he was thinking. She said, "He may not be dead. Don't let her die. And don't be afraid. I'm not." She added, smiling, "Not with any amazement, in fact."

He laughed shyly, remembering the marriage service and old Matthias's trumpet-voiced injunction. Being afraid, especially of yourself, was not good.

"I'll do it. I'm sure you're right."

# Chapter 4

HE walked through gray woods, neutral-colored in the brief twilight. A quiet western wind soughed in the branches far above his head. The earth was dark and the trees tall in the river valleys. Behind the wind the afterglow of day warmed the sky, but ahead the light was cold. He used no paths, walking easily and quickly between the trees, swinging round the little village of Kahari and heading directly for the river. The fall of the light gave him direction, and here in his own district he could have felt the lay of the land in an evening darker than this. Often jungle fowl had led him off into the forest, and then it was he, not his gunbearer or the local shikari, who found the way back to the horses.

He wore a white loincloth and a white turban. A dirty gray blanket flung round his shoulders kept off the bite of the approaching night. His chest and legs were bare, and his skin—every square inch of it—had been stained by Mary and "the woman of the patel's house." He knew her name but thought of her in that phrase, the ordinary one used by Chandra Sen and every Indian for his wife. No wife ever mentioned her husband's name either. To do so meant that she had renounced him, or her religion—or her life.

"The woman of the patel's house" was small, middle-aged, and dumpy, suety of complexion from the good living of her husband's fields. Voluble as a sparrow, she had worked with Mary to apply the stain on him, both of them giggling while he shivered in the loincloth.

Now he grinned sheepishly at the memory. He looked down at his feet, scuffing over the thin jungle dust. He wore high-ankled Bandelkhand slippers. Chandra Sen did not think Gopal the weaver had worn anything on his feet, but William's soles were soft and European and he could not have walked the distance barefoot.

Chandra Sen was sure the slippers would not be noticed, and if they were that no one would think them strange.

Chandra Sen had offered to tie his turban, but he had done that himself. He began to rehearse under his breath what he was going to say when he reached the funeral pyre.

More self-confidence, that's what he needed, they told him—Mr. Wilson in so many words, George with circuitous, mannered politeness. Now that he was alone in the jungle and on his way to do what was right, he was not at all confident that it was right, or that he would succeed. Mary had all the confidence in the world, and more brains than other women thought proper. Why had she accepted him? *That* was confidence, all right.

He saw a leopard's pug mark on a crossing game trail and knelt to examine it. That was not in character; a village weaver would not hunt leopards; he would be hunted by them, or would hope not to be. Gopal would have looked briefly, recognized, and hurried on, glancing over his shoulder as if the black rosettes even then padded along behind him. William rose quickly and walked forward. It was absurd; the jungles were empty.

He thought he heard a rustling under the trees to his left and stopped quickly, his mouth dry, but there was no sound, nothing to see in the gathering dark. After a minute he swore aloud softly, to reassure himself, and walked forward.

Farther on, a pile of bloody dove's feathers littered the earth beside a lonely bijasal; but that had been the work of something smaller than a leopard, perhaps a hawk. He did not stop again.

The sun was altogether gone, and the night upon him. He knew he was near the river. Close ahead the wife of Gopal the weaver waited for death; her pyre would be ready. He hurried forward until he saw the night-polished black of water ahead and the red touch of fire in the treetops. Surely he was not too late?

He sniffed the air uneasily. It was a small fire, dissected by the intervening black trees into vertical bars of light. A dozen men stood around it, and a woman sat on the grass.

He moved to his left, to come into the open between the fire and the Bhadora ferry site downstream. The lights of the village shone on the far bank. They flared dimly in the corners of his mind and eye; he shuffled forward, his attention focused on the square-built pyre on the grass. It was four feet high, made of fine logs cut square and laid longwise and crosswise upon each other. Garlands of red and yellow flowers lay on it.

He stood behind a tree at the outer limit of the reaching light. He dared not go closer because he had never met Gopal and did not know how far he could trust his deception. Some of the men by the pyre had hoes or pointed staves in their hands, and one a rusty matchlock. A group was chanting quietly in ragged, quavering unison. The priest of Kahari stood by the smaller, lighted fire. A faqir had wandered in from somewhere and stood apart, wild-haired, ash-streaked, his total nakedness made obscene by the mechanically lengthened penis hanging down to his knees. A heavy stone hung suspended from the end of it on a leather thong.

The woman sat on the ground beside her pyre among a cluster of earthenware jars—clarified butter, to make the wood burn furiously. Lonely flowers, dropped from the garlands, littered the grass among fallen leaves, twigs, goat droppings, and refuse of the river's last flood. She was dressed in white, and her pale brown face was turned toward William. She was young and wide-eyed; her lips curved delicately, and a spot of high color stood out in either cheek.

He saw with sick dismay that she had torn her clothes. Some of the brightness at her feet was not flowers but firelight reflected from small jewels and gold trinkets. She had broken all her ornaments and cast them off her. She had ripped her bodice from neck to waist so that her young breasts forced out. She had torn down her hair, and it hung about her shoulders. Her large eyes strained up to see something in or above the treetops.

William tightened his fists. By these acts she had cut herself out of society. To the men about her she was already dead.

The chanting stopped. Above the tinkle of the river the voices were clear.

"My child, he may not be dead . . ." That was the priest, speaking solemnly. What did it matter now? The woman on the ground might exist, alone, but she had no place here, except the pyre. She did not seem to hear the priest but looked upward still. Another, older, grayer man said, "Wait. It is no sin to wait if you do not know."

26

The woman shook her head triumphantly. "I know, I *know!* Gopal is dead, Gopal my husband, Gopal is dead, my Gopal!" She shouted her husband's name over and over again.

That was the last, unanswerable defiance. She was dead.

Two men shuffled over to the heavy jars. They lifted one and began to pour. The ghi gurgled out and splashed on the ranked logs; the river murmured, the priest droned a prayer. William found his voice, pitched it hoarse and deep. He took a step forward.

"Ohé, *wait* there!"

The men at the pyre held the jar between them and looked round. The jar fell from their hands and broke on the logs. The ghi ran out over their feet. The people fell back, leaning forward but edging back, as though their feet willed them away against the fearful curiosity of their eyes. Their faces were drawn, terrified, expectant. Here in the jungles of India nothing was impossible.

The priest, pressed back with outflung arms against a tree, quavered, "Are you man or spirit? Do us no evil!"

"Man!" William said.

The woman at the pyre raised her head. She moaned once, but could not find strength to move. A dark blush suffused her face, she grabbed the torn sides of her bodice and held them together in an agony of embarrassment.

William ground his teeth in shame. "It is I, indeed. Enemies have laid a plot. They say I killed a merchant in the Deccan. The English are after me. I did not do it. There are proofs, and I must get them."

The woman at the pyre covered her face with her hands, tried to get up, groaned and fell back. She said, "Are you hungry? Ill? Hurt? Let me come with you. I have no place here. See . . ." She held out her arms to him, bare of ornaments, and scooped up the scattered bangles and let them fall again. "Take me with you. I am dead here. See . . ." She tore back her bodice once more.

William spoke huskily; he could not hold his voice steady. "It cannot be. I must go. Do not tell anyone—none of you! Await my return, in our house, and live well."

He turned and ducked into the trees and ran blindly away,

27

away from the shrieks of the woman at the pyre. He heard her screaming form words. "I can't! I'll wait here for you! Here, here!" The sound faded, and he heard nothing but the crash of his feet. He ran through the black jungle, seeing with cat's eyes, sensing the thinly spaced trees before he came to them.

What had he done? The woman would not return to her house. Chandra Sen could see that she was fed. But her face was vivid before him; the heat of its love burned him. For her there was no life without her husband. She would not live. She would exist only, there by the stacked wood. Men secretly sent by Chandra Sen would build a leaf roof over her to shelter her from the June sun and the drifting August rains and the December dew. He had not come instead of death to her; he had put on another guise, and that guise was death. Gopal would never come back. She would sit there forever.

He slowed to a walk, gasping for breath. He did not know whether he had done good or evil.

# Chapter 5

THERE was something wrong with the light. The rising moon cast its shadow ahead among the trees; it should be shining on his right cheek. He turned right and headed north. The Bhadora-Madhya trails lay half a mile ahead in front. When he reached them he would know where he was, know which way to turn for the track to Padwa and Chandra Sen's house and Mary. Tugging at his loincloth, he swung forward.

A dry twig broke with a distinct crack not far off. He thought of the leopard's pug mark. That had been quite close to this place. But leopards did not crack twigs underfoot if they were hunting. Pressed into the shadow of a tree, he stared in the direction of the sound. He saw nothing, heard nothing.

A man's voice close by said, *"Ali bhai salaam!"*

*Greetings to Ali, my brother.* Ali was a Mohammedan name. But how, in this mottled darkness, had the stranger recognized him for Ali, whoever Ali was? Did he look like Ali as well as Gopal?

Not knowing what to say, he did not answer. Between two trees fifteen feet off he could make out the shape of the speaker. The man had a dagger in his hand.

In a sudden spurt of anger William forgot who he was supposed to be and what clothes he was wearing. He stepped out toward the shadow and said sharply in Hindi, in his ordinary voice, "Who are you? What are you doing here? Put up your knife at once!"

The stranger edged back, keeping fifteen feet of distance between them. He was slightly built and wore the usual white loincloth and white turban.

William repeated, "Who are you? Who is Ali? Come here, and let's have a look at you."

The man said quietly, "Who are you? You are not Gopal the weaver."

William in turn stepped back into black shadow and said gruffly in his hoarse, assumed voice, "Yes, I am."

The stranger did not answer and did not move. He sucked in his breath through his teeth and seemed to be making up his mind what he should do. He said at last, "I have been following you— Gopal. I heard you speak to save the woman of your house. I, too, am in danger of my life."

"Have you killed someone?" William said quickly.

The man evaded the question. "It is not the English who are after me. I have done nothing to harm them directly." He put a light emphasis on the word "them."

William's slow brain grappled with this new problem. How could he get away before the stranger's questions probed too deeply into his disguise? The woman at the pyre still hovered in the background of his thoughts. This man seemed to know Gopal; he might know where he was, and William would like to find out; but any question would give away his deception. Also, what had the fellow done? Who threatened his life? William was responsible for law and order here. If the man had committed a crime he should answer for it; if he had not, it seemed that he was flying from private vengeance, a vendetta of some sort, perhaps. For eight years since they took over these territories the British had fought furiously to put down all the lawlessness rife in the old Mahratta empire. They had succeeded. He should arrest the stranger, take him back to Padwa, and there make him tell the truth.

But he could do none of these things. His own deception held him in a stranglehold. He was not William Savage but Gopal the weaver, who was thought to have killed a man and was on the run from English law, and from William Savage who represented it.

He must get away. He began to creep silently backward, tensed to start running, feeling behind him with his hands.

The stranger said, "Don't go. I want to show you something."

William kept moving.

The half-seen shadow said, "I must go back to the river, then, and tell her at the pyre that the man who came was not Gopal."

William cried desperately, "I am, I am! Let me go!"

"Come and prove it. Perhaps you are, after all. She can ask a couple of questions which would tell at once. Or there may be some little mark on your body which she would know. But why go? Come with me. I want you to see something. There's nothing more important in the world for you—Gopal—because you looked at the leopard's pug mark, because you didn't want to let the woman die."

William drew in a deep, angry breath. He did not like being pushed. He strode forward heavily, an angry English official; but his slippers sounded so strange hitting the earth that he shuffled to a standstill, paused, and muttered dejectedly, "All right."

"Good. Follow me. Be quiet. And, above all—Gopal—do not cry out or move away from my side, whatever you see. Do you understand? Otherwise your neck will look like mine." He laughed bitterly and came into moonlight. His head was tilted slightly to the right on his neck. "Like mine, only more so—so much more that you'll never feel it."

He had put up his dagger. He passed William without looking round, and William, after a last brief hesitation, followed in his footsteps.

The man moved easily, and after ten minutes William knew that the cross trails from and to Bhadora must be close; simultaneously the lopsided man ahead slowed the pace.

In front, the light of a big fire glinted among the trees. William started, wondering whether he had lost his sense of direction altogether and they were back at the river and the pyre there had been lit. The shape of the trees ahead was familiar, but these did not stand beside the river. He remembered where, off the bullock-cart track west from Bhadora, there stood a large grove of shade trees, and in the middle of it a banyan. The grove was not beside the track, but a few hundred feet back to the south of it. It was a favorite place for travelers to pass the night—eastbound, if they expected the ferry ahead to be shut down for the night; westbound, if they had crossed the river too late to proceed farther on their journey toward Madhya.

The lopsided man held out his arm as a bar. They could see

31

nothing for intervening bushes and trees, but the man listened and seemed to hear something that satisfied him. William heard only the faint crackle of the fire. The stranger gestured to the right and, said in an extraordinary, almost soundless voice that yet had none of the sibilance of a whisper, "This way. Keep low."

They moved on. William's heart tightened with unwilling excitement. The bushes grew thick in their path, and they crawled the last ten yards on their stomachs. The grove opened out before them. Still another yard the lopsided man inched forward and placed himself so that the roots of a bush spread across his face and broke up the firelight and shadow on it. William crawled up beside him and lay still, quietening his breath.

Back there he might have said he had smallpox, or plague. Then this man would have kept away from him. But these ideas always came too late. Now he could only lie still, remember the man's face, and see what happened. He glanced sideways, and after two minutes pursed his lips and knew he could not describe his companion at all. Apart from the slight tilt of his head he was nondescript, indescribably average: brown skin, dark eyes, slight body; lips, chin, nose, hands—nothing to say except that he had them. William turned his head carefully to the front.

From the middle of the grove the big fire painted moving designs on the trunks of the trees and dusted the undersides of the high boughs with pink light. Eight or nine travelers, all men, huddled about the grove in irregular grouping, the fire reddening their faces or silhouetting them against the lighter background. They peered out into the darkness from time to time, their eyes aglint with fear of the road.

Light blinked from cooking pots and brass lotahs. Rolled blankets and shapeless bundles threw black shadows on the grass. As William's eyes became accustomed to the great fire he picked up other tiny fires sparkling among the trees. Two men squatted apart from the others and apart from each other: Brahmins, he thought. Across the big fire sat a man with a ruddy, healthy face; the complexion, the tightly curled beard, and the manner in which the turban was tied told that he was a Sikh from the north. A slim boy of about ten stepped out of the darkness and stood beside the Sikh. "Father, our food is cooked."

32

It was clear that these people were not all of one party, but William could not yet see how they should be grouped: the father and son obviously; the two Brahmins probably, although they ate with their backs to each other; the others in the grove were lumps of shadow, small movements, low voices, half-seen faces.

The ruddy Sikh farmer stood up and looked about him. Lifting his voice, he said, "Our food is ready. I am of the Khalsa, as you can see. We have good food—chupattis and dal. Who is hungry, that may by his religion eat from our hands?"

The Brahmins took no notice. A voice from the outer gloom called nervously, "I thought you had a companion with you to share your food."

The farmer stared from left to right and lifted his shoulders. "So we did. A Mohammedan we met on the road. I could have sworn he came in here with us, but he must have gone on his way."

The anxious voice said, "Perhaps he is a bad man, planning to destroy us. What do you know of him? What do we know of you?"

The Sikh lifted his head indignantly. "*I* am Gurdial Singh Garewal, of Qadian Mughlan by the Beas. This is my son, my only son, who will inherit many acres of fine land when they come to burn me." He squeezed his son's shoulder, looking affectionately into the boy's level eyes. The son was nearly as tall as the father.

Then, remembering he was a Sikh and had been insulted, at least by inference, he continued haughtily, "As for my companion, I know nothing. I met him down the road, not five miles the other side of Bhadora. Poor company he was, too. Perhaps he is a jewel carrier."

"Aah, tst!" The man under the trees sighed and clucked his tongue, as if to say that that explained everything. "Perhaps you are right." His voice dropped to a whine. "We are poor men. We have no gold with us, or anything of value. We are mortally afraid. You have a gun, but who can prevent the tiger eating his fill?"

The farmer spread his shoulders. His son piped in a clear treble, "See, here is the gun. We are Sikhs. Don't be afraid." He dragged an old heavy musket out into the firelight. The farmer ran his hand up under his curled beard and smirked with father-

33

pride. William felt his own face loosening in a smile. The farmer loved his son so much, and in a few sentences, a few attitudes, had shown so much of his character. And the son—Mary would bear him a son one day, as fit for pride as the boy out there, white instead of wheaten gold.

The boy brought chupattis on a maul leaf, kneeled to place them before his father, then went off and returned with the bowl of dal. Father and son broke off fids of chupatti, stirred them into the dal, and picked them out all green, hot, and dripping. They threw back their heads together, dropped the pieces into their mouths with their right hands, and chewed noisily.

William shifted impatiently. He was getting stiff. The man beside him did not turn his head or move his lips, but said in that far-off voice, "Do not move. Wait."

When the farmer had eaten, and belched his satisfaction, and sat back on his haunches, a new voice spoke out of the semi-darkness beyond. "You go north, sirdar-ji?" A man waddled out into the light, a fat man with a gray face and protruding brown eyes. William saw he was a Hindu merchant but could not tell where he was from. He had traveled certainly, because he knew how to address a Sikh.

The Sikh answered the question. "Yes, north. Toward Allahabad. Thence, Delhi. Thence, to my house. And you?"

"In the opposite direction. I hear the ferryman at Bhadora is a villain, who demands much money or he will work one evil. You must have crossed there. Is it true?" He leaned toward the farmer, his eyes popping in the firelight and his lips moving, like a rabbit's, on an invisible green stalk.

The Sikh stuck out his chest. "He tried! Right in the middle of the stream he and his sons stopped the boat and asked for money. From me! I offered to cut their ears off!" He whipped a twelve-inch dagger, the Sikh kirpan, from his belt and held it out. "We reached land safely."

The fat man nibbled furiously. "All Sikhs are warriors. But what can I do? I am a poor man." His face shone with the grease of good living. The farmer snorted under his breath, and his son giggled. Beneath the bush William smiled.

The fat man continued earnestly, "A poor man, I say. Are we

34

not all poor on the road, if we have any sense? Heavens, this middle land of Gondwana is a wild and terrible place. We have jungles in Bengal, but the ground is flat, and not rocky, and there are more fields between, and the people are civilized. Here"— he leaned farther over—"there are savage jungle dwarfs, with blowpipes and poisoned darts!"

The farmer said thoughtfully, "It is strange. Here, for a few hours, we meet in the jungle. We have never met before. We eat our evening meal in this grove together. Probably we will sit around this fire until it is late, and tell stories of our homes and our travels. Tomorrow, pouf! we will be gone. Who can tell that we ever met? that we ever existed? I wager that one who was with us, the jewel carrier, could tell tales."

"Could but won't," said another, who had come up to join the circle in the firelight. "Men of that profession do not talk."

"You are right," the fat merchant said. "I have had occasion to employ them, and they are secretive fellows."

"You?" said the farmer. "You, sending jewels? Now I had an idea you were a poor man."

The merchant joined in the laughter and raised his hand to signal a hit. It seemed that, as he overcame his fears, he was not averse to letting these strangers know that he was a power in his own place. He nibbled at nothing still, from some nervous tic, but his eyes crinkled, and William liked him.

William's chin rested on his hands, and he felt strangely relaxed, considering the circumstances. The smell of food made him hungry, and he would have liked to crawl out and join the travelers. He wanted to find out more about the ferryman at Bhadora. It was a disgrace that these extortions should go on in his district, and something of a slap in the face that he should not know of them. It was worth lying here in discomfort and eavesdropping from this hiding-place under the bushes just to have found out that one fact. More: never in his life had he been among Indians without their knowing it and adjusting their talk and their attitudes accordingly. They had not seemed to, but he knew that they had, and what he saw now proved it. The travelers in the grove were not acting any parts. He was glad to be here, below the surface of the district. He was learning something.

35

Mary should see him now. She'd have a strange vision of him, but a true one, to set against the coming actuality—her husband at work with exasperating slowness over the revenue records and the convolutions of the written law and the logarithms of land survey. In his office the dusty, massed tomes of judgments seemed to lean forward in their shelves and threaten him: *Be careful!* His clerk, so quick and smug, always gave him the right reference before he had thought to wonder where to find it. Brown-stained, dressed in alien clothes, hiding under a bush—he was more comfortable here than there. Perhaps it was the cool night air, or the nearness of the road he loved to travel, or the rough earth under his hands.

The farmer's son threw a dead branch on the fire. His father said to the merchant, "I am going to Madhya. I will report the ferryman to the English sahib there. I hear that most English officials will give justice without a bribe."

The merchant laughed. "You do not know the English, sirdar-ji. In your land your own king still rules, I think? Now, if a man such as you were to make a complaint against a ferryman such as this one is, what would your king cause to be done?"

"If the complaint was made by a man such as I, a man of good reputation and a good Sikh," the farmer answered slowly, "our king, the Lion of the Punjab, would send soldiers and cause the ferryman to be trampled under an elephant. Perhaps he would first have the ferryman's hands cut off, perhaps not."

It was true enough, William thought wryly as he strained to hear.

"So! That is true justice," said the merchant.

"Provided always that the accuser is a gentleman of good reputation, and a good Sikh," the farmer added quickly.

"And that is just, as I was saying," the merchant went on. "But here! *I* am a man of some fame in my own place, too. Are not we all, in our degrees?" There was a murmur of agreement round the fire and from the shadows under the trees. "Yet where the English have their grip they treat all men as equal, the blackest damned sweeper from Comorin, the palest twice-born Brahmin. The English Collector in Madhya would ask you for proof. He would keep you there many days while he sent to fetch the ferryman. Then he would appoint a day many more days ahead for the trial. He would keep all who speak against the ferryman. The ferryman, meanwhile, would gather men to speak for him—perjurers to swear that they, too, were in the boat at the time and that your story is a wicked lie. At the end, when many pages have been written down, there is no judgment. Conflicting evidence! Of course," he added, throwing out his arm in a vehement gesture, "it is quite other in *civil* cases. Then a clever man with a good pleader can keep a case going for months and years in the English courts. One can so cloud the issue that perhaps the other side, the bad ones, can be worn down by the expenses so that they are glad to settle the case out of court."

He rose heavily, hitched at his loincloth, stretched, and yawned. "I am going to sleep, my friends. I am tired."

"Ah, the night is cold." A voice spoke from the darkness.

William's brain registered the *non sequitur* of the remark. He felt his companion's hand grip his elbow. He saw two men flanking the Sikh boy crouch forward. A dirty gray cloth flashed momentarily and jerked round the boy's neck. One of the men tugged at it, the other forced the boy's head over to one side. For a fraction of a second, through a blinding mist of disbelief, William heard the merchant's transfigured, fierce voice. "*That* one, quick!"

The farmer lay on the ground, his head twisted round at a right angle, his eyes bolting out at his son. The two were sprawled at the edge of the fire, among the ashes and the soiled leaves which had been their supper plates. Shadowy men ran, crouched, grunted, swore. The fat merchant was on his feet, a cloth in his hands, pointing, gesticulating.

William gasped aloud and scrambled to his feet. The branches of the bush caught him; the man at his side grabbed his feet and said furiously, "No, no! You promised!" William tore loose and ran forward, shouting in Hindi, "Stop it, stand still! I am . . ."

A face popped up from nowhere and the neck fitted into his outstretched hands. His fingers closed with a snap. He felt the strength surge into them as he lifted the man and dashed his head against a tree. The man lay on the ground and did not move. William stood panting over him and glared round the grove.

Suddenly he realized he was alone among murderers. The fat

merchant had picked up the musket and was trying to steady his aim. Other men moved around in the shadows behind him. The lopsided man had vanished. The Sikhs were dead.

William bounded over the fire, smashed his fist into the merchant's face as he passed, and ran out into the darkness. He stumbled among the trees, falling, bursting through thorn scrub, fighting away from the firelight. Men ran after him. He heard the crackle of leaves under their feet. The bright moon scurried through the treetops to his right, keeping pace, holding him fixed in light. A sharp thorn ripped his cheek. Another tore off his turban.

They were close. He threw himself down under a fallen tree and caught his breath. They were loud behind him. He heard them stumble past and run together. They muttered challenge and greeting: "Ali bhai ram ram!" "Ram ram!" Ali again! The little treacherous swine—he would break his neck.

The anger died, and he lay cold as death under the trunk. Insects began to crawl over him. Dead twigs crunched to the left and ahead. They could not be more than twenty feet away. They moved back and forth, met together, whispered, moved away. Silence. Faint sounds from the direction of the fire behind him. Its light filtered among the trees. It was going out, dying to the accompaniment of chunking and slithering. Digging? Smothering the fire? Were they all there? Had they left a pair of men lying here, as silent as he?

After two hours he was trembling so violently that the tiny chatter and stir among the leaves sounded like the march of an army. He began to edge away on his stomach, moving one arm and leg at a time. Drops of blood from his face plopped steadily onto the leaves. A nightjar set up a sudden appalling shriek of alarm. The darkness moved by his right side. Orange light glared on white teeth and popping eyes above him. The explosion rocked him.

He was not hit. They would have to reload the musket. He jumped up and ran, crouching. The surface changed underfoot, the shadow splashes fell away, he saw the moon. He was on a road, and a man stood on it. Two men. Moving, but they had heard him. His throat burned, and he was frightened. He would never escape them.

38

He turned back into the jungle and ran. The men behind did not call out but came after him. The merchant with the gun was somewhere ahead still. And others. How many?

He slammed into a tree, turned, and ran crazily back toward the road. Human arms reached out for him and he swung his fist. Some noisy thing fell into the undergrowth, groaning. The road again. He began to run down it.

He was not young enough for this, or fit enough. They would get him. He saw the turning to Padwa, ran well past, jumped off the road and lay down. They had lost him for a minute. He got up, crawled through onto the Padwa trail, and ran.

# Chapter 6

THE moon rode high above the knoll and the village. The silence of the fields hammered at him, and the sky swung round the moon. He hurried under the orange trees planted on the side of the street and screamed suddenly when a fruit fell on his shoulder. The two dogs began to bark furiously. All lights were out. He had no idea what time it was. He sagged across the courtyard wall, his heart heaving, and could go no farther. He croaked, "Ooh, Chandra Sen, come quickly."

Inside the house nothing stirred. He remembered dimly that they were to leave the door open so that he could creep up the stairs and into the house without knocking. No one must see "Gopal" return to Padwa. He pushed himself upright and stumbled forward.

Under the house the dogs went crazy. He heard a chain snap and the jangling of the broken end as it came over the stones toward him. The dogs were at him; teeth closed in his leg, and the weight dragged him down. He seized that dog by the throat and began to throttle it, while the other tore at his bare stomach. He kept calling, "Chandra Sen! Your dogs! Hurry, hurry down!" The watchman should have been here, but wasn't. Chandra Sen must have sent him on an errand to keep him out of the way.

The door of the house burst open, the light of a torch flooded the courtyard, and Chandra Sen ran down the steps, a big staff in his hand. He called the dogs by name and beat at them with the stick. William had loosed his grip on the dog's throat, and it lay retching at his feet. After a few seconds it crawled away, while its brother began to attack it.

Chandra Sen grasped his staff firmly and held up the torch. "Who are you?"

"Sav—Gopal. Put the light down." It would be too much if

someone saw him now and word went to the woman at the pyre. All his terrible evening would go for nothing.

He dragged past the patel, across the courtyard, up the steps, and into the house. Inside, his legs would not hold him and he sank slowly to the floor. A tall mirror, cracked, and framed in heavy gilt, stood against the whitewashed wall. He saw himself in it and did not wonder that Chandra Sen stared with open mouth.

His brown-stained skin was torn and bleeding. Deep scratches scored his bare shoulders, and the flesh of his stomach was torn. Froth bubbled on his lips. He mumbled, "See, I am Gopal!" and laughed, and cut the laugh short, winning control of himself.

Chandra Sen lowered the torch; its flames dimmed and sprang up again; black smoke wisps curled to the ceiling. He cried, "It is! It is! What has happened, lord?"

William sank back against the wall and told his story. He dared not glance toward the mirror while he spoke, or he would have burst out again in mad laughter. He finished, suddenly uncertain, "I think—get your men out, patel-ji, quickly. Perhaps we can catch these murderers. Where is my wife?"

Chandra Sen slipped off without a word. Mary's quick feet, light and firm, came down the passage. She saw him, and checked her step, and ran forward and flung herself on her knees beside him. "Oh, darling! William, are you all right? Quick, bring bandages, slaves!"

The house awoke. Voices muttered everywhere. William rested his head on Mary's arm. "It's nothing much."

"Did the people try to kill you? Is she safe?"

"She? Who? Oh, yes, she's safe. It's something else. I can't tell you all now. Can't we stop everyone coming in here? They'll all know it wasn't Gopal, but me."

An old woman with her veil awry, who smelled of cozy sleep, shuffled in and squatted down beside him. From the door Chandra Sen said, "Do not worry, sahib. No one will tell. I vouch for them." The old woman washed away the dirt, felt his cuts and bruises, and muttered to herself.

Mary said suddenly, "Must you go out again?"

"Yes."

41

She did not try to stop him, as he had half expected, but said, "Then we must get this color off. The lotion's ready. We made it while you were out."

The room filled, and William's impatience mounted. The patel's wife rubbed the spirituous lotion into his face and hands with a cloth. It stung fiercely, and he bit his lips against the pain, but the color came out. The old woman grunted and grumbled and went on, sure-fingered, with her work. At last Mary bandaged his stomach. He stood up, supporting himself for a moment on her shoulder.

"I'll get your clothes," she said and ran off to their room at the back of the house. The patel and his wife and the old woman left. Mary came back, and William jerked on his English clothes. Horses' hoofs clattered in the yard now, and arms clashed. He was ready. He glanced in the mirror—wild eyes, cuts, otherwise all right. He said, "There's no danger now. Don't be afraid for me."

"I'm not—not for you. Kiss me."

He dabbed a kiss hurriedly on her lips, then turned again and sank his mouth on hers. "Oh, Mary!"

Chandra Sen waited for him outside. "Do we need a big party, sahib? That will take more time. I will have to get the men from all over my estates. But we are six here, not counting your honor."

"That will do for now. But I think you had better send out to warn the others that they may be needed in the morning. . . . You have? Good."

Five horsemen waited in the yard. Two carried sabers, two muskets, and one a pike. The pikeman was his own butler, Sher Dil. His groom was there too, holding his horse, and the pistols were ready in the holsters on the front arch. A young boy, Chandra Sen's son—about the age and size of the boy William had just seen murdered—held the bridle of a seventh horse. The veiled shadows of women murmured shrilly from the lighted doorways and windows of the house.

William gathered his strength and swung slowly into the saddle. He raised his hand. "Your master has told you what has happened?" The riders muttered assent. "Good. We will go first to the grove where the murders were done. If we find nothing there, we had better spread out and search the roads."

"How will we know the murderers, sahib?" said Chandra Sen.

William stopped short. What *did* they look like? They were nondescript: two Brahmins, four or five others. The fat merchant —his face was clear enough. Two of the others were Mohammedans; he had known that from their turbans. One was old; he remembered the wrinkled face. One was young—no, that was one of the Brahmins. But had some of them been among the murdered? The Sikh and his son were not the only ones who had been killed. Or were they? It had happened too quickly. Then he ought to describe the lopsided man; he too must be caught: but it was impossible to describe him, except for that bent neck.

Haltingly he told the party what he could remember. His confidence ebbed away, so that with his hurts he felt sick and ready to vomit. He was not sure now that he would recognize anyone except the fat man with the popping eyes and nibbling lips. Men would be brought roped to his jail, and he would not be able to swear to them. What would the laws of evidence say? What would Mr. Wilson say?

Chandra Sen gathered up his reins, looking at William keenly. "That is good enough. We will catch them if we have to arrest every traveler on the roads."

William jerked his shoulders, as though he could by that gesture shake loose his worries, and pushed his horse into a fast canter. One behind the other, the six horsemen tore down the street after him, then onto the path between empty moon-bathed fields, then into the jungle where the horses' hoofs struck loudly against the tree roots and sparks flew back from Chandra Sen's torch into the faces of the riders behind.

The grove of murder was silent. In the dying moonlight the shadows lay differently, and William was not sure that this was it. By day it was recognizable easily enough; but there were other groves. He did not know . . . he was not sure.

He reined in his horse. "Chandra Sen, this is the place—I think."

Chandra Sen raised his torch, holding reins and naked sword in the other hand, and looked across at him with—what? compassion? Damn them all, it *had* happened, just as he described.

The riders jostled forward, and the horses blew softly through

43

their nostrils and bit one another's necks. A man coughed, another cleared his throat of dust, spat, and swore under his breath. Sher Dil said officiously, "Silence!"

William thought this was the place. He did not know what to say or do now, and was silent, tongue-tied.

Chandra Sen cried, "You three, go back down the road, all the way to Madhya. Tell the police daffadar what has happened. Bhimoo, Sher Dil, accompany the Collector-sahib and me. I think the villains may have gone on, sahib, and crossed the river."

"They won't have used the ferry, anyway," William said dully. "It will be closed down."

"Yes, but the merchant might have lied to the Sikh about the direction he was traveling in. He might have crossed the river earlier in the day. And the man, the Mohammedan who had been with the Sikh, *he* crossed with the Sikh and his son apparently. Let us go and find out what we can."

"All right."

Chandra Sen swung round and, followed by William and Sher Dil and the grim watchman, galloped for the ferry. They reached the west bank of the river in a few minutes and did not pass anyone on the way. The bank was deserted and silent; the houses of Bhadora opposite were dark; a single small light burned in the ferrymen's hut. Chandra Sen shouted, and shouted again, and at the third time a surly voice grumbled across the water in answer.

"Who the devil are you? Wait there and sleep till morning. Any man who travels at night is a damned fool."

"It is Chandra Sen, patel, who speaks, and with him is the Collector-sahib from Madhya," said Chandra Sen in a quiet, high voice that carried over the dark water and echoed back from the houses. There was a long pause. Then the ferryman, his voice a loud whine, "I come, your honor. I come as fast as I can."

Listening, they heard him swear at his sons, heard their grunts and oaths. The lamp moved, water splashed and gurgled, the faces floated closer across the river. When the bow touched bank the ferryman came, stooped forward. He peered shortsightedly at them, amazement written on his coarse face.

"It is indeed the Collector and the honored patel. But—but—how has the sahib been hurt? Is it—"

44

"Never mind that," Chandra Sen answered curtly. "There has been foul murder committed near here. The sahib saw it done." He gave the futile descriptions of the men. "Do you remember any of those people crossing in your boat today, yesterday?"

"Yes, your honor!" The ferryman grew voluble. His sons stood behind him, eying William. "The Sikh and his son crossed an hour before sunset—I remember them. He was tightfisted and gave us a miserable baksheesh. And now he's dead!" He sighed sententiously, his bloodshot eyes vindictive and triumphant in the guttering torchlight.

"Yes, he's dead," William snapped angrily, "but not before he told something of your little ways which will be of interest to my police. Now, about the lopsided man, the fat merchant, the others —do you remember them?"

"We don't remember, sahib," the ferryman whined, clasping his hands together and bowing his huge, knotted shoulders. William noticed how the "we" shared with his sons the blame for what had not been remembered, while the "I" of the previous sentence assumed all the credit for remembering the Sikh. This ferryman of Bhadora was an unpleasant person. "We don't remember—"

Chandra Sen interrupted, "Very well. Try to recall the men we have described. If any of them come this way, seize them."

The ferryman began to protest, whining. What could he do against murderers? He was afraid. He was a man of peace. Chandra Sen said gently, "You have four sons, do you not? Your boat rests its bow on my land now, does it not? Do you want to be driven away from here?" The ferryman clasped his hands and was silent.

William and Chandra Sen and the two servants turned away and rode back a little distance. William sat his horse, the others surrounding him, and thought, Where might the murderers have gone? What had they done with the bodies? If he could find those it would at least dispel the doubts he saw behind the patel's politeness—doubts of his sanity. The watchman too was looking at him as though he had gone out of his mind and must be humored. Sher Dil was worried for him. Those two did not know just why or how he had seen the murders. They never would. Upstream the little fire at the burning ghat had gone out. The woman was there, waiting.

Heavily he said, "Shall we rest here till dawn, patel-ji? Then we'll go to the grove and look for the bodies. We'll want the rest of your tenants probably."

Chandra Sen told Bhimoo the watchman to return to the house and bring the larger party on as soon as it was light enough. "Ohé!" William called as the man trotted out of the torchlight. "Make sure they bring all the picks and shovels they can. We may have to dig."

William and Chandra Sen dismounted, tethered their horses, and lay down to rest. Chandra Sen seemed to sleep soundly, wrapped in his loose clothes, but William could not sleep. The lap of the drifting stream hurt his head. Sher Dil stood on guard and murmured with the ferryman and his sons. They had built a fire, and the light played on the tangled leaves above his head. Their low voices rattled in his skull.

He thought of Mary. Damn, he ought to have sent word to Madhya. He had a patrol of eight mounted police there, under a daffadar. He did not think quickly enough. He remembered then that Chandra Sen had done it all, and he turned over painfully on the hard ground. As he stared at the fire and the men hunched round it, it became another fire and they other men. The Sikh boy who was dead stood beside him, offering him food.

The murderers formed a dangerous band, and they had come into his district at a time when travel was at its peak. Scores of defenseless travelers were at their mercy. The band could not survive uncaught for long—or could it? The jungles of his district were wide and contained many places of refuge: forgotten water holes, caves among the hills, deserted Gond villages. He prayed suddenly that the murderers would leave his district and go into someone else's. He bit his lip and tried to think of Mary again.

A more terrible idea flowered in the mesmerizing fire. Murder was difficult enough to punish in India even when the murderer was taken standing over the corpse with a reeking knife in his hand. But it might be years before another such chance as last night's would even cause anyone to think that murder had been done. On the road none knew where a traveler came from or where

46

he was going to. A man left his home to visit relatives, a two-month journey, to stay there three months and return. At his home they would not become alarmed until a year had passed. Then they might make inquiries. But how? There was no way. They could only accept that the traveler had vanished—snake bite, tiger's fangs, cholera, something—unless the missing man was a jewel carrier. Then the bankers would take a hand. What had happened to that fellow with his head on one side? Who was he? Who was Ali?

Chandra Sen stirred, and William saw that he was not asleep. He said, "Patel-ji, I can't sleep."

"Nor can I, sahib."

"I was thinking about this Ali. I did not tell you that he's someone's brother. The lopsided man thought I was he. And the murderers were calling him when they were after me. We might be able to find out who he is because there are not too many Mohammedans in the district."

The patel's sad eyes turned away and looked at the fire. "I do not know. He does not live close to here." A long silence. "Sahib, you remember you told me that the Sikh said that a Mohammedan traveled with him to the ferry?"

"Yes."

"And the Mohammedan left him about the time he entered the grove?"

"Yes. We asked the ferrymen, don't you remember? They did not recall him, and we don't have any good description."

"I think he was the same man who led you to the grove, the lopsided man."

William stared at the patel. It might be true. If it was, the lopsided man had crossed the ferry in company with the Sikh and his son. That mattered, because it would give the direction in which the lopsided man had been traveling.

He climbed to his feet and walked stiff-legged to the fire. The ferrymen stopped talking and stood up. He said to them, "I asked you about a lopsided man who carries his head on one side, remember? We think he may have been with the Sikh when he crossed in your boat. Now do you remember him?"

The old ferryman half closed his bloodshot eyes and screwed

47

up his face in an ostentatious effort of memory. His hands trembled, and William thought he must have been in an opium sleep when Chandra Sen's summons awakened him. At last he said, "I—we're not sure, lord."

The eldest of his sons, a man of about forty, broke in, "I saw the man the sahib describes. He was with the Sikh. I remember now, because he stood just in front of me in the boat. I'd forgotten him—even his neck. He was so ordinary."

William returned to his resting place. Chandra Sen had heard the exchange. The lopsided man must be found.

In an hour light began to glint on the leaves and draw gray and silver stripes across the water. A low bank of mist covered the river, and brightening ripples showed where fish rose. The dawn breeze sent a horizontal streamer of smoke creeping along the grass from the fire. William got up and stretched. Chandra Sen was already afoot. Sher Dil stood by the smoking embers. The ferrymen had fallen asleep and lay like twisted corpses on the grass. A group of early travelers with a cart creaked down the opposite bank. William walked to his horse and mounted. Chandra Sen and Sher Dil followed him back along the road.

He recognized the grove at once and turned into it. The fire had been there; he had lain here, with the lopsided man beside him; one of the Brahmins' fires had been there, another there. A dozen men trudged up the road, digging tools in their hands.

"This is the place?" said the patel.

"Yes. Here." He pointed out where everything had taken place. Chandra Sen called, the tenants crowded close and sucked in their breath and muttered, "Horror!"

"Let them spread out," William said to Chandra Sen. "Let them search the whole grove for signs of recent digging. The bodies must be buried here somewhere. And look for marks where they might have been dragged into the jungle. Let them search well."

The party split up at Chandra Sen's quiet direction and walked through the grove, peering at the ground. William went to the place where the big fire had been and put down his hand. Someone had scattered earth loosely over the ashes. He picked the earth

48

away with his fingers until he had uncovered the ashes. They were still warm.

The light grew, and the tall trees began to throw shadows across the grove. The searchers came back one by one. Nothing, nothing, no sign. William stared past them. They were waiting for his next orders. There was only one place anyone could have dug here and not left a trace.

"Dig under the fire, here."

"Very good, sahib," Chandra Sen said. "As you wish." He indicated the fire with his toe and repeated, "Dig here."

"Here?" asked Bhimoo the watchman. "Under the fire? They have thrown earth on the ashes, which is a wise precaution at this season against jungle fires. But no one has disturbed it otherwise, except the sahib just now."

William hesitated. They were looking at him oddly. Sher Dil's face was loud with anxiety that he should not make a fool of himself. He said shortly, "Dig here, dig deep." He flushed and turned his back.

Chandra Sen's body-servant spread a roll of carpet and brought out and prepared a hookah. William and Chandra Sen sat together, puffed in turn at the hookah, and watched the men digging. The patel pushed away the mouthpiece. "That man with the twisted neck, sahib—I think he is the key to this. I wish we knew more about him."

"Yes." William thought back. "All we know is that he's a Mohammedan, if this Ali is his brother. Besides, the Sikh said he was, supposing your theory's right, and he is the fellow who accompanied the Sikhs as far as the grove and then vanished. But"— he stopped and put his head in his hands—"all the murderers were calling on Ali as their brother, and they were certainly all not Mohammedans. The fat man was a Hindu, a chaudhri."

"You know, sahib," the patel said quietly, "sometimes people use the word 'brother' as a greeting to a friend."

"Yes, of course. Well, this lopsided man—the Sikh suggested he was a jewel carrier."

"Ah, that's very interesting."

In the preceding sixty years of anarchy, jewels, especially dia-

49

monds, had increasingly taken the place of other currency. As the gem market fluctuated in different parts of India, bankers and brokers sent jewels around the country. They employed professional jewel carriers for the purpose. Although scores had died or been robbed on the road, no one had ever heard of a jewel carrier betraying his craft.

Chandra Sen continued, "Do you think he saw through your honor's—h'm—disguise?" He handled the words like delicate china.

"I don't know. He might have. He seemed to suspect I wasn't Gopal."

"Men of that profession survive only by keeping their eyes open. But they usually also keep their mouths shut." The patel sighed lightly and called to the diggers, "Have you found anything yet? How deep are you?"

"Three feet and more, patel-ji, and nothing yet. The earth hasn't been turned here though, not for a long time."

William set his face and limped to the edge of the hole. As he watched, a man swung down with his hoe. The earth came away cleanly and showed white beneath. Men ran up and crowded round the hole. The earth flew; every few minutes fresh diggers jumped down to replace the men in the pit.

They handled the bones reverently as they uncovered them and placed them out in a row on the grass. William stared down at them with a sense of fright. These bones were dead and gray-white, picked clean by worms and ants. The diggers found vestiges of cheap leather shredded into the soil; and discolored patches of cloth, already half earth, which crumbled at the touch; and five cold skulls; but no hair, no skin, no flesh.

The sun beat down. Sweat ran down the diggers' backs. Their faces were strained, for this was the desecration of an ancient grave, perhaps, that they were committing. In times of great calamity, or after battles, when the survivors had no leisure to cut the wood and no oil to make the wood burn, Hindus were sometimes buried in common graves like this.

Chandra Sen's long face was solemn. "These died a long time ago."

Plague might have done it, or cholera, or smallpox, or famine, or war. William wiped his forehead. He had a splitting headache and sat down suddenly to ward off an attack of vertigo. He must go on and find out.

He said, "Get *all* your men, Chandra Sen. Dig up everywhere. Dig up the whole grove, especially where there are the marks of old fires."

For a long moment the patel hesitated. The expressions of the men working set sullenly. At last the patel bowed his head. "It is an order." The digging began again.

The nine mounted police from Madhya arrived in a loud clatter. They were all the police William had for the whole district, and they were in reality only semitrained cavalrymen, with little knowledge of police duties. He sent them out at once to search the roads for the merchant and his companions and the lopsided man.

An hour later Mary came. She slipped down from the saddle, gave the reins to her groom, and walked toward him. He got up quickly and hobbled over, holding out his hands. "Don't look, dear. It's ghastly."

She took his hands and held them. He saw that she was looking over his shoulder at the lonely bones. Her mouth set and she turned her eyes to his. He was afraid to meet them. She said, "You were right. I knew they thought you were seeing things. And now you can show them—Daddy and all the rest of them!"

He looked up in astonished wonder. "I was right? Show them what?"

"You've found out something really big. Oh, it's horrible, but you have discovered it, because you wouldn't let that girl die!"

His mind whirled. He had not been thinking in that fashion. She went on, "Now you're going to catch this gang. They must be a gang. And you will save so many more people's lives." She looked straight at him, and her eyes were like sapphires. With her, he would succeed all right, and make George Angelsmith smirk the other side of his scented, damned face!

She said in a businesslike voice, "I've sent the bullock cart with our baggage on to Madhya. I've brought blankets on the horses, and some food. How long do you think you'll have to stay here?"

"I don't know."

"I'll stay with you. Here—" She gave him brandy and a cold chicken and warm chupattis. She brought out salve and bandages and patched the wounds showing on his face and hands. Then she sat beside him and held his hand and did not speak.

The digging continued through the afternoon and evening. Grumbling women arrived from the scattered holdings, bringing food. They set lanterns on the ground and held torches. The men dug. There were places where no one could dig, where the tree roots grew thick together; but in all the open spaces they burrowed into the earth. Travelers passed along the road; the police brought more in; William scanned them all closely and asked them questions. None had been among the party of murderers, he thought. Their recollections of other travelers were vague and useless.

On the ground the row of skulls and thigh bones grew longer. A second row had to be started, a third. Some of the bones were older than the first they had uncovered, so old as to be pockmarked with the small holes of organic decay. Some were so fresh that the maggoty flesh still clung to them, and the strangler's mark was clear on their necks. They had all been mutilated. Where flesh survived, great driven holes showed through chest and belly. Every major joint had been broken back on itself. Big men, so smashed and folded, took no more space than a child; children, broken, became small square bundles. There were no women recognizable. The strong sweet smell of death filled the grove. The diggers dug with the ends of their turbans flung across their mouths and spat frequently. Mary watched with lips tight and blue eyes afire in the lamplight.

As the second dawn broke, Chandra Sen's face was as gray as the light, and his hand lay cold on William's arm. "I am sorry. You were right."

William counted. There were sixty-eight bodies—rather, sixty-eight skulls. None could tell now how many bodies there might have been. Some had lain here years beyond reckoning, two centuries perhaps. The newest was not more than a week in the earth. The bodies of the Sikh farmer and his son had not been found.

The strength had gone out of William's legs. Sher Dil helped him onto his horse. "Chandra Sen, let your men rest," he said feebly, "then bury all these again. Cause Hindu and Mohammedan prayers to be said over the grave. I will send back the priest from Kahari as I pass, and the maulvi from Madhya."

His head sunk on his chest, he let the horse walk at its own pace down the road. Miles passed and he did not speak. He did not feel the burning sun, or hear the robin in a tree, or see the cheetal stag arching across the path ahead. He did not notice the travelers on the road who stared up at him, or the men in the fields, and he did not know that his wife was at his side. He remembered her; she had tried to cheer him up yesterday, when only a few skeletons lay on the grass. But this—this was monstrous. He had believed her then, believed in himself. But all the warmth had ebbed away as the picks swung.

A mile out of Madhya she touched his arm gently. He started in the saddle and turned to her. Her eyes were full.

"William."

"Oh! You . . . I'm finished. In disgrace." He had not slept for two nights, and the road swung like a pendulum in front of him. "I thought I knew everyone, everything. I could have said, I have said, that not a thief can move in my district without my knowing it. For three years I've sat here thinking that whatever sort of a fool I was at books I knew my people and I looked after them. Meanwhile sixty-eight of them have been murdered not a day's stage from my headquarters."

She held his arm tightly and the horses pushed together. "It's not your fault. It's not! Most of those poor people were killed years ago. No one can blame you."

He shook his head, shaking off the excuse. "Yes. But a gang of six—seven, perhaps—has been committing wholesale murder during my three years here, and I've known nothing! I've made lots of mistakes, and I can face them and myself only because I thought I knew the way ordinary people here lived and moved and died. I thought I could help them."

He did not speak again until they reached the bungalow. Dismounting in silence, he gave the reins to the groom and turned to laugh harshly in Sher Dil's worrying face. "Sixty-eight, Sher Dil! You counted?" The bitter laugh echoed behind him down the bungalow's central passage.

Mary ran after him. "William, won't you lie down? Let's talk about it later, when you've had some sleep."

"I've got something to do first."

53

In his study at the back of the bungalow he reached for a sheet of thick parchment, found the quill, and at the third try dipped it into the ink. She watched the trembling in his hand die slowly away. His wrist and strong fingers grew rigid. The black letters marched in slow time across the paper:

To: The Agent to the Governor General for the
Kaimur and Mahadeo Territories.
From: The Collector of the Madhya District.
Sir, I much regret to report that I have this day . . .

He lifted his head. "Your father will like this. After what George Angelsmith has told him he'll be expecting to hear that the woman at Kahari became suttee, but this is even better. This is just about what he's always been expecting from me, isn't it?" He bent again over the paper. She did not answer but sat on the other chair and her tears fell into her lap.

54

# Chapter 7

"SMILE for me please, William," she said, an early morning two weeks later. "You don't know how nice you look when you smile. George won't arrive till the afternoon, and even when he does there is nothing to worry about. You're such a serious old thing."

"I'm old all right, compared with you."

"Nonsense. I feel sometimes that I'm the old one! I believe lots of wives do." In a rush of words she tried to hide her chagrin at touching one of his many raw spots. They were standing side by side on the veranda of the bungalow, looking out over the garden. George Angelsmith was coming from Sagthali with some message from Mr. Wilson. William did not know what the message was, but he could guess, and did not find it easy to smile today, even at Mary.

She said, "I'm dreading his coming too, really, you know, because we won't be alone then. I love this. George seems to carry a whole station around with him—all the rivalries and attitudes and habits."

William nodded, and a smile came of its own to his lips. She had been too young to remember her first three years in India. Born in a little place in Bengal, she had gone home at the age of three with her ailing mother. Her mother died in England. A year ago Mary had arrived out here once more, to join her father, so all she knew of India was Sagthali. Sagthali was a "station"—a place where, beside but apart from the Indian community, there had grown up barrack cantonments for the army and bungalows and offices for the headquarters of the civil administration. In a station there were never less than ten English families, and often many more. Sagthali had over forty.

In a station, suburban England enclosed you, and you saw India only through those windows of the mind that you chose to scrub clean and look through. In the outlying districts it was different. One

55

Englishman, the Collector, to whose charge the civil government of the district was confided, lived alone in a headquarters town, such as Madhya. Madhya had a population of five thousand, all Indian. If the Collector did not like Indians, he liked no one. If he despised India, he despised everything. In a district an Englishman could be alone—and lonely; or he could have a hundred thousand friends. His happiness rested in his own hands, and his wife's if he was married. Many English women hated district life so much that they turned their husbands into embittered drunkards.

So William sighed with relief to hear Mary say out loud that she loved "this." "This" was Madhya—aloneness but no loneliness; work without rivalry; the honored place but no aloofness. Two weeks was not very long to judge by, but he knew she meant what she said. For their happiness she had to mean it, because he was changing. His unsure dependence on himself was becoming an interdependence, he on Mary, Mary a little on him.

His smile faded slowly. He did not know how strong this new thing of love in marriage was. George was coming, and with him the threatening shadows of Mr. Wilson, and the Governor General in Council. Trouble was coming. Many people—especially women, he'd heard—fell away from you if you went into disfavor. George's presence did something strange to Mary. She hardened visibly and began to fight something—or for something?

He walked slowly at her side through the spreading garden. She was talking about Sher Dil. A feud had grown up between them, the inevitable one between the new wife and the old servant, the old friend, who has served when his master was a bachelor, and borne all the responsibility, and known all the happy days and the sad days and has not had to share them with anyone else. Sher Dil obeyed Mary with wooden correctness, when he understood what she was saying. That was not often, although William knew that in nineteen years of service Sher Dil had picked up enough English to understand any message he wanted to understand. William had hoped, among his other worries, that this could be resolved. He did not want to lose Sher Dil. But Mary was so young and impatient; even now she was saying that she found Sher Dil's manner intolerable. At any moment the underground struggle would break into the

56

open. Then Sher Dil would have to go, to find another bachelor and begin all over again.

"William, dear, who darns your socks? I see holes in them, and then the socks disappear when I'm ready to mend them."

"Sher Dil."

She laughed. "I thought so! Cobbles them would be a better word. I'm surprised you don't get bruises on your feet."

They stood beside an oleander, and William carefully put his arm round her waist. She leaned back against him and dropped her head on his shoulder. A score of sparrows were out dusting themselves in the garden path. Solomon came out on the back veranda of the bungalow and stared at the sparrows; from the corners of their eyes the sparrows watched him. Solomon was a young cat, furry, gingerish, and unnaturally long of tail. He could not control his reflexes, so that as he watched his jaw muscles tightened and he gave out a trembling yammer. Then, one paw at a time, he slid down the steps and pressed himself flat on the lawn. The grass was an inch high; the ginger cat's tail lashed and his jaws worked. Mary whispered, "Isn't he sweet, and silly? He'll never catch a bird in his life. Do you know, you never told me you had a cat?"

"Didn't I?" He knew perfectly well he had not told her. He was afraid she would expect him to own a pair of large, exuberant hounds. Sometimes people didn't understand a man who lived alone with a cat and a carpenter's bench.

Solomon crept to the flower bed and lay down eight feet from the sparrows, his head sticking out between the flower stalks. The sparrows ruffled their feathers and shouted "Cat, cat, cat" more loudly to each other. Solomon bounded out of ambush, all his claws spread. The nearest sparrow flew chattering into a tree; the others moved a yard farther down the path and sneered volubly.

Mary stood away from the oleander and gripped his hand hard. "Come on in. Breakfast's ready. And after that you're not going to sit in your study and wait for Mr. George Angelsmith You're going to give me another Hindustani lesson."

"All right." He took a last glance up the road, turned, and walked at her side to the house. She was wearing white, a flowing high-waisted Empire gown, almost transparent, so that the shape of her

57

long legs showed through. He had tried to make her wear a bonnet to protect her head from the sun, but she laughed and shook out her short hair, and said, "I'll look just as nice in freckles—or just as dreadful!"

After breakfast he sat down at the escritoire in the drawing room with Mary beside him. Teaching her Hindustani was rather like schooling a spirited young horse. She had the will to learn and a quick, determined mind; she picked up the rules of the language and a large vocabulary far quicker than he had all those years ago; but she did not have his ear, the coordination between ear and tongue which could repeat a phrase, once heard, just as it had been said. She was determined to make the words go *her* way. It warmed him inside to watch her fighting the language as if it were an enemy, to be subdued by sheer will power.

He said, "Now, do you remember about postpositions?"

"Yes. There are no prepositions in Hindustani. They are postpositions. They follow the word they govern. 'For the cat'—you say, 'the cat, for.' *Billi*, cat; *ke-waste*, for; *billi ke-waste*, for the cat. The most common postpositions are *ka*, *se*, *ke-waste*, *ke-uper*, and so on and so on. Darling, I want to learn how to market, how to ask prices, and tell them it's too much."

Did he hear a horse? He cocked his head. It was the waterwheel. He said, "What? Oh, yes. But it's better in the long run to learn the language properly."

She smiled affectionately. "I know you're right, but I do want to know how to say, 'That's too expensive.'"

He recognized that this was going to be ammunition for her feud with Sher Dil. He said, "*Woh bahut mahngga hai.*"

"*Woa bote mengga hi.*"

"No, that's not quite right. Listen: *wvoh b'hote mahngga hai.*"

"That's what I said. You're not listening, William."

He pushed his chair back and stood up. "I'm sorry, Mary. I—want to work in my shop. I won't need any tiffin." He hurried out of the room.

His shop was a wooden hut with a straw roof, standing at the side of the garden behind the bungalow. In the wall opposite the door five saws hung from wooden pegs above a long, wide teak carpenter's bench. The light streamed in through the windows and

58

shone on the bright, lightly oiled surfaces of his tools, the shiny edges of wooden planks and blocks. The floor was clean; a wooden box under the bench held sawdust and wood shavings. George was on the road, and on George's saddle the displeasure of England, and they were coming down on him together behind shortening shadows. Who said it was not important to stand well in the eyes of your fellows? Only cats were impervious to blame, praise, affection, doubt. He had watched Solomon for hours on end but could not see where the strength came from.

A heavy block of sal wood lay on the bench. He moved it with one hand, one motion, under the vise; one twist with his left wrist and the well-greased screw spun round and checked on the wood; his left forefinger steadied the toggle, pressed, the vise held. He took a scaleboard plane in his right hand, touched the block of wood lightly with the fingers of his left hand, pressed the plane down and forward. The plane bit whistled, the scaleboards rose and curled and passed into his left hand, and were laid on the shelf, each exactly one-sixteenth of an inch thick. The plane whistled, and the sure strong shuttle of his hands took him away from here.

"I think I hear him coming." Mary stood in the door. The sunlight had moved off his bench. He put down his tools and followed her across the garden to the bungalow. From the road a voice called in Hindi, "Way there, make way for the sahib!" The clip of hoofs was loud. "That's him," William muttered and put on his hat. "Don't you come out now, Mary. Three o'clock. This is the worst time for sunstroke."

She stood on the veranda, her head in the shade, her dress shimmering bright in the diagonal sun. William walked down the steps. George rode slowly up the drive, followed by a running groom. He waved his hand in greeting and William waved back, looking at him half in admiration, half in envy. That was the way a man ought to look—tall and fair, immaculate as the morning, riding a wide-nostriled Arab with a long tail and long mane. George showed no dust of the road, no strain of the journey, no hint of the unpleasantness of his errand. George had a wide mouth, soft golden whiskers, and gray eyes. The sun struck the royal blue of his coat and reflected up, glowing and softening, under his chin.

William's grooms ran out and held the Arab by the snaffle. George swung down from the saddle in a single graceful movement. He swept off his hat in salute and smiled with a flash of white teeth.

"Morning, William. How's our bridegroom? Recovered from the excitements?"

"Yes. I'm all right. Fine. Come in. Have a peg?"

George ran up the steps and bent over Mary's hand, brushing it with his lips. His glittering silver spurs hung just correctly loose, so that their chains clinked and jingled musically against the stone. Mary pulled her hand away. "Good morning, Mr. Angelsmith. I trust you had a nice journey."

"Very pleasant, ma'am. And how do I find you?"

"Very well, thank you. Would you care to eat soon?"

"I had a spot of chhota hazri at Bhadora, ma'am, but to tell the truth I could do with a real meal and a little something to go with it."

"Good. I thought you might. Dinner is ready."

George chattered amiably as he washed his hands in William's bathroom. William answered in monosyllables and shuffled his feet. The shadow had come and lay over the house.

The dining room was cool and dark. The sweat which had broken out on him when he saw George began to dry cold under his coat. Sher Dil served the meal; Mary's deep, pleasant tones rang like a bell in the high ceiling; the bell was a little insistent. George's light tenor rose and fell. Plates and dishes clattered softly on the sideboard. The waterwheel at the foot of the garden distantly chunked and gurgled. George and Mary held up the conversation.

They made a superb pair, one fair, one dark, both young and alive, both effortlessly capable in their spheres and sex. Two thoroughbreds—with Dobbin the *tertium quid*. He watched them secretly, trying to see them both in full focus at the same time; but he couldn't, because George was on his left and Mary opposite. George and Mary reacted on each other, and a tension grew wherever they were. He could not tell whether it was dislike that strained them or—the other thing. He cut little pieces off his steak and could not swallow them; and drank the snow-cooled claret thinking it was water.

George drank down the last inch of wine in his glass and touched his napkin to his lips. Leaning back in his chair, he said, "A magnificent—" But William could stand it no more. He jumped to his feet, the chair legs scraping agonizingly, and said in a loud voice, "Well—er—I expect we have a lot of business to get through, George, don't we? I mean, we'd better start."

George rose. "Too true, too true. Pray excuse me, ma'am."

Then they were in William's study, and William closed the door carefully. The windows onto the veranda were open. The sparrows had gone up to rest in the trees; the gardener was plucking weeds under the wall; the bullock walked round and round in endless circles at the well; the door of his carpenter's shop needed a new coat of paint. He closed the windows.

Searching in the drawers of his desk, he found a box of cigars and held it out.

"Cigar, George?"

"I think I will, old boy. Thanks."

Solomon lay asleep on the desk among the papers. William lifted him gently and put him on the floor. In silence the two men cut their cigars, pierced, lit, drew, puffed. William sat down at the desk. George stood by the mantelpiece, examining his cigar as if he found something of more than passing interest in it. William sat up. He had dreaded what was coming, but now that it was here a needle of anger pricked him. Damn them all, he'd done his best.

"Well, what is it? A severe reprimand? His Excellency's displeasure? What?"

George shrugged and waved his cigar. "You take these things too seriously, William. It's not as bad as that. And if it were, who cares? The Old Man's not pleased, not pleased at all. No mention of official sanctions, old boy, nothing like that. But he's muttering to himself about you."

George moved away from the mantel and sank into a chair, all in one of his single, easy movements. William clamped his teeth on the cigar.

George said, "But seriously, none of us can understand how this—er—massacre has not been discovered before. No reflection on you, you understand. The Old Man appreciates how well you know the natives, how good you are at keeping them happy. But there it is. He wants to know. Everybody wants to know."

William sprang up and trod on Solomon's tail. The cat howled, and both men started, then relaxed, and laughed. William sat down again.

"I don't know. I've sat here racking my brains, trying to think what I could have done, and Reeves before me too, I suppose, and the Saugor Pandits before that. They can't have wanted the gang to murder people in this territory, can they?"

"Maybe. Get a percentage of the loot. The Old Man doesn't though! Well, there it is. The murders are bad enough, old boy, but we all know murders can't be entirely prevented here. What upsets the Old Man is that you don't even know when one's been committed. Old Griffin happened to be in Sagthali when your report arrived"—Griffin was the Collector of the Khapa District adjoining William's to the south and west—"you know what a livery old lecher he is. But he's about the Old Man's age, and they were cronies before they came to the parting of the ways—rum." George lifted his elbow twice. "The Old Man still has a high opinion of him in some respects. Griffin said, 'Nothing like that could happen in my district. If it did, by God, I'd know the next day!' "

William stared out of the window. "Nothing like that in my district." He should hope not; the scale of murders was appalling enough; and the gang itself must have been kept alive for a century and more by new blood, by descent from father to son perhaps. It was unthinkable that two such bands should be operating in adjoining districts at the same time. One was enough for the smell of scandal to permeate up to the Governor General. It was his own bad luck that the unique horror flourished in the Madhya District.

He said, "Perhaps Griffin would have found out if he'd been here." He remembered Mary at the grove, her driving anger, and her determination that he should root out these murders. She might be listening outside the door. He would not put it past her. He said, "George, I'll catch these people if it's the last thing I do. I'll go out after them. I'll cross examine every man who lives here or passes through, if it takes me all my time for the next two years. You didn't see the bodies. I'll get them!"

For the first time George seemed embarrassed. He blew out a slow cloud of smoke and said carefully, "William, I don't think that would be advisable."

62

William frowned in bewilderment. "Not get them? Why not?"

"No, not spend all your time on it. You know, the Old Man really sent me down to talk to you about your Deori revenue assessment, and one or two other things."

"What other things?" William knew the answer without asking but spoke to gain time to think.

"Well, what happened at Kahari? Did that woman burn herself in the end? You forgot to mention it in your report."

"No, she didn't. I don't have to report women who think they're going to become suttee and then don't, do I?"

George eyed him speculatively, a tiny flush of color tingeing the sunburn of his cheeks. "No. Well, of course, I'd happened to mention it to him, so he wanted to know. How did you stop her?"

"The husband came back."

"To stay?"

"No. He disappeared again." William was bogging down and growing angry. The woman waiting at the pyre came often into his thoughts, never bidden, always to torment him: right or wrong? He said, "What else?"

"Oh, that case—*Sohan Lall* v. *Manohar Dass and Others.* Someone's complaint about the grazing rights in the Taradehi forests, I think it was. Thakur Mall's appeal came up, and the Old Man allowed it, and wrote a lot of rude things about your original judgment. Reversed your finding and annulled your sentence, in fact."

"But Thakur Mall is guilty!"

"You and I know that, old boy, but the law, the evidence! There were irregularities. You didn't do this and you did do that. In fact" —he stood up and walked slowly down the room—"in fact the Old Man says you would be well advised to study your law books afresh; to finish the revenue statement before the end of the month; and dispose of all the outstanding civil causes you have on your hands." He softened the message by imitating Mr. Wilson's measured manner of speaking.

William didn't want sympathy. He wanted Mr. Wilson and the Governor General in Council to understand what it was like here. He pounded the table suddenly and raised his voice to a shout. "*I'm doing my best!* Why won't they give me time? Have they forgotten what it's like in a district? If I spend my time in my office I can't meet the people and find out what's really going on."

George Angelsmith cleared his throat.

William finished savagely, "Oh, yes, I see! I don't sit in my office, I don't do any paper work, and still my people are murdered by the score under my nose! Look here, I've been thinking. This is obviously an emergency, something quite exceptional. If I can have an assistant, an Englishman, and an appropriation of a few thousand rupees—just for this year—for about forty extra mounted police, I'll get this straightened out."

George replied at once, as if the request had been foreseen and its answer prearranged. "Not a hope, old boy, not a hope. We're all shorthanded, and there's no money to spare. We're not collecting as much from the district as the Mahrattas did. Dash it, you keep writing in to say the land revenue collections should be lowered."

"I know, but I do have a special problem here, don't I?"

George shrugged his shoulders in answer and came to a halt beside the desk. William sat flushed and angry, staring down at the scattered papers. It was not really true that he had a special problem here. He had the ordinary problem, much intensified. Apart from the nine mounted police at his headquarters there was nothing—nothing but the villages, each with its patel and watchman, and the zemindars and jagirdars with their occasional posses of armed tenants and servants. Crime in a village could be detected because the watchman knew everyone's comings and goings. Open armed robbery by strong roving bands—of which the Pindaris had been the archetype—could be put down by cavalry. But this that he had stumbled on was something between: too small, secret, and tenuous to be caught by cavalry; too large and mobile for the watchmen, who were in any case chained to their villages and could not know anything about the travelers who passed by on the roads.

In a single moment of inspired vision William saw his district as a living, breathing thing, an angel's reach of earth, watered, peopled, sucking in this air, sleeping under these stars. The Road, arterial, venous, million-branched, was a living thing which required that men should walk free along it, as the winds blew free across it and the rains fell free upon it. His work lay there. He must find a way.

64

There had been a long silence. The papers under his hand seemed far off and very small, as though seen through the wrong end of a spyglass. George was looking at him, a little puzzled, a little contemptuous.

George said, "Cheer up! I'm going to Khapa. I'll be in the same boat as you by the middle of next week. Then we can foregather at Chikhli when all is blackest and together throw ourselves into the murky stream."

"Are you? You'll find it's the only life, far better than that social rot in Sagthali." He saw George's smile and went on, "I know you like all that too, and you're certainly good at it. But you'll be good at this. You'll pick it up in no time. Mr. Wilson won't have any trouble with you. What happened to Griffin?"

George lifted his elbow again, and William nodded. "Dead?"

"Strait jacket. The day after his talk with the Old Man."

"Oh, good. I mean, not so bad!"

They smiled together. William could not dislike George without envying him. And when you envied something, you wanted it. So you'd be disliking yourself. Perhaps you would, if you were George.

William said, "Let's split another bottle of claret. You'll come out after partridge this evening?"

"Love to, William. The bride coming too?"

"Yes. She's fond of shikar."

Talking and smiling, William followed his guest to the drawing room. The worst was over. With Mary in his mind he had faced it and seen it through. It really was no use being afraid.

In the drawing room Mary stood against the light, her head drawn proudly up and the skin taut about her eyes. She saw his face and relaxed; her eyes smiled at him. He said, "All finished. All well."

She stepped gracefully away from the window and across the room. "A drink? A cup of tea?"

In the night William lay still for a long time and listened to Mary's steady, deep breathing. He could not sleep. He slid out under the mosquito net and walked across the rush-matted floor. Mosquitoes whined in his ears and settled on his bare wrists. His muslin sleeping skirt swished faintly against his legs.

He had made a decision and now faced the problem of executing

65

it. Deciding had been hard; this might be harder. He could not catch the band of murderers unless he went out on the roads after them. He could not go out after them without neglecting his other work. If he did that, he might be dismissed from the service.

The same problem would face his successor. The roads, at this time, required constant observation, and something more—love, perhaps, or understanding. Without a special devotion to the task, effort would go astray.

He looked out of the window onto the starlit grass and the bulky, shadowed trees. They had the same outline as those trees beside the Seonath where the wife of Gopal the weaver sat on the ground beside her unlit pyre.

Mary's whisper made him start violently. "William, please come and talk to me."

He climbed back into bed, and she curled up against him, lying with one leg between his and one breast pressed softly on his chest. "Darling William, can't I help?"

"You have. You don't know how much. . . . I know what I must do. I must go out on the roads." He tried to tell her of the reasons for the decision; but they were in part mystical, and he could not, with his halting tongue, make his vision of the Road shine out in this hushed English bedroom. He tried to tell her of the difficulties facing him.

She said, "Is that all?"

"Isn't that enough?"

"William, you are right. You are *always* right, in yourself. You have only one real task now: the murders. What does it matter if Daddy gets cross?"

"I'll be dismissed."

"I don't believe it! And what does that matter? They'll only send you back to your regiment."

That they would—send him back, marked "Failure." It was the loom of failure that made him fail. If a man did not care about failing, he usually succeeded. He had seen that plenty of times.

Mary went on whispering (why did married people whisper in bed in their own houses?), "I was thinking, while you were in the study with George." (Ah, of course, George was in the next room. He had forgotten: she hadn't.) "Listen, you throw the onus on Daddy.

66

Catch the murderers. If he wants to dismiss you after that, he has to tell the Governor General that it's because you were doing something important and he wouldn't give you any help. That's not failure!"

He lay without stirring, and muttered, "I don't know where to begin."

"We must get more people on our side, see that everyone knows and is on the alert. I'm positive those men murdered Gopal the weaver! It wasn't just luck that led you to them. We must have lots of police on the roads and give rewards for all and any information. Every village ought to be made responsible for the roads and trails past it. Why don't you put police posts on important roads to check travelers in and out of the district? No, that wouldn't work."

She was leaning on one elbow, talking urgently. Her forcefulness flooded through him. His voice in reply was sharp, almost snappish. "Of course I can do some of that, but I can't scratch the surface without more men. They won't give them to me."

"Raise a corps of volunteers! Compel all the important men in the district, Chandra Sen and all the others, to subscribe to a fund for paying more police. Threaten everyone with extra taxes. Hint that you'll decide cases against anyone who doesn't give money or spend a day a month patrolling the roads." The starlight sparkled in her eyes, and William gulped nervously. She was riding at a gallop through every sacred rule and principle of the Honourable East India Company's administration.

"But—but—"

"I've got some money. Quite a lot. Daddy gave it to me as a sort of private dowry. He made me promise never to let you have the handling of it." She laughed cheerfully, and so loudly that the bedroom rang. "We'll use it to raise new police, tomorrow!"

Still he was silent. He had been alone too long, too long reliant on his own insecure self. His eyes pricked and hurt in the darkness. Mary's warmth against him dragged up his loneliness, and he turned to her with a cry. She opened her arms and engulfed him.

"There, there, my dearest husband . . . William, there, there . . ."

# Chapter 8

THEY rode together down the road, rolled cloaks on their saddle bows. The horses' hoofs sank deep into the soft surface, throwing up clods of earth as they came free at each pace. Mud splashed the horses' legs from fetlock to belly and soiled the riders' clothes. The heavy air deadened all sound, softened all outlines. The sun shone in a deep blue sky among drifting white masses of cloud. The Collector of Madhya, accompanied by his wife, was returning from a tour of his district. The town of Madhya lay ahead among distant trees.

Other things marked the passage of time: a certain ease in the way husband and wife rode together; the manner he had now of turning to her; an unashamed affection in his eyes and voice. It was late in September, 1825.

He said, "Nearly home. It was a useful trip."

She nodded. Every year, as soon as the slackening of the monsoon made travel feasible, the Collector of Madhya went out on a brief tour of his district. This time he had been on the road for two and a half weeks, and Mary had been with him. Through fifty little villages they had discussed crops, taxes, and local disputes with headmen and peasants. In its direct purposes the tour had been successful. But beyond that was their campaign to find the murderers, and in that battle the tour, like all their previous efforts since March, had produced a net result of nothing.

In March they had begun their campaign. In June the rains broke, the little streams became torrents and the roads deserted ribbons of bog. In September the rains lightened their grip on the land and travelers girded themselves for their journeys. A new season of travel would begin formally with the Dussehra festival in three weeks' time.

For all their searchings they had found nothing, and no more

68

murders had come to light. William could see no comfort even in that—rather the opposite. Dussehra was close, and he feared he was on the wrong trail.

He looked ahead. Already the travelers whom it was his duty to protect were out on the roads. Half a mile in front, a score of men and women walked toward Madhya behind a big flock of goats. He strained his eyes, saw they had no baggage, and knew they were only going a few miles between villages. Tiny in the softened distance beyond the goats, a solitary man approached from the direction of Madhya. Turning in the saddle, William saw two mounted travelers half a mile back, and with them five servants or followers on foot, all heading for Madhya.

He returned to his thoughts. Early in March he had enrolled four extra squads of mounted police and appointed one man in each squad to be daffadar. Some had come with horses, which he hired as he hired the men. For the rest, he had sent a coper through the bazaars of the north and west to pick up likely animals.

He had stationed one squad permanently by the ferry at Bhadora, and they reported that the woman still sat by her pyre. Unknown hands had built a shelter over her before the rains came. Unknown hands placed food beside her on leaf plates and every day filled a cracked jar with water. In the dark she moved to the riverside, the police said. She kept alive.

The other four squads William had sent out to patrol the roads and trails of the district, the men working in pairs. They had seen nothing and heard nothing—partly, at least, because travelers were more afraid of them than of any unseen danger. The anarchy of the Pindaris was not far back: armed horsemen were objects of terror still, whatever ragged travesty of British uniform they wore.

All the while the village patels brought in stories of suspicious characters seen, uncanny noises heard. William had spent hundreds of hours investigating. Most of the tales turned out to be rumors and nothing more; a few were by-products of local feuds; the remainder had been thought up out of whole cloth. The patels, eager to please and impressed with the gravity of the situation, seemed to feel that suspicion would fall on them unless reports of strange incidents were occasionally made from their areas.

And while William fought against the murderers, the slow ponderous anger of the government bore down on his back. He had neglected its other business, and it was displeased. In May Mr. Wilson had sent him a formal reprimand. In June, when the monsoon broke, William and Mary and the clerk had worked furiously together and succeeded in clearing some of the arrears of paper work. Mr. Wilson's fusillade of notes, inquiries, and orders slackened as the monsoon strengthened. The rain poured down and beat on the roof. William worked at his desk until his eyes hurt, then found refuge and short hours of peace in his carpenter's shop. Sometimes he talked with Mary in the drawing room when the rains made it so dark that the lamps had to be lit at midday.

Once she had said, "You know, I think the government doesn't want this story uncovered." It had shocked him at the time. But Reeves, his predecessor here, was now a Commissioner somewhere in Bengal. The Agent before Mr. Wilson had climbed to new heights. The smell would rise high and wrinkle many mighty nostrils.

Mary's horse shied at a stone, and he grabbed her reins in alarm.

"It's all right, William. I'm not made of porcelain." She pushed out her lower lip at him, and he shook his head and grinned contentedly. The baby ought to be born in April.

The lone traveler from Madhya drew level with them, almost past. William was looking at his wife, and the affectionate smile lingered on his face. Mary blushed and turned down her eyes.

Without moving her head she said, "That man's neck is bent on one side."

Five seconds later William realized what she had said. He swung his horse round with a shout. "Hey, you! Stop! Come here!"

The man, seemingly lost in the reverie of the long-distance traveler, started back, looked up at the towering horse, and began to run toward a thin line of saj trees bordering the road. Beyond the trees a field of turned red earth showed plain and open. The man saw that he could not escape from a horseman that way. He stopped, turned, and came cringing forward, his hands in front of his face, palms joined.

"Great lord, great lord, what does your lordship want of a poor man?"

The grooms ran up; Mary spurred forward to cut off his retreat. He was trying to hold his head upright, but he had to bend the upper part of his body in compensation. William looked down between his horse's ears and felt a grim triumph flood through him. Someone had been bound to pick this fellow up, sooner or later, if he traveled in the district. He was glad the chance had fallen to him—through Mary.

He said, "What is your name?"

"Hussein, great lord."

"Profession? No lies, now!"

The man hesitated and looked furtively up and down the road. "I dare not tell you, sahib," he said, eying the grooms meaningly.

"Where are you going, where have you come from?"

"I have come from Balaghat, and I go to Agra."

"On the twenty-seventh of February you traveled to the Bhadora ferry, westbound, in company with a Sikh and his son?"

The man cringed deeper and moved his shoulders, clasping his fingers together. "How should I know, sahib? I travel much. It is my business. I am not an educated man. How should I know the time and place?"

"You would remember a Sikh. We do not see many here."

The man screwed up his brow. "I think I recall them, perhaps. I am not sure."

"That's enough. You come with us. I want to talk to you." He spoke to the grooms. "Watch him closely, you two. Here, give me my gun."

They rode on toward Madhya, Mary's blue eyes alight, William carrying his loaded fowling piece across his saddle. Ahead of them the lopsided man trudged through the muddy puddles, a groom at each side.

In Madhya, Mary went to the bungalow and William took their prisoner direct to the tiny mud-walled jail. He called the jail watchman and took from him the keys of the cell used for dangerous criminals. The gallows stood in the courtyard outside the barred window. William did not have the power to award sentences of death; the gallows were a relic of the stern days of martial law eight years ago, when sometimes twenty Pindaris at a time had been hanged here and afterward displayed in chains on the roadsides.

71

He pushed the man into the cell, followed, and locked the door from the inside. The watchman protested, but he told him curtly to be quiet and sent him away.

Surveying the lopsided man closely and in a better light, he confirmed his first impression. The man—Hussein, he'd said—was quite nondescript. He had no particular features except that small inclination of the head. On entering the cell William had been triumphant and angry. Those emotions were already evaporating. He remembered something this man had said in the forest near Kahari: "There's nothing in the world more important for you—Gopal." It had been the truth. But it implied that Hussein had *then* expected murder, and that Hussein had *then* known he was not Gopal but an English official.

Hussein squatted on the floor and kept his eyes down. At last William said quietly, "That Sikh and his son were murdered. You left them just before they fell in with their murderers at the grove by Kahari." He dared not mention anything about himself yet.

Hussein looked up. "There was someone with me that night. After I left the Sikhs I saw a man hurrying through the jungle. I followed him. He did not walk quite right. Later I went close to him. I have sharp nostrils. Weavers cannot afford to smoke expensive cheroots, so that the after-smell lingers around them."

William thought slowly. Hussein was trying to corner him, make him admit that he had been Gopal. Why? He said, "That's very interesting. If you did meet such a man, why did you take him to see murder committed? And afterward, why didn't you come here and tell me, the Collector, what had been done?"

Hussein half turned his shoulder and seemed to be wrestling with himself.

William continued quietly, "You're a jewel carrier, at least part of your time, aren't you? Don't you realize those murderers are still at large? That one day they may rob and kill you? Help me to catch them and bring them to punishment. I will keep your professional secrets, if you are innocent of murder. If you are one of the band, turn informer."

The gallows stood stark against the gathering darkness. Hussein could not see them from where he squatted on the floor with the window high behind him. But the last of the light threw the shadow of the upright onto the wall opposite him. As darkness swept down the shadow lines of bar and scaffold faded. The man nodded his head slowly.

"It is an omen. Kali's? Who knows?"

William did not speak, not being sure what the man was talking about. When Hussein spoke again William jumped, for the voice was not the same. A load of fear weighted it now, and an inner purpose fought against fear to hold it steady, and it was not obsequious.

Hussein said, "Do you fear our gods?"

William thought, and shook his head. "No."

"Then how can you rule us, know us? I must speak in riddles because until you fear our gods you cannot understand me—or believe me. The goddess Kali, who is the Destroyer-Goddess of the Hindus, has given the roads of the world, and all who travel the roads, into the hands of her servants. Her servants must love no other than her I was one of them, until my band fell in with a girl, the most beautiful I have ever seen or hope to see. Kali gave her omen, which was an order to kill the girl and her companions. All night I struggled with myself, and in the morning I knew I was not a true servant of the goddess, though I had eaten her sugar of communion. I loved the girl more than I loved Kali. I did not want the girl to die. I tried to save her. The band would not agree. Then I fought for the girl's life, and the band broke my neck, and killed her, and left me for dead."

The little man's voice was low and far away, not a whisper. William said, "I don't understand. What band? How did Kali order you to kill the girl?"

"I can't explain yet. You have to learn to fear our gods—fear Kali. . . . For a year since then I have lived in fear and have had no place. The servants of Kali think I am dead, and it is better that they should. I was with the Sikhs when they came to the grove. I saw who was there already, so I slipped away. It was not my old band in the grove, and those men would not, perhaps, have recognized me—my home is not near here—but they might have, and I do not take risks. I slipped away. Then I saw the man hurrying through the jungle." He looked up intently. "I saw him stop and examine a leopard's pug mark. I followed, and followed, and

73

learned that he too did not want to let a woman die; that he would even do wrong to save her, for lying is wrong; and that he was not Gopal the weaver. He was an Englishman. Watching him, it came to me that only the English have the power to fight the servants of Kali, and put me in a safe place, and protect me. And it came to me that they had the power because they did not fear our gods, but that they could achieve nothing until one of them, at least, learned that fear. I made a plan quickly. I asked the Englishman to promise to say nothing, do nothing, whatever he saw. And I showed him the servants of Kali. And didn't he break that promise, and spoil my plan, and nearly get me killed, and send me on the run again?"

"But, Hussein, there were only about six of them. If you had come to me—the Collector—afterward, and told me what you knew, we would have caught the murderers by now and hanged them in Sagthali, and you would have nothing to fear."

"Six?" Hussein laughed shortly. After a long silence he said fretfully, "How can I make you understand? None of you understands, yet it's all round you, always has been. You're blind, because you have no fear as we have fear."

He stood up slowly, shaking his head. His hands moved, something soughed in the air and locked round William's neck. A hard knot pressed under his ear. He could not speak, and opened his mouth to breathe but found no air. Hussein's eyes were close to his. He hit out with his fist, and Hussein stepped away. The grip on his neck loosened, he sucked in breath and fought down a dizzy nausea.

Hussein squatted on the floor again and said evenly, "I'm sorry. I had to show you. I should have been behind you, really, so that you couldn't have punched or kicked or stabbed." He tucked a large square of cloth in his waistband. "That's how it is done."

William stopped the trembling in his legs and began to swear, but Hussein cut in, "Listen. I have thought of something. We can begin again, as we were at the Bhadora ferry, only this time you'll know more. I should have told you then, but I hadn't time. I still can't explain everything, because you do not fear our gods. You have to move forward, a pace at a time, and come to understand

74

before you can act. Do you remember a group of travelers who passed on the road today while you were arresting me?"

William thought back. The little convoy—the two riders, the five men on foot—which had been behind them, had come up while he was questioning Hussein. He had a vague picture now of an inquisitive, rather self-satisfied face passing behind Hussein's shoulder. Hadn't the grooms waved the party curtly on?

He said he thought he recalled them. Hussein sniffed in the darkness. "You *think!* You ought to know. That is a rich man, a thakur from Moradabad. He came through here four seasons back and must now be repeating his journey. He likes the world to know that he is an important fellow. But he is not so rich or so important that his disappearance would cause much remark. He and his party will rest tomorrow here in Madhya. Have them observed, noting carefully the color and distinguishing points of the horses, the shape of their saddlebags, the pattern on the charm round the thakur's neck. It is held up by a flashy necklace of gems. They are stones of the fourth grade, I saw, but not everyone will realize that. Observe, note down. When they leave here, follow at a day's march behind. No closer, or nothing will happen. Do not take a large party, but take your memsahib. She has a sharper eye than you, and a quicker mind. And let me go. Already I can feel the breath in my mouth."

William said, "What's going to happen?"

"Murder."

"But who's going to murder, who's going to be murdered? And how do you know?"

"The thakur's going to be murdered by some servants of Kali. I don't *know*, but it's very likely. That will give you a start, and a little understanding. But you've got to let me go. I must find out something. I want to know where Gopal the weaver really is. I'll come back, then we can take the next step."

William said shortly, "I cannot let the thakur be murdered, and I cannot let you go. You don't seem to realize that you are under suspicion yourself, and everything you say makes it worse."

For a long time the man on the floor was silent. Twice he began to say something, and twice cut it short with a groan. At last, as

75

if he had found a new line of argument, he said, "Why do you think I am doing this?"

William did not answer. He had no idea.

Hussein burst out, "You've been in a uniform all your life—red coat, fine hat, sword! You've been one of a band! All the English here are a band. You've had a place in the Company, been sure of friends, sure of help when you wanted it. So was I, until a year ago. Since then I've had no company, no friends, no place. I want to be with other people and like other people. I suppose it was that which made me desert the goddess for the girl. I can go back to Kali, but I don't want to. I am afraid. Please understand. I want a red coat, I want to be safe in it. And I can't be unless you help. That's why I followed you in the forest. It was only an idea then, and I wasn't sure of it. Now I am. Now I have a plan. You must let me go. I'll come back after the thakur's been murdered, I promise."

William paced up and down the narrow floor. He'd have to have time to think about the thakur, and what to do. He'd have to talk to Mary. He'd like to trust this man all the way and let him go. There was something very ordinary, and therefore genuine, about him. The sort of murderers he had mentioned, "servants of Kali," could not be ordinary.

Then Mr. Wilson's stern presence looked over his shoulder. "Releasing an accessory to murder! Wasting six months chasing moonbeams! Letting slip the one vital witness when he was at last caught!"

He said unhappily, "I can't let you go, Hussein."

The lopsided man sighed unexpectedly and seemed resigned. He said, "Very well, you can't. . . . What is the pay of a chuprassi at your courthouse?"

"A chuprassi? Four-eight a month."

"And the red coat and red sash—does he get them provided or does he have to pay for them himself?"

"The Company provides the first ones. After that the chuprassi has to keep them up for eight years and three months out of his pay, and mend them when necessary. Then they are supposed to have become worn out by fair wear and tear and are replaced free. But what on earth—"

76

"Have we not been talking about red coats?"

William had thought before that the man spoke in symbols and wanted any form of security. But he saw now that this was a direct and very literal mind, and that all the great abstractions of security, peace, a place among fellow men, were for him enclosed in a red coat and a red sash.

Oddly moved, he unlocked the door, slipped out, and relocked it, leaving the lopsided man squatting on the floor in the cell. He hurried down the smoke-scented street, past the guttering lights in the shops to his bungalow. Mary was in the dining room.

"Well," she said eagerly, "what did he say?"

"He has a rather frightening story. It isn't a story, either; it's just hints, 'through a glass, darkly'! It's difficult to believe him, but somehow it's more difficult not to. It's not only his words, it's an atmosphere or something."

He ate, and between mouthfuls related what he had been told in the jail. Mary said, "Servants of Kali . . . ordered to kill . . . something we don't know about and will never understand unless we learn to fear their gods. It *is* frightening. Or it's a rigmarole of lies to get him out of jail. That's what Daddy might say."

"I know. I couldn't write a sensible report on it."

And yet the lopsided man's short sentences, spoken under the twilight loom of the gallows, were like a dim lamp suddenly lighted behind a curtain. The light itself showed nothing, but it threw shadows, and the observer could guess at the shape of substance from the shape of shadow.

Mary said, "I understand why he wants a red coat, somehow, without understanding anything else. I think you ought to let him go."

William nodded. That was what he really wanted to do. In Mary's tone was the unspoken addition, "Do what *you* think is right. It doesn't matter what Daddy thinks."

When Mary spoke again she came round the table and put her hand on his shoulder. "And, my dear, you'll have to do what Hussein said about the thakur. Otherwise we will never find out anything."

"We will be murdering him." William pushed his chair back and stood up, his hands at his sides. Mary did not answer. Her

77

eyes were wet. William saw the young Sikh boy's face, blackened and dead in the ashes of the fire. He said curtly, "All right. I'll let Hussein out of jail in the morning, but I won't let him go. We'll take him with us when we follow the thakur. I'll put someone to watch that party at once. Sher Dil!"

"Huzoor?" Sher Dil ambled in.

"Send the boy down to fetch Daffadar Ganesha, please."

# Chapter 9

IN the early morning William awoke to the urgency of a man's voice calling in the compound. He heard the word "escaped," jumped out of bed, and pulled on his boots and shirt and trousers. He had not slept well, and the thakur had haunted his dreams. Was it the thakur who had escaped from the death lying in wait for him, and from William and Mary Savage, his murderers?

He ran out into the passage. He met Sher Dil coming in at the back of the bungalow and, through the open doors, saw the jail watchman gesticulating on the veranda.

"What's the matter?"

"The prisoner in the jail has escaped, sahib," Sher Dil said. "The watchman has come with the message. He says the prisoner half strangled him."

The watchman fell on his knees in an apparent agony of abasement and fear, so that the huge keys at his waist jangled with his trembling. Not so long ago he would have been thrown off a tall building onto a spike for this. Custom still demanded that he crawl and tear pieces out of his ragged beard. If he behaved calmly it would strengthen people's suspicion that the sight of a little gold had blinded him to the escaper's intentions. People always distrusted policemen, irregular cavalry, and jailkeepers.

William said quietly, "Get up, man, and tell me what happened." He sensed Mary behind him.

"Protector of the Poor, at first cockcrow the villain called for a lotah for purposes of nature. I took it to him. I was not going to let him out of the cell, of course. He flipped a handkerchief through the bars and around my neck. Aiiih, it was quick, quicker than the eye can see, and as the Presence knows I am nearly blind in the service of— I continue, I continue, Presence. He held me there so that my breath was stopped and all my past rose up

79

before me and the night went black. It was a dark night. He whispered, snarled through the bars, and I pressed up against them with my senses flying and a pain like hammers in my head! He said, 'Let me out or you die!' I struggled! The noose tightened! Tightened!"

The watchman, kneeling on the veranda, seized his own neck with both hands and jerked his head in fierce pantomime. He had seen in William's eye that no severe punishment hung over him. His eyes rolled. The wings of his narrative genius carried him aloft. Sher Dil's mouth was set in a disbelieving, silent sneer.

"Look!" The watchman raised his head, and on the thin old neck William saw a livid circling weal. "I was afraid. I opened the door and he came out, and—and I do not know what happened next. I fell to the ground and knew no more until the morning on my eyelids awakened me, and I had a great headache—which I still have."

William eyed the old man dispassionately. The first part of the story must be true. He felt his own neck and remembered the terror in that square of cloth. The second part? A small jewel had probably changed hands, in consideration of which the old jailer remained senseless till daylight, time enough for Hussein to get well away.

It was good, because Hussein might so easily have kept the cloth taut and saved himself a jewel—and lost a red coat. Now two people had been in that lopsided man's power, and for the sake of a red coat he had let them both go.

William said to the jailer, "Take heart. There's no great harm done this time. Here's a rupee. Go and buy some toddy, and be more careful in future."

Sher Dil did not conceal his surprise at the calmness with which William took the affair and went away, shaking his head. William turned and re-entered the bungalow.

Mary said, "Are you going to go after the thakur just the same?"

"Yes." He put his arm around her, needing her warmth, and they went into the bedroom to dress properly.

In the evening Daffadar Ganesha came with his report. Sher Dil let him into the bungalow and slammed the door of the study behind him. Sher Dil knew by now that another journey was in prospect; excitement filled the air, which he was not to share and must not talk about; and once more he would be left behind while the new young woman went with William.

Ganesha shuffled his feet uneasily and kept his arms tight by his sides, as though he feared to knock something over if he moved an inch. He was a dark brown, heavy man with a wrinkled forehead, much animal courage, and few brains. By question and answer William dug the story from him. Mary listened, took notes, and sometimes asked for translations of phrases she had not understood.

The traveler's name and title was Thakur Rajun Parsad. On the road he wore a white turban, a blue silk robe embroidered with saffron yellow trimmings, white jodhpurs, and red slippers. He was a thakur and a small landowner. He lived near Moradabad and was on a journey to Nagpur. In Madhya he had bought some provisions, but not a great quantity, not enough to carry his party on to Khapa, which would be the next place of any size in the direction he was going. William heard that item with relief: it would be easier to trace him if he bought food at wayside villages. In his party was an older man, name unknown, whom the thakur always addressed as "Hey, you!"; overheard phrases indicated that the other man was a poor relation who depended on the thakur's generosity for his bread and butter, paying with flattery and the service of minor errands. There were five servants in the party: a bearer, a groom, a sweeper, a cook, and one bodyguard armed with a matchlock. They were going to set off at dawn.

After a long hesitation William decided that the daffadar and one policeman should accompany him and Mary on the trail; and that both police should wear native clothes but carry concealed horse pistols. Many people would think it strange for the Collector to travel in this manner, but to the casual observer it would be less conspicuous, and the policemen might be able to get more information from wayside villages.

Now there was another day to get through, and another night, if he was to obey Hussein's injunction and keep a day's march behind the thakur. He could not work, and all day and all night hot and cold ripples moved over his skin. The curtain of the unknown shook in the wind, ready to part for him. The thakur and six innocent men were going to their deaths, and he was cold with

81

the cold of their graves. He wrestled with himself, and in the end, as at the beginning, knew he had no choice.

On the fourth day they reached the Nerbudda River at Chikhli. The ferrymen were sure that no one of the thakur's description had crossed the river. The night before, a plowman on the hillside above Taradehi had been sure that he had seen the thakur. The thakur and his party had vanished between Taradehi and Chikhli.

William and Mary and the two policemen turned their horses and rode slowly back up the trail. The killing had been done in daylight, and if they looked they must find a trace. There must have been a struggle.

Tall trees closed their branches overhead. They trotted along a dark green tunnel, damp and hot and loud with the bells of a wayside stream. Three miles up, Ganesha, at the rear, stopped and raised his voice, to be heard above the water.

"Blood, a spot on a tree—here."

Low down on the trunk of a sapling a single splash of blood had dried matt black against the shining pale bark. They looped the reins of the horses on a branch and began to search carefully. Casting round from the blood-marked sapling, they forced through springy bushes and into the jungle. Something glittered at the foot of a big tree. William bent, stirred the soggy leaves, and lifted up a small, bright pickax, very sharply pointed, well oiled, and apparently little used. A painted pattern of whorls and triangles writhed up the haft. The prints of bare feet showed faintly near the pickax, where the leaves did not cover the earth.

Scraping leaves aside with her hand, Mary called out, "Here— the earth has been disturbed." William's heart bumped, but it was not a big or deep patch that they found. Ganesha dug quickly, forcing his fingers into the soil. When the hole was a foot deep he fumbled in the dirt and slowly brought out a rupee. Sticky brown stuff mixed with dirt clung to the coin. Ganesha felt it, smelled, and said in astonishment, "Sugar!"

There was nothing else. William wrapped the rupee in a handkerchief, put it in his pocket, and led the way back to the path.

He was suddenly very tired, and overborne by silent, insistent voices muttering, "I am dead. Who am I? Where am I? You

82

killed me." A lowering gloomy heat oppressed the shadows. He flopped down on the ground and jabbed the point of the pickax with aimless anger into the path.

"A spot of blood. Sugar and silver. *This!*" He jerked the handle of the pick. A clod of earth came up and crumbled where it lay. A bright yellow thread shone in the hole. The three stared down.

Ganesha said stolidly, "The thakur's coat."

Mary whispered, "Right in the path—under the feet of every traveler. Oh, William, these are the most evil, cruel people in the world."

Up and down the winding path foot marks and hoof marks overlapped in profusion. No one would think to dig here. William himself had not dug; he had stuck in the point of a pickax and found a saffron thread. Hussein had told him to note and remember every detail of the thakur's dress. Otherwise it would have been only a thread in the path. He picked it out and put it in his pocket.

He said to the policemen, "You two stay here. Let no one pass. Hold any who come. The memsahib and I will ride to Chikhli and bring men."

"*Achchi bat!*"

William climbed into the saddle and, with Mary following, galloped south.

Late in the evening, his body aching and his head swimming, he could have sworn that this was the grove by Kahari, that time went backward. Here were the same flares and lamps, the same doubting, patient peasant faces, the same flash of pick blades in the light, the thuds as they struck the earth. Two late travelers tried to pass and were brought to him. He stared dully into their faces, made the shy woman draw back her veil. He had not seen them before. He waved his hand wearily, "You may go." This road was little used.

Ganesha supervised the digging. The trooper-policeman lay snoring in the path. The lamps shone on the sweating backs of the diggers. Of a sudden their heads came up, and their faces were not doubting now but incredulous and fearful. They dragged out a foreshortened brown body, crying aloud with sharp exclamations of compassion and horror.

83

William was sitting a little way back with Mary, but not far from the digging men. The forest that had been his friend for so many years was not friendly these days.

All seven of the thakur's party lay under the path. Ganesha came at last and asked him respectfully to come and look. The bodies lay in a row beside the lamps.

The thakur he thought he recognized; he had learned so much about the man. The beautiful coat was stained and torn; the empty saddlebags had been under the corpse and now lay beside it. In another's bloodstained secondhand clothes he saw written, "Poor relation"; and the expression on that face had remained obsequious even in the frozen amazement of dying. Here were the marks of the servants of Kali—a weal round every throat, the broken joints, the great wounds in chest and stomach. In these newly killed victims the bellies gaped open, and the entrails, bursting out, were heavy with loose dirt and slimy with mucus. Cut stakes, the points sharp and bloody, had been there in the pit with them, and a log and a club. The thakur's necklace was there, round his neck, and the charm on it. "Fourth-grade stones," William muttered to himself. *They* knew.

He was turning away when a digger at the end of the trench cried out, "Another!"

William stammered, "Th-there were only seven. What—what do you mean?"

The man held up a whitened skull.

William's knees had no strength in them. He covered his face. "Dig."

The bodies coming up now had been dead a long time. None of them had any flesh on the bones. Soon, as the minutes crawled by, twelve skeletons lay beside the seven bodies. William's mind balked at the scope of the horrors. He did not hear Ganesha at his side. Mary shook his elbow gently, and Ganesha repeated his message.

"That is all, sahib, we think."

Mary jumped to her feet. "William, we must go to Mr. Angelsmith at Khapa at once. Don't you realize that this is in his district? We passed the boundary near Taradehi, you told me. We can find

84

out at Chikhli who *did* cross the ferry. We can catch them if they're still together."

He thought it over. He was glad Mary had made him think. He said, "There are other ferries down river—Kerpani, Barmhan. These murderers might have used one of them after they did—this."

"Perhaps. But let's try Chikhli first. And—oh, William, it's dreadful to be relieved about anything now, but don't you see this means that the murderers are working in other districts as well as yours? That Hussein was speaking the truth?" Her eyes were blazing.

"I suppose so." He rose to his feet. He'd have to get George's help. He'd have to cross examine the ferryman at Chikhli more closely, follow his nose, and see where it led him. It was no good trying to explain to George about the "servants of Kali" yet. George would not believe him. He'd have to treat it as plain murder until Hussein came back and explained further—if Hussein ever did come back.

He said, "Ganesha, leave the trooper here on guard, tell him to see that no one touches the—great God, he's still asleep! You come on with us."

They galloped down the path under heavy clouds, the branches whipping their faces.

# Chapter 10

THE chuprassi squatting in the shade of a tree outside George's courthouse rose uncertainly to his feet when he saw them riding up. It was about ten o'clock in the morning. At last, recognizing William for an Englishman, he ran into the building. A minute later George Angelsmith strode out through the waiting crowd of pleaders and litigants. Hurrying without seeming to hurry, he ran down the steps to seize Mary's bridle and helped her to the ground.

"What in heaven's happened?" He looked from one to the other. They had crossed the river and ridden twenty miles through the last of the night and the first of the day, and they were tired and very dirty. "Is—is there an uprising?"

William stretched his aching thighs. "No. Murder. Same people. More of them."

They were walking up the steps through the standing, inquisitive-faced crowd. George slowed his pace and stared at William. "Murder? The same people? But what—"

He cut short the query, and Mary said, "It's in your district this time, Mr. Angelsmith."

Only then did William suspect that George had been going to ask what concern the murders were of his. George said, "Oh!" and pushed through the door into his courtroom.

"Court adjourned till tomorrow. Get out, everybody," he snapped curtly. The pleaders adjusted their steel-rimmed spectacles, bowed, gathered up their quills and ink bottles and files, and straggled out of the courtroom. They peered curiously at William and Mary as they went.

In a high-ceilinged chamber behind the courtroom George pulled up a chair for Mary and sent a chuprassi to fetch brandy and food from his bungalow nearby. His nostrils seemed a little pinched, and there was a tiny tremor and tightening at the corner of his mouth.

William hurried through his story, glossing over how he came to be following the thakur, and at the end sprang out of his chair and limped stiffly across the room. "George, the ferrymen at Chikhli gave us fairly good information about the people who crossed the day before yesterday. There were twenty or so in all—"

"Any horses?"

"No. I don't know what the murderers did with them; sent them round by Kerpani or Barmhan with their own horsemen, I suppose, or back along the north bank toward Sagthali. But the men at Chikhli remembered four of the travelers very well, for one reason or another."

"But we don't know any of the four were in the murdering gang, do we?"

"Some of them must have been! And we have nothing else to go on, so we must follow this. Mary and I were only a day behind the thakur when he was murdered. We've lost another day searching and digging. That means the gang is no more than forty-eight hours' march from here. Within fifty miles, say, at the outside. That's all in your district, isn't it?"

"Practically."

"We've been talking it over on the way here. Our plan is this: send gallopers out with the descriptions of the four men; have the roads scoured, at once, by the Lancers. They're not out on maneuvers, are they?"

"No, they're here."

William saw a fire of impatience glowing behind Mary's eyes. He said, "Get the whole regiment out, George, every man! Put parties on every main trail in the district, twenty or so each, galloping to the district boundaries—"

"Farther, if necessary!" Mary snapped.

George looked at her in amazement. He seemed to be speaking to himself. "Ye-e-es. There's a chance there. But, William, it's not a military responsibility. We're not encouraged to call on the army in a criminal case of this sort. You know that."

"What does that matter?" Mary broke out. "Any decent officer would send his men out when he heard the story."

87

George's eyes widened. He drummed his fingers on the side of his chair. "Yes. And of course we will get the credit still—I mean, the departmental credit. I suppose you're sure the new murders actually took place in my district?"

"Yes. At the foot of the hill below Taradehi, less than four miles from Chikhli."

"But they might have been killed in your district, and—well, carried into mine."

Mary whipped out a tiny handkerchief and blew her nose with extraordinary violence.

William said, "Well, I suppose it's possible, but—"

George stood up, flushing. "It doesn't really matter. The point is that we have discovered the new murders within twenty-four hours of their being committed, and the old ones date back to before I—we—came here."

He sat down at a small table and scribbled a note. "Chuprassi! Take this to the cavalry lines. It is for the colonel or the adjutant, in person. Run quickly."

While they waited they ate and drank. Through the window William saw that Daffadar Ganesha had bought a bowl of rice from somewhere and was leaning against the courtyard wall, eating fast.

After half an hour a lieutenant colonel of Bombay Lancers, followed by a lieutenant, rode up in a shower of flying mud clots and strode into the room.

"Damn my bloody old eyes, what's it all about, Angelsmith?" the colonel bellowed. "Oh, good morning, ma'am, beg pardon. Well, what is it? The regiment's standing to."

George began to explain. The colonel, a large man with yellow whites to his eyes, studied the wall map and breathed stertorously. The lieutenant fingered his curling ginger mustache, listened, and looked at Mary from the corner of his eye.

"Good. That's all clear," the colonel shouted at last. "Now, what if my lads recognize one of these cutthroats?"

"They are to arrest the whole party and escort it back here for interrogation."

"A soldier has no powers of arrest! There'll be lawsuits, damages, claims of assault and battery, God knows what! I know. I locked up a thieving bastard of a groom—sorry, ma'am, beg pardon—

locked him up in my stables for three days, and he sued me! Ate the mare's goddam oats too!"

George paused and looked thoughtful. "Of course, that's true, Colonel. Any officer or regular soldier acting in this case might be sued for unlawful constraint. I would get a departmental wigging, perhaps worse. You are the senior civil official present, William. What do you think?" He began writing absently on a piece of paper.

Official displeasure was to William a physical, human thing, an old man in a ribboned coat who settled on his back and weighted him down and shouted "Careful!" so loudly that he could not think. As George spoke he found himself muttering, "Yes. Yes. I hadn't thought of that. We'll have to be careful."

He met Mary's eye. She was not angry with him. A current of force lifted him above his doubts, and swept away the old man with the purple ribbon. He heard his own voice. "The department can go to hell. I'll grant temporary powers of arrest to everyone engaged, on my own authority."

"You might put that in writing, would you, old boy? Ultimately it is still my responsibility in this district, but it would help if you agreed that—oh, something like this: 'Apprehending an immediate danger to life and property, I direct that etcetera, etcetera.' Here, old boy, I've written it out. You just sign it."

William seized the quill and scrawled his name at the foot of the paper. After signing, he read it. The paper gave the necessary authority in two lines at the end, following a longer preamble which stated that Mr. Angelsmith, Collector of the Khapa District, was acting on the urgent advice of Captain Savage, Collector of the Madhya District, in a matter of which he, Mr. Angelsmith, had no direct knowledge.

"That's good!" George tucked the paper away in a drawer. "Now, let's start. Split up your officers among the various roads in any manner you think suitable, please, Colonel."

The two soldiers clanked out of the room. William stood up. "George, we think that the bulk of this party is likely to be on the road through Singhpur, Harrai, and Tamia, heading for Betul and the southwest. Either that, or they'll have branched off at Harrai for Chhindwara and Nagpur. I'm going with the lancers allotted to the Harrai road. Who are you going with?"

George began to cut a cigar. He took a long time over it, doing the job with none of his customary fluent ease. Mary watched him closely until he answered, speaking through the blue cloud of tobacco smoke.

"You know, I don't think I'd better go out at all. Someone must hold the fort here, be ready to direct reserves, question prisoners brought in, and so on. And who is going to look after Mrs. Savage?"

William started. Without thinking, he had supposed that Mary would be at his side. But there might be some danger ahead, and husbands were supposed to be keen to keep their wives out of danger. He did not feel that at all. He wanted Mary to be with him, always. He said, "I think—"

Mary interrupted, "Yes, darling, I am tired. You must go though, alone." She looked at him with an unfathomable expression. "You can do it, alone. Mr. Angelsmith and I can look after each other. I can help him write his report to Daddy in Sagthali."

George glanced quickly at her and away again. William swore at himself. He was a selfish cad to have forgotten the baby; but, looking at her, he could have thought she had too. This was nothing to do with the baby.

Trumpets screamed from the cavalry lines to the west. William jammed his shako on his head. "I must go. Er—good-by, Mary."

He ran down the courthouse steps, calling to Ganesha, and together they mounted and trotted down the narrow street. They caught up with the lancers in a walled lane on the southern outskirts of town. Forty troopers rode jingling southward, led by a young cornet. A somewhat mystified eagerness animated the soldiers' faces. The cornet was too young to hide his excitement, as a proper officer of cavalry should. He saluted. "Mr.—Captain Savage? I have a fresh horse for you."

"And one for my daffadar here, Mr.—?"

"Harrison, sir. Yes."

"Good. South, Mr. Harrison, please. We will split our forces at Harrai."

At Harrai in the burning afternoon they divided up. Mr. Harrison took Ganesha and twenty lancers and rode on south toward Chhindwara. The other half accompanied William southwestward on the rocky trail toward Tamia. In direct command of William's group was a middle-aged Lance-Daffadar Rikirao, a slight man with high cheekbones and a tight mouth. At midnight William rested his group for four hours. Then he pressed on, and in the dawn reached the top of the escarpment at Tamia. This was the southern boundary of the Khapa District. One step more, and the protests would come flying in from Sir Richard Jenkins, Resident at Nagpur, on behalf of the outraged Bhonsla sovereignty.

William rode past the boundary cairn, and the lancers followed —only ten of them now: two horses had foundered; the rest of the men William had dispatched in pairs along important trails branching off to right and left. He had seen or heard nothing of the band of murderers, or of any member of it. He wondered if the others had had better luck.

With the dawn a hill storm broke and drove rain in their faces. The dust on them turned to mud. Mud flying from the horses' hoofs spattered the blue uniforms and obliterated the gold facings. By ten in the morning they were not to be recognized as soldiers of the Company, or as any kind of soldier.

At a corner below Tamia, where the road fell away in winding curves and the angle gave a long view, William saw movement far ahead. With his hand he sheltered his eyes against the rain. It was a big party, moving well closed up together. His stiffness vanished, he shouted, "Gallop!" and swept down the road at the head of the wetly flapping lance pennons.

Ten minutes later he rode out onto a plateau and saw the big party close to. A man at the back of it turned as he watched, and stared, and ran forward shouting. The travelers became agitated, like ants in a disturbed nest, and scurried back and forth. A black puff of smoke rose and the sound of the report followed. Three hundred yards—no ball could cover that distance. William stretched his fingers on the reins and smiled in relief. This must be his quarry. Why should anyone else attack Company's cavalry?

The travelers, now in a loose circle, each man facing outwards, edged back from the road toward the broken ground of a water course and thick scrub jungle on the right. William surveyed the discipline of the movement and was confirmed in his hopes. The lancers, in a formation no better than a mob, unslung their lances, burst forward without orders, and rode across the plowed field at the travelers. More smoke puffed out, balls sang in the air. A lancer slid quietly over his horse's tail to lie face down in the mud. Tiger grass and thorn bushes and the twisted gullies of the water course swallowed the travelers. The lancers eddied about and yelled to one another and waved their useless lances. Rikirao hit one of them in the face, shouted a single bitten-off order, and herded them back to safety under a desultory fire.

William rode forward alone. "O travelers! Stop shooting! Come out! We are Company's cavalry."

A musket ball droned past his head. A harsh voice cried from the scrub, "Go away, robbers. You cannot deceive us with bazaar uniforms, all mud-spattered, and homemade lances and imitation Englishmen! You are murderous Pindaris. Go away!" Then, after a pause, and in a wheedling yell, "Find someone else to rob. If you go away, we promise not to tell anyone we have seen you!"

William trotted back out of range. It was only too reasonable that travelers should mistake his men for Pindaris. Seven years ago Lord Hastings, the Governor General at that time, had taken the field against those freebooters and, using the entire enormous force of the Company, had destroyed them. They were bandits, and in their heyday had ridden in hordes together, sacking whole provinces. Since 1818 that power had gone, but small bands of survivors still roamed the road, especially south of the Nerbudda. And the uniforms of the lancers were very dirty.

Rikirao said, "I'll take four of these young lunatics round to watch the back of the scrub"; and he added apologetically, "They've got no discipline yet. I'll charge if those people try to escape the back way. Come on, you, you, you! Take that silly grin off your face! Follow me!"

A maddening battle began, and for three hours crawled south along the flank of the Betul road. The band of travelers edged onward through jungle and thorn brake, always in disciplined formation, always firing at any close approach of the cavalry. The rain stopped, the sun climbed, and William fumed with impatience. He was certain that the particular men he wanted were slipping away and shedding stolen jewels in caches in the scrub.

Near one o'clock the travelers made their first error. Encouraged by the fear their muskets apparently threw into the cavalry, they attempted to cross an open space between two patches of heavy bamboo undergrowth. Across the road William saw the movement, waved his arm, and screamed in sudden excitement, "Inward wheel! Charge!"

From both flanks the lancers galloped down. The travelers closed their ranks, men among them ran out and jabbed pointed stakes into the ground, muskets boomed, the lance points leaped forward. William guessed there were about forty travelers with a dozen firearms among them. A lancer fell to his left, a wounded horse screamed and kicked to his right. Then he was in it, lashing out, and realized he had only a whip in his hand.

A face, pale and long, rose up before him, and he drew back the whip. The face was Chandra Sen's. He gasped, and in the effort of holding his stroke fell off his horse. "Chandra Sen!" he cried as he fell.

The travelers closed in over him, the cavalry swirled all around, hoofs thudded and clashed. Chandra Sen stooped over him; a knife shone in his hand; his eyes stared down into William's. William had been sure that the patel had recognized him in that instant before, when he had held the stroke of his whip; but that could not be; Chandra Sen was going to stab him. He cried again, through someone's smothering, sweaty hand, "Chandra Sen! It's Savage!"

The patel paused, and his long bloodhound face set in amazement. Then he stood back, dodged a thrusting lance, and shouted, "Friends, stop fighting! It is our most excellent Collector-sahib from Madhya, and my friend! What have we done? Stop, stop!"

The travelers rested their arms and closed in round Chandra Sen. The cavalry surged among them, the horses' long manes tossing and the lancers shouting angry words and hitting the travelers on the heads with the butts of their lances. Rikirao jumped down from the saddle.

"Are you hurt? Harrison-sahib will not forgive me."

William rose wearily. "No. I'm not hurt. Tell your men to let the travelers be. I'm terribly afraid that we have made a mistake. My fault though. Don't you worry."

# Chapter 11

LANCE-DAFFADAR RIKIRAO said, "It's no mistake. Look at their discipline! I'll search them, and then we'll take them all back to Khapa. Some loot may be in their baggage."

William himself was too shaken in his judgment to have given the order; but he could not countermand it once Rikirao had spoken. The lancers pushed the travelers into a line at the edge of the plowed field and began to search their belongings. The travelers wailed in protest, and William looked at them individually and closely for the first time. As his eyes moved from man to man his heart began to bump. Two certainly, and perhaps three, tallied closely enough with the detailed descriptions given by the ferrymen at Chikhli and with the vaguer recollections of informants in the villages north of Taradehi.

Chandra Sen stood aside between two servants who had been carrying his kit. William recognized one of them as the surly watchman Bhimoo and was momentarily surprised. A village watchman was an employee of the community, not a personal servant of the patel. Then he recollected that watchmen usually shared their duties and their salaries with members of their families. There was no reason why Bhimoo should not accompany Chandra Sen on his regular winter travels.

The patel urged his fellow travelers to be quiet, not to worry, and to do what they were told. Somehow, without moving, he had changed sides, and by the force of his personality and appearance was now to be numbered with the lancers. The troopers called him "lord" respectfully. Rikirao saw and heard. His hard-bitten little face tightened; he said harshly, "You! Fall in with the others."

Chandra Sen raised his eyebrows deprecatingly, looked at William, and said, "The Collector knows me, Daffadar-sahib-bahadur."

All the specters of official disapproval sprang back onto Wil-

94

liam's shoulders. Rikirao's mouth was set in a thin, hard line. Chandra Sen waited in passive dignity.

William said, "I'm sorry, Chandra Sen, but someone might have hidden something in your kit without you knowing." A shadow, something vague and new, something between a hurt and a threat, clouded the patel's face. He bowed courteously at last, and Rikirao himself began to untie the bundles the servants had carried on their heads.

Soon every unwounded traveler stood behind his spread belongings. The lancers had dismounted and stood opposite; the troop horses were tethered in groups to trees in the jungle beyond. One soldier lay dead in the field and two others were hurt. Four travelers sat on the ground, moaning over bruises and lance stabs. Everyone was exhausted and short-tempered. The sun had dried their wet clothes and steam rose from them.

William got up stiffly and began to examine the baggage. He did not hope for much. Even if some of these men were robbers, they had had ample time during the long fight to throw away the evidence. He found that their baggage did not contain any disproportionate collections of valuables, nor did a search of their persons bring more to light. Rikirao ordered his men to probe each traveler's rectum, which was a common hiding place for gems. Chandra Sen turned white with anger when he heard the order given, and William intervened to save him from this last indignity. With a touch of malice, remembering the vicious dogs, he did nothing to help the watchman. The hubbub from the travelers rose to a crescendo of outrage as they undid their loincloths and bent over.

The searchers found nothing suspicious anywhere. Jewels there were, in reason, and when William asked about them the travelers said, "This is mine . . . this is my wife's . . . that one I bought two weeks ago . . . it is the money for my return journey." He could not disprove what they said.

When the search ended he questioned each man separately, asking who he was, where he had come from, where he had spent the last four nights and with whom, and where he was going. He spoke first to Chandra Sen.

The patel said he was on his way to visit his eldest brother in Nagpur. "As you know, sahib, it is my custom to visit my kin at this season. The village clerk has always borne my responsibilities well during my absence, has he not?" Continuing, he said he had left his house a week before, traveling to Khapa by way of Tendu-kheda, Patan, and Shahpura, where he had stayed the night with friends. His tone, though polite and calm, carried a hint of com-miseration. William's sense of futility increased.

The patel glanced about while giving evidence, and, having made sure he could not be overheard, broke off to mutter, "Sahib, I pray you be, careful what you do. I do not know how many of these travelers are men of influence. I fear that the pleaders in Khapa will get at them if you take them all back there in arrest as I heard the daffadar suggest. They will all think they have cause for suit against you. There will be much unpleasantness. Mr. Wilson will come down from Sagthali as he did in the case of—"

"These others," William interrupted doggedly. "Where did you meet them?"

The patel shrugged. "Some down the road this very morning. That one, certainly, and those two who look like brothers"—he pointed with his chin. "Most of the others in Khapa. That little fat fellow, he says he is a silversmith; he joined me in Shahpura."

"You crossed the Nerbudda there?"

"Certainly, sahib. I have told you I came through Patan, and where else could I cross?"

William groaned inwardly. Chandra Sen, his only reliable wit-ness, had not used the Chikhli ferry, and therefore had not come down the steep path from Taradehi where the murders had been committed. Still, he was glad he would not have to take the patel back to Khapa—or Madhya, perhaps—to give evidence of recog-nition of other travelers.

"Thank you, patel-ji," he said. "Please stay here until we finish this, in case we need your help. Then continue your journey. And I am very sorry we had to stop you."

His questioning of the other prisoners centered on the three whom he had recognized from descriptions given at Chikhli or beyond. He breathed more easily when each in turn denied that he had crossed the Nerbudda at Chikhli. All three said they had used the busy ferry at Barmhan, where three boats were in continuous operation. William's uncertainty and embarrassment began to evap-

96

orate. These men had been positively described and would be positively recognized by the witnesses who had given the descriptions. They had come down through Taradehi and crossed at Chikhli. They said they hadn't. If they were innocent, why should they lie about their route?

Seeing that they were not going to be executed on the spot, the three began to protest with growing anger—they were busy men, they could not wait, they had important affairs to attend to. William held to his determination and, in the face of Chandra Sen's worried headshaking, took the three into formal arrest. The other travelers he released. They packed their belongings as quickly as they could and hurried away south. Chandra Sen and his servants were the last to go. William waved in suppressed triumph to them, and the patel shook his head and waved dejectedly back.

Late in the afternoon, after a party had buried the dead soldier, William and the lancers set out on the long journey back to Khapa. Three of the weary horses had to carry prisoners as well as lancers. Soon after the start Rikirao reined in with a cry.

"Something bright there! Buldeo, go and get it."

A lancer slipped down at the edge of a patch of tiger grass beside the road, gave his reins to a comrade to hold, and walked forward. The grasses waved, and he came out with a disappointed look on his face.

"Only a pickax, Daffadar-ji. Shall I throw it away?"

He held it up, and Rikirao's charger shied from the bright sparkle of steel close to its eye. William called, "No! Bring it here."

The lancer gave it to him. It was bright and clean and patterned like the other. He could not tell whether the two were exactly the same or only generally similar. He would check when he got back to Khapa. He tucked the haft between the holsters on the front of the saddle and rode on.

These pickaxes were of a strange pattern and size, and unusually well cared for. He had never seen any like them before, and now he had found two within a few days. He thought of the broken bodies, and the pits dug for them, and looked at the tool more closely.

They reached Khapa at noon the following day. George's court chuprassi took the prisoners and led them off, loudly complaining, to the local jail. A pair of lawyers' touts woke up from a doze in the courthouse compound and ran after them. The commotion died away down the street.

Mary came out from George's bungalow. Of a sudden William was very tired and rocked on his heels as she held out her hands. He patted her arm clumsily. "I'm all right. Did any of the other parties catch anyone?"

"Yes, six. You've got to lie down. What happened?"

"We had a little battle, and it turned out to be with Chandra Sen." He frowned down at her. "Did you say they'd arrested six more? I have three. We don't have adequate descriptions for nine people. Some of them must be innocent."

Four described at Chikhli. One—say, two—beyond. Four and one make—nine? The ground trembled under his feet and the steps were very steep. Mary supported him until he reached the chamber behind the courtroom and flopped into a chair.

George and the cavalry colonel were waiting for him. They looked concerned, and he heard them speaking but could not understand clearly. The damp heat of the Nerbudda valley brought the high ceiling down to oppress him and squeeze his head. They all talked, he with them, and the talk went in no direction and achieved no object.

They held nine travelers on the strength of descriptions given for five or six. He would have to see them all, but the situation would not change, because he knew that some of the men would look alike. They would have an averageness, so that two fitted every description. The descriptions themselves overlapped; it was not quite clear, now, whether in each case one or two men had been meant.

Of the nine prisoners, only three said they had used the Taradehi cliff road and the Chikhli ferry. The searchers had found no incriminating loot on any of them, or among the parties they had been with when arrested. The horses of the murdered thakur and his relative had disappeared.

William's head rolled forward of its own weight. Again and again he ran his hand carefully over his hair.

Mary said, "All we saw of the thakur's kit in Madhya was what he wore or displayed. We must find out exactly what jewels and valua-

98

bles he left his home with and would have kept concealed in his baggage. Then we can compare the list with what these people have in their possession."

George shook his head. "It will take six months to do that. And how are we to prove the thakur didn't sell some of his jewels along the road? You can't hold anyone six months on no evidence, can we, William?"

A small angry fire began to warm the pit of William's stomach. He was not clever, and that was well known. But if he thought a thing out, and held to himself through every discouragement, and if Mary held to him, he would be proved right.

He said, "Six of these men have sworn they did not use the Tara-dehi road. I am going to take those six back up that road. They'll be recognized—some of them. Those I am going to hold in arrest. I am going to do what Mary suggests. I am going to find out every-thing about them, if they have to sit in my jail for a year, and I am going to find out everything about the thakur."

"That's a good idea," George broke in quickly, leaping to his feet. "And you'll keep the prisoners in Madhya and hold the trial there, what?"

"Yes, that seems the sensible—"

"I thought trials had to be held in the district where the crime was committed," Mary said in a hard voice.

George said with brittle mockery, "You're quite right, ma'am. You *do* know a lot about civil regulations! But, for one thing, these men have to be taken over the road to Madhya anyway, so that the witnesses can identify them. And, for another, a District Magistrate can always ask for a case to be transferred into or out of his jurisdic-tion for good and sufficient reason."

The colonel picked up his schapska and blew the dust off the top. "Talky-talky finished? I take it you want me to provide an escort to Madhya for these rascals?"

William nodded wearily, and the colonel strode out of the room.

William dragged himself to his feet. "Got to . . . examine the three . . . who don't deny . . . they came through Taradehi. Think I'll . . . let them go. They might be murderers too, of course . . . not worth following up . . . this time . . ."

99

Mary took his elbow and shook her head firmly. "Mr. Angelsmith can do that for you. You're going straight to bed."

William was too tired to argue, too tired to notice the sharpening of George's expression. Leaning on his wife's shoulder, he walked slowly out into the heat.

In the morning his party started northward on the road to Madhya. When they reached the village of Andori, on the south bank of the Nerbudda opposite Chikhli, they stopped to rest, and William sent for the ferrymen. The owner of the boat came forward with his three assistants. The escorting lancers stood or squatted in the shade of the big trees. The strong sunlight fell down through the branches and picked out the gold facings on their blue uniforms. The horses rested their weight first on one leg, then another, and ceaselessly swished their tails at the flies.

William watched the approaching ferrymen, and his heart sank. As they shuffled forward they looked about them at the soldiers and prisoners. William saw that their faces were closing visibly, like oysters, and veils were coming down across their eyes. Before, when he had talked to them, they had done their best to help him by remembering what they could. They had given him descriptions. Now the men they had described were confronting them. Perhaps they had never expected that. Perhaps they had invented the descriptions in the first place, to satisfy him and get rid of him. Now it was different. These prisoners had not done them, personally, any harm. The courthouses were a long way off; cases took a long time to reach the magistrate; who would work the ferry? They had written nothing down on paper. The spoken word could be forgotten, disavowed. It was an inborn habit of India's poor, bred over turbulent centuries of intrigue, when the shifts of power made it safer to forget than to remember.

William said to the boat owner, "You remember me. I was asking you three or four days ago about people who had used your ferry."

The old man blinked cautiously, hesitated, and seemed to decide it was safe to recognize the Collector of Madhya.

"Yes, sahib. I remember."

"Look at these six men here. Have you seen any of them before?"

The travelers glowered at the ferryman. The ferryman looked slowly from face to face, obstinate stupidity congealing in his expression.

"I don't think I've ever seen any of them before."

Mary exclaimed angrily, and William bit his lip. He turned and surveyed the prisoners. One of them was not at all average, and, once remembered, could have been forgotten again only on purpose. He hardened his voice. "Look here, ferryman, you said that on that day a short, broad Mohammedan crossed. You described him. You said he had a face pitted with smallpox and no forefinger on his left hand. Do you see that man here?"

The prisoner second from the left wore a Mohammedan kulla under his turban. He was short, broad, and pockmarked. He had no forefinger on his left hand.

The old ferryman looked carefully at each of the resting lancers, then let his glance wander over the prisoners. "That gentleman there is a Mohammedan, I think, and he has no forefinger on his hand. But he is not the man. I don't remember that I have ever seen him in my life before." The other three boatmen whined in chorus, "Nor I, nor I, nor I."

William's temper snapped. He shouted, "You're lying," and turned to the cavalry jemadar in charge of the escort. "Jemadar-sahib, take them into arrest, all of them."

Now no one would be able to cross the river here. Travelers would have to go down to Kerpani or up to Shahpura. Traffic would be disrupted. There would be many complaints, and the tales would be carried to Sagthali. William did not care.

It was the same story all up the road to Madhya. The witnesses who before had recalled faces and quirks of dress now forgot them.

William plowed grimly ahead on the course he had set himself. He had to plumb the depths of the quagmires surrounding him. He experienced a savage satisfaction in acting so far out of character. He had always been reasonable and understanding; it was a delight to be neither. He would not be hanged as a lamb but as an obstinate and furious lion.

He threatened the village patels, browbeat the witnesses, and arrested everyone who had given any information on the case. His column grew, and when the troopers of the escort rode with snaffles jingling and saddles creaking into Madhya, twenty-seven sullen prisoners walked between the files.

There was no place in Madhya to lodge such a crowd. William jammed them into the four cells of the jail, where they set up a great wailing clamor. That done, at seven o'clock in the evening he walked to his bungalow. The townspeople stopped talking as he passed and looked covertly at him to see what kind of demon had taken possession of him. Pleaders' touts ran past him in the opposite direction, toward the jail, and salaamed obsequiously as they squeezed by.

In the bungalow he went straight to his study, sat down at his desk, and pulled out a parchment sheet. Mary stood at his side. He said, "I am not going to let those people loose, *habeas corpus* or not. I am going to send all our police out, to the ends of India if necessary, to trace the thakur's belongings and check against what these prisoners had on them. And now I am going to tell your father what I am doing."

He began to write steadily in slow-formed, large characters:

> To: *The Agent to the Governor General for the
>       Kaimur and Mahadeo Territories.*
> From: *The Collector of the Madhya District.*
> *Sir, I have to inform you . . .*

# Chapter 12

IN the same study, a week later, Mr. Wilson stood in front of the fireplace, his hands joined behind his back. The bungalow had a fireplace in every room, not so much to disperse the raw cold of January and February evenings as to remind the man who had built it of his home in England. No fire crackled now behind Mr. Wilson's coat tails; these were the perfect October nights, warm, earth-scented, and companionable. Mr. Wilson looked out of the tall windows, where the light of bonfires rose up in the sky and flickered on the windowpanes. In the town they were beginning their celebrations of Dussehra, the most important festival of the Hindu year.

Green curtains hung down beside the windows, and between them, as between green pillars, a distant rocket fizzed up into the sky. William's mind jumped out and rode up with the red rocket, where the wind rushed in his ears and he could see down on the town, on the great masonry water tank, on the little Mohammedan temple on the hill. From up there he saw the Hindus' procession snaking through the narrow streets, its banners waving. This year he had managed to prevent the town's three hundred Mohammedans from holding a procession of their own across the path of the Hindus. This year there might be no Dussehra riot. Then again, there might.

He knew Mary was in the bedroom, standing near the open door. Not dignified—but she never worried about dignity; nor did he, any more. She wanted to hear; so when Mr. Wilson had closed the study door, William managed to open it again, a little crack, so that their voices would carry to the bedroom. It was important that Mary hear, because then she would be beside him, and he would know it, and would not be afraid.

Already he had been in here with Mr. Wilson for two hours.

The two men fought a fight, but it was not a duel, because each also grappled with extra, unseen adversaries. William spoke past Mr. Wilson at bulky phantoms of rectitude, which had power but no inner vision. Mr. Wilson wrestled sharply with William, and with the forces that had made William so different a man.

Mr. Wilson did not grow angry. His mind was fixed in its course. A thing was right or wrong; there could be no argument about it, no need for anger. He studied William with intensity, trying to find the explanation of the inexplicable. William Savage would not, could not, have done these things. William Savage might have— William Savage *had*—earned rebuke because of his slowness; but he had always been ploddingly correct. There had been nothing strange about him in the past—just that he was a man perpetually one step behind decision.

But Mr. Wilson had come down to investigate reports of a man running ahead of decision, an angry, intemperate man, a man so little afraid of power that he used it like a shoe. Mr. Wilson stepped cautiously into William's mind to track down the gadfly that had driven him to these acts. Mr. Wilson's daughter too was being carried headlong to disgrace.

"There is no doubt, nor do you deny, that in concentrating on the attempt to apprehend these murderers you have neglected the other affairs of your district . . ."

Mr. Wilson began a severe lecture. William listened, noting dispassionately the things he had left undone. The list was long and black, but no worse than similar lists which he and Mr. Wilson could have prepared for some other British officials.

". . . now this matter of the arrests. You know that you have acted without a shadow of justification in law. I would be inclined to place some of the blame on George Angelsmith, except for the letter you wrote in Khapa stating explicitly that he was acting only at your urgent request. In that affair you misused the military arm —to no purpose. The military are already too apt to think that we civilians are a flock of incompetent owls. You have confirmed them in their opinion. You have failed to catch the real culprits—that is mere ill luck, and not at all blameworthy, though I must point out that it is extremely unfortunate that this man—what was his name?

104

Hussein?—escaped from your custody. But, having failed, why this madness of arrests without evidence and holdings without charges?"

William went close to him and said, "Why? Mr. Wilson, there is nothing more important in my district than to run down these murderers. There is nothing more important in all the territories under your control, I believe."

"That is as may be. But it does not give you power to disregard the law, our law, the justice for which we are striving so hard to inculcate a respect among the people."

"What does justice mean?" William burst out passionately. "Fair trial, the rules of evidence, no double hazard, no hearsay, and so on and so on? Or protection against injustice, against violence? The means, or the end? You've read the report Elphinstone wrote on these Mahratta territories when we first took them in '17?"

"Yes, Captain Savage. I helped to prepare it." Mr. Wilson looked at William with a sort of respect, as if he had imagined before that William could not read. "I think I know to what part of the report you are referring—where Elphinstone wrote that we must consider whether perfect fairness is more important than the prevention of crime? Quite. He pointed out, as I recall, that with the Mahratta territories in the condition they were, the two were incompatible because there existed in the people no respect for law. Well, Captain Savage, we have chosen—if we had a choice, which in my opinion we did not. On the one hand we could continue despotism, under British instead of Mahratta rulers. On the other, we could plant the impersonal rule of law, and with our strength guard its growth through all trials and adversities."

"What does the rule of law matter to the man who gets killed? Or to his wife and children?" William said bitterly. "How can a rule of law flourish where people call themselves 'servants of Kali' and kill because a goddess orders them to?"

Mr. Wilson shifted his feet impatiently.

William went on, "Oh, I know we have no evidence about them yet. That's just what I mean. I tell you, sir, they cannot be run down within our rule of law! Indians aren't English. 'No man dies by the hand of man,' they think, so they won't give evidence because they are not angry with the murderers. They think men who kill are driven by God to kill. And there are too many jurisdictions, too far to go to give evidence, too long to wait. We've got to go outside the law to catch them, to prevent more murders."

"And I will not permit you or anyone else to go outside the law, to prevent this or any other crime."

Mr. Wilson was a massive thing, not human, a great block of granite in front of the cold fireplace. Through the windows the moan of conch horns and the clang of bells sounded faintly in the room. The bonfires brightened the sky and dimmed the lower stars. This Dussehra was the feast of Shiva the Destroyer and of Kali, the dark blue goddess with the disheveled hair and the cincture of bloodstained hands and the tongue protruding from her bloodstained mouth—Kali, who ordered her servants to kill. Dussehra marked the beginning of the season of war and travel. At Dussehra men set out on enterprises of great moment, armies put on their trappings and prepared for war. The throngs pushed huge idols through the streets, the bleeding heads of sacrifices fell into the dust.

William strode to the windows and flung them open. The surge of noise rode in on the October night—deep, uncontrolled, dark with blood and vivid with life, a thing of killing, being killed, dying, living, struggling, spilling of blood, pouring of seed, rotting, bearing. The smell poured in, and the smoke of cow dung and burned powder, and a dead cat in an alley, and the breathing earth.

Mr. Wilson understood. He drew himself upright, not proudly or pompously but like a man standing against overwhelming physical force. Sure of his inner strength, he stood braced against the clamorous, writhing night. He said, "No one, for no reason. The law will prevail."

William closed the windows slowly, the noise beat against the glass, in the study it was quiet. Solomon slipped in with a small mew and jumped up on the desk and began to rub his neck and head against William's hand. William stroked the cat gently, curling his fingers under its ears. The low purring sounded louder than the muted roar of Dussehra.

Mr. Wilson said, "Captain Savage, I am going to relieve you of your position. To save trouble, I recommend you apply for transfer back to the military department, on any personal grounds you choose. I wish to have your formal application before I leave in the morning. I regret that I must do this, but it is right. You are not fitted for employment in the civil administration of India. I must do it, especially—" He did not finish the sentence, but William could have finished it for him—"especially because you are married to my daughter."

Here it was. Here was the worst they could do. It did not feel bad. It did not feel as bad as the nights when he did not know where right was and where wrong was. Now at last he had plowed into the quagmire, and for his people's sake touched the bottom of it.

It would take Mr. Wilson a little time to get a successor for him here; not enough to run down the thakur's murderers though. That job was begun, and he could only leave it to the new man to carry on, if the fellow had the courage. He shook his head, while Mr. Wilson watched him closely. It wasn't a question of courage. From the beginning—and the woman at the pyre whom he had not allowed to die was the beginning—he had been bound to this thing by special, personal chains. It had controlled not only his mind but his heart, and even his hands. Because of the woman at the pyre the little man Hussein had come to him, the man so simple that he preferred a red coat to the embrace of a goddess. No chance for Hussein to get a smart official coat through William's help now.

He said, "Very well, sir. I presume I am to stay until you have appointed a successor and he has had time to come here?"

Mr. Wilson's strong face was almost respectful. He said gruffly, "Yes. It will be a few weeks, I expect. I will move as quickly as I can."

"Thank you, sir." William stopped abruptly and Solomon stopped purring. William said, "India holds us accountable. . . . Won't you go to the drawing room, sir? Mary will be with you in a minute."

He turned his back, pushed open the windows, slipped out, and walked across the garden. The door of his shed was unlocked and he opened it and went in. By the fitful light of flares and bonfires and rockets he found the oil lamp and lit it. He took a large block

107

of teak and a chisel and began to work with single, expert strokes of the mallet. He had Mary, and his body growing in her, and his love in her. All the rest was gone. He would make a cradle, on transversely placed rockers, delicate, to move at Mary's touch, but so heavy and strong it would not tip over whatever the child did.

# Chapter 13

HE did not hear Mary come into the shop but knew in a minute that she was there. He said over his shoulder, "You haven't left your father alone, have you?"

"He's gone to bed. When I went to the drawing room he just kissed me and shook his head and went to bed. I think he knew I'd been listening. He looked very puzzled."

William grunted and went on with his work. Mary did not use much perfume, but an alien sweetness of cologne water had come in with her to mix with the tang of the wood. The shop was so small that she seemed to be looking over his shoulder. He struck a shade too hard with the mallet and muttered, "Damn!" Simultaneously Mary said, "Hadn't we better talk about this?"

He said, "Please leave me alone." She was all he had, but the piece of wood was shapeless still, and she could not see what it would become.

She snapped back, "I'm concerned in this too! We've got to do something, quickly, about catching the murderers, not waste time in here."

He put down chisel and mallet and turned sadly to look at her. She was so young and strong. He ran his hand down the side of his head, over his hair and cheek and neck.

She began to cry, and leaned forward, and burrowed her head into his chest. "I'm—I'm sorry, darling. It's the baby. I want him b-born here in Madhya."

"He? She!" he said softly, stroking her hair.

She jerked up her head, shaking off his caressing hand. He stood away from her, deeply hurt. She was listening to something. After a minute she said, "I could have sworn I heard someone's voice, speaking in Hindustani. Do you think it's Hussein? Oh, I hope he comes! It was so faint it might have been inside my head. This baby!"

She was frightened, and he went over to the door and opened it and looked across the garden. He heard the voice plainly, but so low that he too could not tell in truth whether it came in through his ear or originated inside his head. Yet it had none of the sibilance of a whisper; it was a speaking voice, lower than he might ever have imagined, except that he had heard it before.

"This is Hussein. Have your servants gone to bed, and the Bara-sahib?"

The hairs stood up on the nape of William's neck. The source-less voice chilled him. Could he answer an inner spirit?

Pulling himself together, he whispered hoarsely, "Where are you?"

"Behind the door."

"The servants have gone to their quarters. The Bara-sahib is in bed."

"Go over to the house, the drawing room. This shed is too like a box trap. I'll follow. When you get there, do not light a lamp."

William caught Mary's hand, muttered, "It is Hussein," and blew out the light. They walked mechanically toward the bunga-low, went in through the back door and along the passage and into the drawing room. Mary stood in the middle of the room. William opened the French windows and stepped back beside her.

He was watching the window, but the after-ghost of the lamp in the shop still burned in his eyes and he saw no one come in. He felt Mary start and heard bare feet on the carpet. A bone creaked some-where beside the escritoire. Staring, he thought a blacker human shape squatted against its dark bulk.

The voice came again. "I've come back. I told you I would. You shouldn't have locked me up. I've heard what's happened in the case of the thakur, and I've found out what I went away to find out. Now we can get on with the next part of the plan."

"It's no use," William broke in sullenly. "I have been removed from my position and am only waiting until a new sahib, one better at figures, can be found to replace me."

The voice said, "You have? Already? Good. Better than I dared hope. Now you have nothing to lose and everything to gain. Like me. Do you think the order for your dismissal would be changed if you were to root out the servants of Kali from India?"

"No."

"Haven't I told you it is greater than anything you English suspect? You would uncover a million murders—and end them."

"A million!" William jumped. "In my district? It's not possible!"

The voice was impatient. "Not in your district alone—all over India. I told you—Gopal—that night at the grove by Kahari that this was the biggest thing in your life. Would the Lat Sahib then dare not to give you honor and a higher place?"

"I suppose not."

He was not sure. Organizations as big as the Honourable East India Company did not like admitting mistakes. The bigger the scandal uncovered, the more highly placed the official who would have to take the responsibility. No one would believe it, anyway. It couldn't happen.

"I suppose not," he said again slowly, "but—"

"Will you promise to make me a chuprassi?"

"What's he saying?" Mary broke in. "I'm sorry, darling, but I must know. It is awful just hearing you mutter and whisper—oh, there's a bat in the room!"

"It won't hurt you. He says he will lead me to uncover a million murders if I promise to make him a chuprassi. He's mad."

"Promise me a deed in writing, in fadeless ink, with your thumb mark on it; then I will show you how we can do it."

William stared at the shadow. What did it matter now? He had failed, and the taste of failure was not too bad. He would have to live with it in his mouth and had better learn to like it.

Mary said softly, "He's not mad, William. He sounds very sane. A chuprassi has a lovely red coat with the arms of the Company on it, and is a part of something big, and doesn't have to travel the roads. Find out what his plan is."

William said to Hussein, "What is your proposal?"

The man on the floor was silent for a full two minutes. At last he spoke, beginning slowly, with gaps and pauses, gaining fluency and emphasis as he went.

"First, the thakur is dead. And six men with him. You followed them and found them. Do you believe now that there is nothing more important in the world for you than this task of rooting out the men who did it?"

William said, "Yes," briefly and surely.

"Well, you must see more. When you have seen, and learned to fear our gods, you will understand everything. You will understand why I want above all else to have a red coat and be like ordinary people. You must leave your law behind and become an Indian and take to the road with me. That will be possible because you have dark eyes and can speak good Hindi. We already know that, as an Indian, you look like Gopal the weaver—which will be useful, and perhaps dangerous."

"Why?" William interjected. "Surely Gopal's dead?"

"I don't think so. But he's far away. And he's a servant of Kali. That's what I had to find out. I told you in the jail . . . why I had to frighten your old fool of a jailer and escape. Now you must come away with me. You will be gone five months."

"Five months? What's the need to stay out that length of time?"

"To complete one whole travel season on the roads, from the beginning to the final dispersal of the bands. To understand. Anything less, and you'll just scratch the surface. In all that time you have to keep silence. You will have to watch murder and do nothing; worse, perhaps, and say nothing, until we return and are ready to act. Oh!" His voice changed as he thought of something. "Is it true that you white people eat with a knife and fork because your fingernails are poisonous? If it is—"

"No," William interrupted impatiently. He had heard the superstition before. "We don't like grease and food on our hands, that's all. I can eat like an Indian. Are these servants of Kali called by any special name?"

"Yes. The Deceivers."

The shadow on the floor used an uncommon word, thug, derived from the verb thugna, to deceive. He said it as Mr. Wilson might have said "Satan and all his Angels."

William said, "I've never heard of them."

"Others have. The Bara-sahib returns to Sagthali tomorrow morning, I hear. I will come for you tomorrow night at this hour. We have much to do. We need several days alone in the jungle before

112

we set out, because you have to learn many things, many words. The Deceivers use a language of their own. Will you come?"

William waited for Mary to say something, to urge him on or hold him back. The question had been put in very simple, direct Hindustani: she must have understood. She did not speak. She was there beside him, warm and strong, but she did not speak.

He said, "I'll come."

The man on the floor said quietly, "You had no choice. Language, dress, customs are important, but our first need is a strong spirit. The goddess Kali is our adversary. Are you protected against her? Do you carry your God's sign, the cross?"

William licked his lips. The bat in the room swooped across the open windows. The bonfires to Kali still burned in the town. He said, "I do not wear a cross. I believe my God is everywhere at my side." He supposed he believed that. Mr. Wilson did—but Mr. Wilson would fight Kali in a different way, confronting her with an icy wall of disbelief. He could never understand her.

The shadow bulked higher and came close. William could see better now, and it was indeed Hussein, the lopsided ordinary man, whose eyes gleamed large and intense close to his own. The man's voice was not steady. "Give me a cross, then. Allah and Mohammed his prophet have failed me against Kali. Give me a cross. Your God is a foreigner and does not know Kali's strength, and will fight better against her than ours, who do, and are frightened. We must fear, but we must not fall. Give me a cross."

Mary whispered, "What does he say? What does he want?"

"He wants a cross to protect him in what he—what we are going to do." Mr. Wilson would have called it gross superstition, and it was.

Mary pulled out the tiny cross of English oak she wore inside her bosom, snapped the thin gold links of its chain, and gave the cross to Hussein. Hussein fingered it and muttered, "Wood. I was afraid it would be silver or gold. Wood is better." A spurt of affection for the man warmed William's heart. Hussein too knew what the feel of plain wood meant; silver was something else, subtle, superior.

Hussein tucked the cross away. "Tomorrow. It doesn't matter what plans you make to get away, except that you must let no one,

113

no one whatever, know what you are doing. And you should try and prevent your absence being discovered for as long as possible. And have the paper ready for me about my post as a chuprassi."

He was gone. The voice was silent, the shadow faded. The soundless beat of the bat's wings, felt as a thud in the inner ear when the bat passed close, died as it too flew out and over the drive.

Mary closed the windows and leaned back against them. "Is that man a bat? Now tell me everything. I know you're going somewhere with him and, William"—she reached for his hand and held it tight—"you have to. But I'm frightened. I've never been so frightened."

He told her, and she was silent a long time. At last she said, "To let people be killed in order to save others. We've done it once already. To do evil that good may come of it. I don't know what it will make of us. You'll have to be very strong." She shivered, seeing visions William could not see. She clung tightly to him. "Promise me you will not kill anybody yourself. Darling, you're my husband, promise, promise!"

"Mary, I couldn't murder anyone. You know I couldn't." Her vehemence astonished him and touched him a little with her fear. He realized he was holding her tighter than he knew, because she could hardly breathe. He relaxed the grip of his hands on her.

Other, material fears closed in on him. Armed men roamed the roads, and he would be unarmed. Everywhere men died by violence, or died gently, their blood clogged by snake venom, or died in a ditch, excreting their life in cholera and dysentery. He saw the road now as an Indian saw it, and for the first time knew he would have to find the Indian, not the British, type of courage to face it.

He said, "I will go. I will not kill. How am I to get away?"

Mary's trembling had stopped. She sat down carefully and looked up, a dim face and a white gleam in the chair. Her voice was steady. "That's not going to be difficult. After Daddy's gone, you pretend to fall ill and go to bed. Only Sher Dil and I will be allowed into your room. Sher Dil will have to know you've gone, of course, but that's all. Later we'll give out that you're still weak and going to do the work from your bed. I'll actually do it. Wait! You'll have to have a bad wrist or something so that you can't write. We'll get found out—two weeks, a month perhaps. Then I'll say I don't know what happened. You told me to do it but didn't say why. You just vanished."

Her voice throbbed, and William remembered the baby; and, as he had become an Indian and seen the road, he became a woman and faced Mary's lonely fight. He wanted to speak and comfort her but could not.

She went on, "I'll stay in Madhya as long as I can, even after it's been discovered, so that you can send me messages and I can do things for you, perhaps. I—I don't think it's going to be easy. Later, if I have to, I'll go to Daddy in Sagthali."

She got up and stood close to him, not touching him. "William, I love you. I think sometimes you don't trust yourself to believe it. I don't know what faces me, but I know it's going to be bad. And you, you who are so—so shy, you can become a mad red dog. I'm frightened."

She began to cry and pressed her wet face into his chest.

## Chapter 14

WILLIAM and Hussein walked between fields, and ahead the lights of a little town sparkled through the chilly night. William breathed deeply and wrinkled his nostrils. India was beautiful, above all on this night of the year. It was the Dewali, the festival dedicated to lights and gambling, which fell always on the twentieth day after Dussehra. Hundreds of open lights, in tiny earthenware bowls, flickered outside each house and hut.

Tonight, as for two weeks past, he was truly a part of India. He had worked here all his adult life—nineteen years, the last three in Madhya. As an Englishman he had fallen in love with Madhya, and this central land's pattern of beauty had grown into him—its earthy reds and deep greens, the shading of its still water in old masonry tanks, its rivers that flowed by white and smoky blue villages. Yet always his race had held him back from complete absorption in it. He had been physically unable to see or hear or smell beauty without noticing the dirt and disease that were part of it. Then, when he noticed, his love changed to something else—to reforming zeal, desire to raise up, to alter.

These weeks alone with Hussein, as in the months to come, he had to be Indian to keep his life, and nothing but Indian. He had to make no mistakes in feel or tone; he had not to reform but to accept, not to fight squalor and cruelty but to become part of them. Only by being Indian and thinking Indian and feeling Indian could he hold any hope that he would return at last to his English ways and his English wife. Already they were altering in the perspective of his mind. He knew that the man who had stepped out of the bungalow, clung briefly in Mary's arms, and then vanished in the darkness with Hussein would never go back. It would be another man who returned to Mary, and William did not know what kind of man that would be.

At his side Hussein walked with shorter strides, and William thought of the cross in the little fellow's loincloth. Their second day in a jungle hiding-place, before the lessons had begun, Hussein asked him with sudden aggressiveness, "This god, this Christ of yours, this cross *is* his symbol, isn't it? For *all* his followers? It isn't a trick, a secret sign, to show him which are black people and which are white?" William tried to reassure him, but Hussein was nervous and did not settle down until they set out on the road. Since then they had walked together for six days northwestward on a little-used road east of and roughly parallel to the main Madhya-Saugor-Lalitpur-Jhansi artery.

William looked down. It was dark, but even by daylight he had confidence in his disguise. Those who looked at him saw what the woman by the pyre had seen that February evening by the Seonath —Gopal the weaver. There had been no question of making him up to look like Gopal; when stained, he *did*. His legs worried him a little. The color had taken well and evenly, as it had all over his body, but the shape of his calves was wrong; they were fatter and smoother than the muscle-corded sticks of a working peasant, thinner than the suet curves of a merchant or bannia. For the rest, he was Gopal, plus the high-ankled Bandelkhand slippers.

There had been a strange incident one evening in a lonely place where Hussein was showing William the rumal. It was the three-foot-square cloth the Deceivers used for strangling, and Hussein was instructing him how to stow it in the loincloth, one end just peeping out ready for the hand to grab. William said, "It doesn't matter, of course, because I'm not going to use it, but surely it would be safer to carry it like this." The rumal turned easily in his fingers; he twisted the top corner over and down and back inside the coil of the rest in a loose knot; it was all hidden from sight. "And it's just as easy to get out." He flipped one forefinger into the loincloth, the rumal sprang out in his hand. Hussein leaped away from him, his eyes starting from his head, and stammered, "Who—who taught you that?" William tucked the rumal away. "No one. It's obvious, isn't it?" Hussein said, "All the gods help us!"

William did not know the name of the town ahead, but Hussein did—Jalpura; he'd been this way once, twenty-odd years before. A small lake bordered the road in front of the town, and William

117

stopped, muttering, "Let's rest here a minute before we go in. Dewali's so beautiful."

Hussein answered, "It's not beautiful, but unbelievers like you think it is holy. We will stop, but only to rest."

"All right. I understand."

"Then we will go into the town and look in the harlots' quarter for—them."

The lights rode like swarming fireflies along the houses at the edge of the town. The lake reflected them, and lights floated on the surface of the water. Brighter lights glared in the streets. Light glowed over the housetops, imprisoned in dust. It was November. The rains had long gone and the raw depth of air made a tiny jagged halo around each flame and light.

Soon Hussein trudged forward again; William followed. In the narrow principal street of Jalpura the shops crowded together, standing for the most part closed and shuttered. In one or two the owner worked with abacus and quill to finish the task of closing his annual accounts. Once, glancing down an open passage, they saw a shopman bending in prayer before his ledgers; a lamp flashed on a single bright rupee laid on the topmost tome. Hussein checked his step, then muttered, "You idolaters! I forgot that all the bannias do that at Dewali. Come on."

Groups of kneeling men gambled in the dust at the side of the street, shouting cheerfully and watched by small crowds. Everywhere travelers mingled with townsmen.

Hussein paused at the open front of a spice shop. The proprietor, a young fat man with a cheerful face, was playing cards with three other men and calling bets. Wooden tokens and some pieces of the Company's copper coinage littered the mat they squatted on. Hussein said, "Friend, which way are the women?"

The spice merchant laughed good-humoredly and waved his hand up the street. "Up there, second turning on the right. You can't miss them."

"God be with you."

They pushed slowly on through the crowd. The harlots displayed themselves, each squatting on a cushion, in open-fronted rooms at street level. The rooms were bare, except that in some a small clay

118

image of Krishna stood on a pedestal in a back corner. In all, an open staircase at the side ran up out of sight to the second story. The old retired crones who were the harlots' body-servants leered toothlessly down through half-drawn curtains from the balconies.

Always a dim lamp on the floor shone up under the harlot's chin and into her face, erasing the lines of age and transmuting into living flesh the heavy mask of make-up. Every harlot wore a layer of white powder on her face and circles of violent rouge on her cheekbones; black antimony ringed their eyes. They stared unseeing at the crowds that jostled up and down the narrow slope of street before them.

Occasionally, without fervor or coquetry, a harlot's eyes locked with a man's. Occasionally a man stepped over the low sill and squatted close to the woman inside and talked. The passers-by paused to hear them haggle about the price. The woman gestured unemphatically, the man argued.

An old peasant beside William said clearly, "Thank God my loins no longer squander what my fields produce!" and went on his way, shaking his head. The haggling customer shrugged at last. The woman rose and stalked up the stairs, her head high. The man followed her. Above, the old crone jabbered, pulled her head back, and closed the curtains. Hussein and William moved on.

In front of the next house the crowd pressed thicker. Inside, a young girl sat on the cushion. William saw that most of the staring men were travelers. He noticed Hussein carefully inspecting them. Finally Hussein made up his mind about something and said to one of the strangers, "Greetings, brother Ali. How much does this one cost? She ought to be good."

William had learned that the form of greeting was the challenge and countersign of the Deceivers. Ali was no particular person; the Deceivers used the name in their salutations, adding a Hindu or Mohammedan phrase according to the religion of the speaker. He remembered when he had first heard it and clenched his fists involuntarily. He had wondered then who Ali was, but had since come to understand that an Indian so greeted would not even notice the phrase unless his own name was Ali, or he was a Deceiver. Most sects and many areas of India had their own customary form

119

of greeting; a Sikh would work in the word *Khalsa*, a Mohammedan *Allah*, a Hindu *Ram*.

The man spoken to turned, nodded, and said, "I don't know. She makes my loins tighten. So young! She is like our southern girls before they are blessed by children. Like a boy almost."

Watching closely, William saw that a pair of travelers, on the far side of the speaker, turned to eye Hussein. One of the pair, a small man in his forties, with large bat ears and a sharp face, moved unobtrusively closer. After a minute William heard the familiar low tones. "Greetings, brother Ali." Then, in an ordinary voice, "She is too expensive for the likes of us, brother. Two rupees."

Hussein laughed. "I must wait then, and curb my appetites. That's what the maulvi says: 'What the harlot gets, the servant of Allah loses.' Perhaps there are as lickerous girls farther north."

He turned away as he spoke and moved up the street, William close at his side.

Everyone was talking, not loudly or in excitement, but giving out a continuous clatter of human voices. Lights shone everywhere, lined in rows along the balconies on the second stories, grouped on the sills and projecting lintels of the doorways, in ranks by the fronts of the stores and houses. Glancing carelessly over his shoulder, William saw the lake and floating squadrons of lights on it, but he could not see the men who were the brothers of Ali. Up a side lane lights outlined the black loom of the local rajah's castle, for they were in prince's territory now.

He walked slowly with Hussein, and they talked as everyone around them talked. In this full-smelling noisy place he lost the last traces of his self-consciousness in his role. As he talked the right words came easily into his mouth, and as he walked his hands and feet and shoulders moved as Gopal the weaver's should.

A high-pitched voice close behind him said, "Where is there a good place to eat in this town? We're hungry."

William twisted his head. The speaker was one of the pair from the harlot's shop—the little one with the bat ears. The other was darker and taller.

"Haven't you eaten already?" he said.

Hussein cut in, "I believe there's a Mohammedan eating house up this street, but I haven't been here for some time, and things change."

"They do, more's the pity," Bat Ears said. "Well, I'm a Hindu, and I see your friend here is too"—he jerked his head toward William—"but I don't think you'll worry about that, will you? We won't. Is this the place you mean?"

He led the way, as if he knew it, down a dark alley, through a half-open door, and into a dingy room. The four of them squatted on the floor in a far corner. The owner of the eating house came and slammed down rice and lentils and cold curried potatoes before them, all mixed on brass plates. It was dark in the room, and the few other people there ate without talking.

When they had finished, Bat Ears leaned back on his hams and picked his teeth. His dark, ruminant eyes surveyed them from head to toe. Finally he said, "My name is Piroo. This is Yasin Khan." His tall companion smiled; he had a luminous, priestly calm and always moved slowly. Piroo of the bat ears continued without emphasis, "What are your names? Why are you not with a party?"

If he had been a yard away William would have sworn the man was not talking, just picking his teeth.

Hussein answered, "I'm Hussein. This is Gopal. He sprained his wrist. He couldn't—work. He's not quite better yet. Our party went without us."

Again no one spoke. Piroo looked at them; all the expression had gone from his eyes, leaving them flat and lightless. Yasin Khan turned something over in his mind. William felt that of the two he was the more important, and waited anxiously.

Yasin Khan carefully put his thorn down on the earth floor. "We have some merchandise. Our Jemadar must decide whether he wants you, though. Come with us." He rose to his feet.

Each of the four paid his own share of the meal. They stepped out into the alley, turned left, reached the street, turned left again, and strolled down the hill. In the open country they did not speak to one another but loudly chanted a war song in unison, stopping every few minutes to shout together to frighten away wild beasts that might be following them. It was very dark.

A mile outside the town they came to a grove of trees, such as in

121

India are planted everywhere for shade and for the comfort of travelers. The glimmer of white tents showed that some of the people staying here were rich. Several fires burned cheerfully, and men crouched round them, wide awake and talking. Piroo seemed to shrink in stature as he came to the edge of the firelight. Followed by the others, he crept mouselike to the center of the grove and said to a man by the fire, "Lord, is your master the Nawab back yet?"

The servant growled, "What's it matter to you?"

"Nothing, nothing, lord, except that here are two of our friends —good, honest, strong men, who wish to join the Nawab's following."

The servant spat into the flames. "Every stray dog in the country attaches himself to my master's train." He glared at William. "You needn't think you'll get any scraps of food from us, though."

William joined his hands in wordless servility.

The servant said, "All right, all *right!* Don't hang around here."

William and Hussein touched their hands rapidly six or seven times to their foreheads and scrambled away. Piroo caught up with them. "We sleep over there." He pointed to a large isolated tree in the far corner of the encampment. "Find a place near us. There is room." Then, softly, "The Jemadar of our band will come in the night to you."

William and Hussein lay down at once and rolled themselves into the thin homespun blankets each carried slung across his shoulder. The sounds of the camp died down, to rise again twice more as groups of travelers returned, singing and shouting, from the town. The Nawab came in drunk. They heard him yelling a bawdy song while his grumpy servant tried to put him to bed in his tent. They heard a shrill, brief curtain lecture, and knew thereby that at least two of the Nawab's wives were on the road with him. At last all was quiet, and William fell into a fitful reverie.

He liked the roughness of the blanket under his chin. This life was real and complete to him; in these past few days he had become a part of the road, as much in place as its wayside trees and wandering beggars. The road itself moved, carrying him forward, unwinding a tapestry of India, outstripping the dusty, leaden-footed folios of paper that loaded him down in his office. Here on the road he

122

knew people, and knew himself, and was a full man. He would be happy to spend the rest of his life on the road.

He thought of Mary, and the daughter she was going to bear him, and turned over restlessly. He was not here to enjoy the road but to seek out the Deceivers who ruled it.

On the last mist-deviled borders of consciousness he saw the tree overhead freighted with swinging bodies, and one of them was his own. From the height of a branch he looked down. He swung gently, and the land spread wider under his eyes, and the spacious fullness of power filled him and throbbed in his dangling wrists. The noose did not hurt his neck. He was a great man, and all travelers passing below looked up to him as a man, and bowed to him.

He awoke with a start and a small cry in his throat. A voice murmured in his ear, "Lie still. Is it indeed Gopal? After all these years? I am Khuda Baksh, now jemadar of a band. Look!"

William peered up in the gloom at the outlines of a thin face and a small dark beard. He lifted up his arms automatically and said, "My friend!" and hoped desperately that Hussein would say something. The Jemadar bent down and hugged him as he lay, pressing his beard into William's face from the right and the left. William rolled over, and the Jemadar lay down beside him, holding one of his hands. Hussein did not speak.

The Jemadar said, "Twelve years, isn't it? And you were a young man. What happened to you?"

William licked his lips. "Let's talk on the road when we get a chance. We have so much to remember." He squeezed the Jemadar's fingers. "But tell us how things stand here, so that we can play our part."

"You're right, as usual. You always had a sound head." The Jemadar's white teeth flashed three inches from William's face. "Attend. I'm the jemadar of the band. Piroo buys the sugar. Yasin Khan is the priest. They are our officers. We have a mixed Hindu and Mohammedan crowd. In this encampment here, now, there are nine of us and eleven beetoos . . ."

The Jemadar spoke rapidly, using many words of the Deceivers' own language. William understood most, but not all, of what was said. Since leaving Madhya, Hussein had spoken mostly in this language to him. A beetoo was an outsider, an ordinary person, anyone not a Deceiver; just as Yasin Khan's reference to "merchandise" in the eating house meant "travelers."

The Jemadar continued, "There are four more of us on the road in front, whom we shall overtake the day after tomorrow. And six more coming up behind. I'm dropping off one of the men to tell those six to move faster, so that they also will come up with us the day after tomorrow—except the messenger, of course. He must not appear again. With you two that'll make twenty-one for the job, against eleven. There's a good killing ground"—the Jemadar used the code word *bhil*—"on this road two days' march from here. Maybe we'll do it there. Maybe the day after. There's no great hurry."

Hussein had talked like this sometimes, preparing him for what he would hear. But the thing itself, put out in matter-of-fact sentences, chilled the ground under William's blanket and dried his lips. He muttered, "That is all clear."

The Jemadar said, "Yasin told me about your wrist. You'll let me know when you can work again, won't you? What of your friend here?"

Hussein was awake. He said, "Strangler, second grade, nineteen expeditions, seventy-four, fit for duty."

"Good." The Jemadar rose and bent over William. "By our Kali, I'm glad to see you! There's disaster in the air this season. I heard a rumor that two parties going south to a rendezvous lost their pickaxes." He shivered, squeezed William's hand, and was gone.

Hussein muttered, "You got through that well. And you are Gopal now!"

William pulled his blanket completely over his head in the Indian manner. The suffocating cold under it clogged his throat.

Hussein's numerous hints at the demon behind the curtain began to take shape. There was no clarity yet. Words were not clear, not spoken in daylight. But the truth was not in clarity. The truth was a bearded man lying beside him in the dark and whispering of death in an old, secret tongue.

Hussein knew that language well. He had been a Deceiver— "nineteen expeditions, seventy-four." Seventy-four? *Seventy-four?* William ground his teeth together. It was impossible to understand Hussein or to trust him. Or not to trust him.

*Beetoo*—an ordinary person, hence, one about to die. He began to think of the man with the aching loins who had admired the young harlot in the window. He had seemed a pleasant enough fellow, cheerful and not too well off. If he was here, he was about to die. The Nawab whom William had not seen was here, and therefore about to die. The noises he had made on his return painted him so that his character stood out. He was youngish—from his voice; happily irreligious—or why should he defy the commands of his Prophet and drink strong wine? good to his people—the sullen note in the servant's voice had changed to one of fatherly indulgence while he was putting his master to bed. And they were about to die, master and servant, killed by William Savage.

He was not going to use knife or rope or rumal on them. He was going to murder them with his voice, by not using it to say a word of warning. A shadow cast forward from that coming moment onto his spirit must have sent the vision of himself hanging by the neck. For the travelers, he was as much Death as the stranglers were. Back there in Madhya he had thought of this, but it was not like his anticipations. It was Death. What had Mary understood—everything or nothing?

"A band of six murderers . . ." Six? He remembered Hussein's little laugh and stifled a groan at his own stupidity. This was so powerful it would need a squadron of cavalry to crush it. More—several squadrons. And the squadrons could do nothing unless a spy saw all, and remembered, and guided them.

Shivering in the three o'clock cold, the compulsion grew strong in him to run out in the grove and shout, "Save yourselves! These men are murderers!"

But he did not know, except for the three officers—Jemadar Khuda Baksh and Yasin Khan and Piroo—which would be murderers and which victims. If he shouted, everyone would yell and everyone run. The beetoos would run, but they could not escape death, because it was everywhere—four ahead, six behind, how many more ahead again?—and himself.

He could not lie still against the prickling intensity of his thoughts, and the leaves and tiny twigs crackled under him as he shifted restlessly. Hussein muttered, "Lie still, fool!"

The epithet stung him. He was a fool, and he could not afford to be. He must harden his heart. Tonight he would have to carry what he had learned in his head. Tomorrow it would go down on the wafer-thin sheets of paper in his scrip. Once a week he would bury the papers under a tree and mark the trunk. Everything would be there—names, minute descriptions, past histories and future plans, routes traveled, methods of working. Under the marked trees would lie such a wealth of evidence that no one, not Mr. Wilson, not the Governor General, could ignore it. No one, ever again, would call him a fool.

In Madhya the myriad lights of Dewali twinkled along the streets. Sher Dil was a Mohammedan and did not allow any idolatrous lights on the bungalow itself, but the grooms and the tire-woman and the gardeners and the other servants had ringed their quarters, roof and floor, and made the compound a smoky labyrinth of gnomish lights.

In the bungalow Mr. Wilson stood in front of the fireplace in the drawing room, his hands clasped behind his back. A log fire burned in the grate and warmed him. He twisted his fingers together, clenching and unclenching them, his head bent a little forward. Mary sat in a chair opposite him, a piece of sewing on her lap.

Mr. Wilson said, "Mary, you promise me you do not know where he has gone?"

Mary did not look up. "I have no idea where he is, Daddy." She bit off the end of a thread and pushed it carefully through the eye of the needle.

"But—but you do not seem to care."

She kept her head down. "I care, Daddy. I don't have to burst into tears and have hysterics to care, do I? That won't help."

Mr. Wilson brought his hands forward and smashed his right fist into his left palm with sudden violence. "He is mad! He was under no disgrace. You heard what I said—you need not imagine that I failed to notice the open door." He gained control of himself. For a moment he seemed inclined to emphasize that he was an Agent to the Governor General, but he looked at her, saw his daughter, and said quietly, "Do you think that he has done away with himself?"

126

Mary began to cry when her father changed the tone of his voice and did not answer.

Mr. Wilson shook his heavy head and looked out at the beautiful Indian lights, which floated so mysteriously through the raw night, though never moving. His face was gray and his eyes tired. He had ridden from Sagthali in triple stages, foundering two horses, after the incredible rumor reached him. He said, "We will return to Sagthali tomorrow. Then, if you insist, you can wait with me as long as—until . . . The poor fellow! I fear the worst."

Mary kept her head down still. "I'm not coming to Sagthali, Daddy. I'm staying here."

Mr. Wilson exploded again. "You are not! Think of your baby!" He looked at her. No sign of her pregnancy showed: it wouldn't, of course—a first baby and not due for five months yet. She was very beautiful now. To clinch the matter he said, more calmly, "You cannot stay, because I have ordered George Angelsmith here. He will arrive tomorrow or the next day. The affairs of Khapa can wait for a new Collector. Here they cannot."

"I'm going to stay until my baby is born," Mary said quietly.

"You cannot, Mary. Do not be ridiculous! What will people say if you live here alone with George Angelsmith? Your poor mother—"

"I am going to stay, Daddy. William may expect me to be here. From Madhya I can't hear people's gossip in Sagthali—and I don't care, either."

"But Angelsmith—"

"Mr. Angelsmith will not worry me," Mary said, stitching busily, the needle clicking against her thimble, her head bent.

Mr. Wilson was filled with a frustration that he had not known since her mother left India to die. It had been frequent then, and just as mysterious. It was something to do with women, something to do with the baby, perhaps, and he could not be expected to understand. The power of his personality, the power of his office, became tangled and useless in his hands. He did not say another word but stalked heavily out of the room.

When he was gone Mary's needle hand stopped its steady shuttling. She sat still, not moving hand or finger or head or eyes, seeming not to breathe.

# Chapter 15

THE Nawab sang through his nose as he rode, his weak, handsome face altering with every moment. William and Hussein walked together, close on the off side of the Nawab's horse, ready to run his errands and applaud his singing. The grove by Jalpura lay two marches behind them, the sun was low on their left, and the road ahead twisted by many channels through rock-strewn grassy jungle. Ridges of basalt rose up on either side, set back a little distance, for the valley floor was half a mile wide. A small stream meandered back and forth, accompanying the pathway and the travelers north. In places it gurgled beside the track, in places the other side of the valley; for three or four hundred yards it would run level, slow and deep; then at a fault it would plunge over a ledge and for the next half-mile scamper down in angry shallows, turning the rocks in its bed slimy brown from the deposit of the soil it held in suspension.

The various groups, walking and riding, which composed the whole party of travelers, were now well spread out. In the mornings they started in a close bunch, like so many courtiers surrounding the Nawab's horse. As the day wore on, and men and animals grew tired, they straggled. The party had increased somewhat in size too, in spite of the one young fellow who had stayed behind in Jalpura for another round with the bazaar harlots, he'd said. This midday someone had recognized an acquaintance among four travelers resting at the wayside. The four had joined the column to the usual accompaniment of curses and grumbles from the Nawab's old servant. The Nawab himself had waved his hand largely in welcome.

There had been a few other people on the road, but most of them scurried by and seemed almost to avoid the mob now constituting the Nawab's entourage. Then, just an hour ago, six men had ridden up from the south behind the column. The Nawab stopped singing and invited them to join his following. They refused with brusque courtesy. They were in a hurry, they said, and must press on. The Nawab shrugged petulantly, and in ten minutes the six were out of sight and their dust had settled, leaving no trace of their passage.

Piroo sidled up on the Nawab's near side and said, "Great maharaj, where is your highness going to encamp tonight?"

The Nawab looked down superciliously. "I don't know. Soon. Ohé!" He raised his voice. "Who knows of a good camping place near here? Our friend Bat Ears has sore feet." William and Hussein cackled with laughter, as they had done a hundred times today and a hundred times yesterday.

Two men pushed forward, both speaking at once. Both said they had used this road often, but they had different opinions about campsites. One urged the Nawab to go to a grove about two miles on; the other recommended a place a mile and a half farther on, a place where, he said, there was a small village and good fruit to be had.

The Nawab stroked his chin. "Fruit? What sort? Peaches from Kandahar—all this way? Pomegranates from Kagan? I like pomegranates."

"The nearer ground is the more desirable, maharaj," the first man shouted. "I know them both. Cannot one of us, or your servant, go and get fruit from the village for your highness and all who want it?"

"Why, yes, I suppose so. But I'll take a look at this first place before deciding. If it's as good as you say, we'll go no farther. At least I won't. You gentlemen are free to go where you wish."

His audience laughed sycophantically at the notion that any of them would give up the honor of being in the Nawab's train, or desert the protection of his name and his servants and their guns and the pistol in his highness's sash.

The sun touched the western ridge and the valley widened out. A small track led off to the left, and the first man, walking beside the horse's head, cried, "It is down here, great maharaj. See, I think someone is there already." He pointed to a trail of smoking horse dung on the ground and the jumbled imprint of hoofs in the dust. The Nawab frowned dubiously and peered down the little track into the depths of shadow cast by a stand of towering bijasal trees.

The would-be guide broke out anxiously, as if some award of money rested on the Nawab's choice, "It is a paradise down there, maharaj. Running water, shady trees, cool grass under the trees—"

"Any girls?" said the Nawab, and again all within earshot burst out laughing and held their sides and nudged one another happily. The stragglers drifted up and formed a humble group, waiting at a little distance for the great man to make up his mind.

While the Nawab picked his nose thoughtfully and fiddled with the red leather embroidery on his reins, a man walked out of the hidden grove. Pausing, he raised his head, and then made a graceful salaam to the Nawab. He carried himself with dignity and his manner made clear that he was greeting an equal. William recognized him as one of the six men who had galloped past in such a hurry.

The Nawab returned the salutation, and the stranger said, "Sir, it is a pleasant place in there, where we are. May we not have the honor of your company? An hour ago we had to refuse. We meant to go much farther"—he shrugged—"but a horse went lame. What can one do?"

Helped by his body-servant, the Nawab slipped off his horse and bowed. "It will be a pleasure to converse with you, sir. These others, my friends"—he waved his jeweled hand at the crowd, sneering at the word "friends" as he said it—"they are good fellows all, and my companions of the road. But they are not, for the most part, either intelligent or amusing."

The crowd muttered in a mild chorus of self-abasement, "No, no, we are uneducated people."

The traveler who had wanted to go on and camp by the village drew nervously away and joined his palms. "Maharaj, maharaj, I must go on. I have business to transact in that village, and I have come two hundred miles for it."

The Nawab's lip curled. "I expect we can survive without you, O dealer in rats' droppings. Now at least we know why you lauded that place. It's probably a filthy hole, but what would you care? You would have been inside the village. Go!"

"We will go with him, maharaj." Three others spoke in whining unison from the outskirts of the crowd. "We too must move fast. We are near our homes. Is there permission?"

The Nawab shrugged his shoulders. "You, too, hurry? To surprise strange men putting out fires in your marriage beds? There is permission."

He jerked his head irritably. On the road much of a man's importance was assessed by the size of his following. The four deserters shuffled quickly away together, each obviously relieved that he would not have to cover the mile and a half alone. The crowd threw a few sneering taunts after them.

The main group of travelers entered the grove behind the Nawab and his new friend. Under the great trees they spread out and sought places to cook and sleep. A happy, tired clatter and chatter arose. Men unloaded the Nawab's packhorses and set up his green silk pavilion and the curtained annex that was his wives' portion. The horses were watered and tethered at the downwind end of the grove, and their riders and grooms cut grass and threw it down before them.

William laid his belongings by the bank of the stream, collected dry twigs and leaves, lit them with flint and steel, and knelt to blow on the infant fire. Yasin Khan the dark man passed by, stooping to pick up firewood. With that distant softness he said, "After food. The Jemadar will give the signal: *The stars are shining bright.* Prayers now, for selected stranglers only. You come. Up that way. Three hundred paces."

William gave no sign that he heard and went on with his blowing. Yasin Khan moved slowly away, lending his sacerdotal quality even to the task of picking up sticks.

The encampment did not seem to empty, but William was on the alert and watching carefully. Here and there a man would drift beyond the vaguely defined boundaries of the grove, drift back a minute later, and soon wander off once more, this time not to return. Unless he had been devoting his attention to it, and unless he had known whom to watch, he could not have said whether any particular man was present or absent. He damped down his fire and followed their example, mooning carelessly about at the edge of the grove and at last walking unhurriedly into the jungle.

131

Outside a dense thicket three hundred yards in, Piroo was bent beside a game trail, picking up twigs. He jerked his head to the left. William turned and scrambled through thick scrub into a small clearing. A stunted neem tree stood in the center of the clearing. All around the leaves were thick, enclosing the tree within a high green wall. A small stone idol lay on its face in the grass. It was very old; several centuries of sun and rain had weathered it and smoothed out its shape. Often William came across these fallen images in the jungle, and always, when he asked about them, received the same answer: They were kings of old time, turned to stone in battles against the heroes of the Mahabharata. But the men in the clearing ignored the idol. It was the tree, the dark evergreen neem, to which Yasin Khan made a short obeisance. William and the others followed suit. He saw with relief that Hussein was here, and the Jemadar, and five more.

Yasin said, "We have no time to waste, Jemadar-sahib. Shall I begin?"

"Yes."

Yasin fumbled under the blanket draping his shoulders and brought out a folded white sheet and a small pickax. The pickax had been hanging, haft downward, in an extra loop of his loincloth. William remembered that every day of the march Yasin had carried the pickax in that manner, and that he had seen it every day, and the pattern of whorls and triangles on it, and had not till this moment remarked the fact, or connected the pickax with those others he had found on the trail of the thakur's murderers. True, many travelers carried tools and weapons. . . . William rubbed his hands across his eyes and shivered.

Yasin spread the sheet on the grass, first removing twigs and loose dirt from under it. He glanced at the sky, where the stars were beginning to prick through dusty blue twilight, and laid the pickax on the sheet, its point toward the north, the direction of the band's travel. Then he took position behind the sheet, facing west. The Jemadar and the rest arranged themselves in a line behind him.

Yasin joined his palms together, raised his eyes to the sky, and sighed, "O Kali, thy servants are waiting. Grant them thy approval, they pray."

132

They stood with heads bowed, their faces purposeful and religiously calm. William heard his own heart beating and felt his nerves tightening with theirs. While Yasin spoke, he wondered what power made the Jemadar, and Yasin himself, who were Mohammedans, bow down and pray to the Hindu Destroyer-Goddess Kali. But whatever they waited for, whatever the reason or superstition that held them, he waited with them, and was held as they were held. Faintly through the trees he heard the sounds of the encampment, the whinny of a horse, a woman's faint call. He waited long minutes, and in the clearing no one made a sound.

A jungle-fowl, frightened by an unknown enemy, rocketed into the treetops out of sight to the left. Catching the alarm, another rose, to the right.

The Deceivers sighed, breathed out, and relaxed their stiff shoulders. William let go his breath in a gasp. Yasin cried, in the voice of a warden of holy writ, low and awed and triumphant, "Kali, we hear! We are thy servants! We obey!"

He took up the pickax and tucked it into his waist, folded the sheet and hid it under his blanket. All the men, except William, pulled rumals from their waistbands and ran them once or twice through their hands. Yasin moved down the line and gave each man a new silver rupee, murmuring a blessing as he did so. Then each man tied the silver coin into one end of the rumal, made a knot there, again ran the rumal two or three times through his fingers, and tucked it back into his waistband. All except the Jemadar and Yasin left a tiny corner showing. William felt a little spurt of craftsman's pride: he could pull out the rumal without leaving a corner ready to his hand. That total concealment, he now knew, was the mark of a strangler who had been formally taught by a professor; it was the strangler's doctorate. He had not been taught, but his hands had known without being told.

One by one the men left the clearing. The Jemadar turned to William. "I think that'll do, don't you? Kali will accept the prayers of us few as a token?"

William said, "Yes, I'm sure she will."

The Jemadar took him by the arm. "The wonderful omens! I know they were granted because you've joined us." He embraced William happily. "This is the first time I've really had a chance to

133

speak to you alone. You haven't changed a bit. You always were marked out for Kali's special favors."

The affection of an old friend lit the Jemadar's thin face. He had a pleasant voice, and a small curved nose with wide nostrils, and wore the green turban of a man who has made the pilgrimage to Mecca. William had examined him covertly on the road and could easily imagine that they had been friends. He smiled now and returned the Jemadar's embraces, hug for hug.

The Jemadar said, "I'll wager you haven't lost any of your skill either, though you may be out of practice. Now I *know* we will have a good expedition. When we set out at Dussehra the omens were good. But since then we've fallen in with only two likely travelers, and they were miserable wretches—suspicious faces, sharp knives, and no money. We thought Kali was angry with us for some reason, and had given us the good omens only to lead us more surely to destruction. Allah knows the Deceivers aren't what they used to be. But you never told me—what have you been doing all these years?"

William thought of the woman at the pyre by the Seonath. Gopal the weaver, whose personality he had assumed but whom he had never met, had tried to give up the goddess Kali for a woman. In the end, the goddess had come and reclaimed his spirit, so that he returned to her. William understood very clearly now; the woman at the pyre would haunt him forever; he had chained her to a memory of her man; and her man had chained himself afresh to Kali.

William understood nearly everything. His brain worked with facile, unhurried speed. Never in his ordinary life had he found it so easy to think. His plan and his immediate action sprang up like obvious milestones before him.

Smiling, he answered the Jemadar's question. "I got married."

The Jemadar clapped him on the shoulder. "And couldn't leave her day or night for so many years? Well, well! You're back now, and still one of the greatest. You just need a little practice—and in the speech too. Only practice makes perfect. Even you will have to pay for those years in bed!" He laughed, winked, and slipped out of the clearing.

Two minutes later William wandered back toward the grove,

134

thinking hard. When he came near the first big trees Piroo rose up from nowhere, touched his arm, and pushed a bundle of twigs into his hand. "What have you been doing all this time, away from the camp? Are you so great you can ignore all common sense?"

William looked down and saw that the little man was furiously angry, his large ears trembling and red. He became angry in his turn and answered shortly, "I wasn't collecting wood. My bowels are loose."

"Then where's your lotah?"

Piroo glowered at him, and his heart sank. That would indeed have been a foolish explanation to give to any idle questioner. He remembered that Piroo had not been in the clearing for the prayers. As an officer, it was probable that he usually attended. Also, William saw that Piroo used a black rumal, and the corner of it showed; so Piroo was self-taught. Piroo had been relegated, because of him, and Piroo was very jealous.

He wanted to apologize but could not find the words, so he took the wood, went to his place, crouched, and began to blow up his dying fire.

Hussein was a little distance off, his back turned, bending over his own fire. William whispered, trying to speak low in the manner of the Deceivers, "Did you hear that in the clearing with the Jemadar?"

"Yes."

"Was it all right?"

Hussein banged a small pot vehemently onto his fire. "All right? It depends. You realize you can't have a sprained wrist forever?" William saw his shoulders shake and thought he was sobbing.

They began to eat. The Nawab ate seated on a carpet beside a roaring fire sixty feet from William's place. The fire was so big that its leaping flames turned the grove into an amphitheater of red light. The clean boles of the bijasals stood up like pillars in the circle, red on one side, indigo blue on the other. The sound of crackling branches dominated the encampment. All the travelers ate, and the only voices to be heard were low and unhurried.

When he had finished, William washed the pans in the water, cleaned them with dirt from the stream bed and ashes from the fire, and squatted down as if talking to Hussein, but Hussein only looked at him with large, sad eyes, and moved his lips, but spoke no words.

The slow twang of a zither tinkled under the trees, carrying out to the travelers the tune of a northern love song. The Nawab reclined in a silk robe on his carpet, the pipe of a hookah to his mouth. The old body-servant squatted at his feet. To the right the Nawab's three wives showed as motionless, featureless shapes behind a screen of gold gauze hung between two trees. From every corner of the grove the travelers drifted across the grass toward the music and the light. William rose to his feet and looked at Hussein. Hussein nodded.

By the fire it was very like the scene in the grove near Kahari, where they had watched the murder of the Sikh and his son. Always at night on the road it was the same, because always travelers rested in these groves and lit fires, and sat around them. But there were more people here tonight, and William knew what would come, and feared it, but could not wish it away. He searched his mind and found no desire to warn the Nawab of his fate. He awaited the signal with gnawing eagerness.

It was the Jemadar who played the zither. The crowd thickened about the fire. Before squatting down, each new arrival made low salaam to the Nawab and in the direction of the gold curtain. The Nawab's eyes were half closed, and he nodded his head in time with the music. The Jemadar was singing softly:

"Moon of the north, thy hands are lotus blossoms,
Moon of the north, thy lips are rose petals,
Petals stronger than steel,
Petals which touch the steel,
And bend it, and make it weak.
Moon of the north, dark eyed, shine on me!
Moon of the north . . ."

His voice wavered up and down the chromatic scale, sliding from note to note, slithering, holding. The zither twanged and twanged, the fire crackled. The audience relaxed in their places and sighed.

At the end they clapped their hands, beating them together at the wrists with low murmurs of appreciation. The Nawab said thickly, "Play on! What is your name, haji? Khuda Baksh? A hum-

136

ble jeweler? You are a bulbul, and worthy of a perch by the King's ear at Delhi. Play on, sing on!"

The Jemadar began another song, low and muted in tone and sad.

"*The bird of the plains sings at dawn.*
*Who shall hear the lone bird in the morning?*
*But you, my love . . . ?"*

He sang a parable of the tragedy of love, despairing and endlessly long. Half the audience dozed off. Others closed their eyes and swayed gently on their heels in rhythms hardly distinguishable to William's ear. The singer sang softer and lower. In time, with the torpor of the song, men moved slowly, like sleepwalkers, about the grove. Two stood entranced behind the Nawab's carpet, three more at the sides of the gold cloth, but not so close that the old servitor would feel it necessary to tell them to keep their distance.

The singer sang so quietly that he could be heard only because there was otherwise utter silence. The fire was quiet. The nasal whine traditional to this music went out of the singer's voice. In the same low key, but in his ordinary speaking tone, he said, "*The stars are shining bright.*"

With the sudden brilliance of lightning the Deceivers struck. Around the fire the cloths flew out, the rumals William had seen consecrated. Men, singly or in pairs, jumped behind their victims. Beside William a small sleepy man leaned forward in a doze; and beyond, the ascetic gentleman who had invited the Nawab into the grove. The gentleman's delicate face froze in murder; he swung a rumal with his right hand. The weighted end, the rupee in it, whirled round the small man's neck into his left hand. The strangler's wrists were turned inward and pressed close together. With a savage explosion of effort he snapped his wrists inward and upward. The small man's head jerked back, a horrible panic mixed with the calm of sleep on his face. The face of the strangler tightened in the firelight, and he drew back his lips and bared his teeth. His wrists cracked with an audible force, his knee drove into the small man's back. A bone snapped, the small man's brown eyes bolted, and he was dead.

Across the fire the Nawab stared with bulging eyeballs into the flames, but he could not see anything, for he was dead. By his feet his servant writhed and heaved in colossal throes that threatened to upset Piroo, the strangler across his back. A knife flashed and blood spouted from Piroo's thigh, staining his loincloth and pouring down over the old servant's neck. The Jemadar called urgently, "Wait! Hold him!" Stooping down, he drove a dagger into the old man's side between the ribs.

The gold curtain heaved and bulged. The three men who had been standing beside it were gone from sight. Except for the Jemadar's cry there had been no sound. William squatted in his place, cold, turned to stone.

The Jemadar came across to him. "You look amazed, Gopal." He wiped his dagger on a leaf, dropped the leaf carefully in the fire, and clapped William's shoulder. "It wasn't so neatly done as it should have been. Quick, to the grave!"

He snapped his fingers at the stranglers, who stood in groups around the fire with exultant, sweaty faces. In pairs and threes they lifted up the corpses and staggered with them across the grove and through the jungle to the clearing where the afternoon's ceremony had been held.

Piroo led the way with a hand lantern, limping slightly from his wound; already he had bound it up so that neither the wound nor the bandage showed beneath his loincloth. He walked across the clearing, under the solitary neem, past the abandoned idol, and stopped at the far bushes. He held up the lamp while the others pushed past him, groaning with suppressed pride at the weight of their loads, and forced through the thorns. In a few seconds the Jemadar stopped under a dense clump of prickly bamboo. William, close on his heels, saw that a circular pit surrounded the bamboo's multiple stems. The bamboo stood on a little island of earth, its murderous spines leaning out over the pit. The earth fill lay round the rim of the pit, and on the earth there were three sharpened bamboo stakes, a thick log, and a short rough-hewn club.

Piroo hurried up and set down the lantern. The men laid the bodies on the ground. Piroo and five others undressed down to the string about their loins and put their clothes carefully on one side. Then the six of them, working in pairs without a word spoken, began to break the victims' joints at knee and elbow. They laid each body over the log and with the club smashed the joints. When that was done they dragged the body to one side, picked up a stake, lifted together, and drove it through and through the corpse's belly. Then they lowered them one by one into the grave.

Stiff-jawed, William stared down at the disarray of the women's clothing; their wide eyes held the same mixed expressions that he had seen in the small man killed next to him. In each pasty brown face panic and disbelief mingled with the woman's last previous emotion. The rapt pleasure at the jeweler's song of love lingered on.

The pit filled and became a welter of bloody cloth, bursting entrails, and staring eyes. The flame of the lamp jumped as the Deceivers moved past it, each time lending the mangled pieces another jerky moment of life. William held to a tree for support and strained to keep down the vomit in his throat. Hussein, crouching the other side of the pit under the bamboo spines, watched him.

A party of stranglers returned to the encampment and came back with the belongings of the dead—the saddlebags and blankets and cooking pots, the Nawab's silk tent and carpet, the women's beautiful curtain, anything that was not worth taking or that might arouse inquiry All went into the pit.

The Jemadar said, "Finished? And ten bodies? That's all, isn't it?"

"Yes."

The Jemadar gave a sign. Piroo threw the stakes, the club, and the log into the pit. Other men worked with their hands to push back the earth fill, covering the bodies and raising a low circular mound around the bamboo. Bending under the spines they stamped down the earth, then smoothed it and spread leaves and grass over it. When all was done they rubbed their hands on the ground, carefully picked up their clothes, and stood waiting.

The Jemadar said, "O diggers, come forward."

More men struggled through the bushes at the side, men William had never seen. The Jemadar said to one of them, "It was well done. Difficult digging here under the bamboo, but an excellent place. We didn't hear a sound. When did you begin?"

"As soon as your prayers were finished, Jemadar-sahib."

The Jemadar repeated, "It was well done. We will check here in daylight, as usual. Move on now to Manikwal. Meet us there. I think—I am sure—that this merits a feast. We'll eat your damned bear, eh?"

The leader of the diggers snickered, as at an old joke, and led his men away.

The Jemadar picked up the lamp and walked back to the grove; the band followed in single file behind him. William walked among them, thinking. Hussein had told him earlier what would be done, and that it was at Kali's command. Why? Hussein did not know. Who could read the mind of the Destroyer-Goddess? But William saw that a broken body took less space than a whole one; that a ripped belly released the gases of decomposition to filter up through the earth, while a whole belly swelled and at last forced up the soil, and caused wandering dogs and jackals to scratch and dig and run away, carrying a woman's arm for all to see. Hussein said that Kali commanded the Deceivers to scatter the seeds of fleawort over the grave, as a sacrifice, but William knew no jackal would sniff twice where those peppery seeds stung his nostrils.

Back by the remains of the great fire the Jemadar turned and raised his arms. "It was well enough done! Has Geb Khan's party come back yet?"

"No," Yasin answered. "I do not think we shall see them until morning. It depends when they found a chance with that fellow, the dealer in rats' droppings." He laughed quietly. "Our little Nawab had a sort of sulky wit."

William realized they were talking about the man who had wanted to go on to the village. The three who had accompanied him were all Deceivers. That man would not reach the village. He, at least, would never report that a large party, including the Nawab-sahib of Dukwan, was coming up the road and might be momentarily expected. The goddess Kali gave her children a long sight as well as a strong hand.

The Jemadar said, "We'll divide the spoil now. The sentries are out?"

"Yes," Yasin answered, "beside the main road. They say they cannot see the fire through the trees. They can smell it, though."

"It's after midnight. We'll risk that. Let's begin."

The band ranged themselves on one side of the fire. Piroo borrowed the pickax from Yasin and turned the earth at his feet

140

where the servant's blood had spilled out. He and the other five body smashers had washed themselves in the stream and put on their clothes.

Yasin spread two blankets. A sentry who had remained by the fire threw the loot in handfuls onto them. Rings and bangles, jewels and necklaces, showered down. The Nawab's sacks of gold mohurs poured out in a flashing torrent, and the fire became dim against the brilliance on the blankets. The sharing began, among good-tempered argument. The more valuable jewels were set aside in one heap, the coin and the lesser trinkets distributed.

William's hands hurt. He looked down and saw that he had pressed his nails through the skin of his palms. The pain nagged him, dragging his mind away from the glittering dreamland in which he sat, and forced him to think. The animation in his companions' faces and the cheerful rasp of their voices made him realize who and where he was. For the last six hours he had forgotten. From the time he entered the clearing and saw the broken idol and stood among the Deceivers in that anxious ceremony, he had been an acolyte in an old religion. Once, by the pit, he had tried to summon up again the shame of those previous nights when he had counted himself guilty of murders then uncommitted; but the shame would not come, only the embarrassed nausea of the new comrade, of the fledgling doctor. An aching half-religious lust had possessed him, to see what would happen next and be a part of it.

He clenched his teeth and sought to justify himself. It was only that he had been eager to get back to his notes and write down all the wonders and mysteries of the proceedings—that was all. The memory of the dead women wrenched him. Only one of them had been over nineteen. There had been a child of four and a smaller baby. One of them might have been Mary and her child.

The Jemadar was saying, "And my friend Gopal shall take part in the initial five per cent share-out to active stranglers. Of course he must also have the share allotted to all stranglers-by-rank in the general distribution."

"He can have the general share, if he *is* a strangler-by-rank," Piroo muttered sullenly, "but he has no right to any part of the five per cent unless he actually strangled this time. And he didn't. The rules are clear."

The Jemadar said coldly, "Who are you to talk to me about the rules? Kali gave us this haul just because she loves *him*, not through any part of your bungling."

"Perhaps," Piroo grumbled, cowed by his leader's fierceness.

"In fact, my friend," the Jemadar continued, "I am now going to appoint him to replace you as the assistant-jemadar, and you had better get used to the idea. You can buy the sugar still. But, tomorrow, stay behind here as daylight check-up man. That might help to teach you manners. You have the fleawort seed? Good. Here, Gopal!" He passed a palmful of gold and a few mohurs to William. William took them, murmured his thanks, and tucked them away. Hussein nudged him and gestured almost imperceptibly with his head. William rose to his feet.

"I'm going to sleep now, Jemadar-sahib."

"All right. Get your wrist well quickly. Thanksgiving is at first light, in the clearing. Then we'll get on to Manikwal. Do you want one of the Nawab's horses?"

"Ye-es." William hesitated. "Don't you think they might be recognized?"

"No. We'll sell them in Manikwal, anyway, and get others. Sleep well."

William salaamed again and walked to his blanket. As he prepared for sleep he muttered to Hussein, "Thanksgiving is the ceremony of communion with Kali, isn't it, when we all take the sugar?"

Hussein said, "Yes. I don't know what god to pray to but Kali, and she's laughing at me. Please, Gopal, keep off the blanket tomorrow if you can. Don't eat the consecrated sugar. Eat of the other, the part that is put aside before consecration. . . . What's the use? You'll have to, or Piroo will get more suspicious than he is already. And he can ruin us if anything makes him try. We're trapped." He looked up suddenly and said, "I know. You *want* to eat the consecrated sugar."

William tried to laugh, but the laugh choked in his throat. At last, lying in his blanket and feeling hot and cold at once, he said, "I don't want to, Hussein. I just don't care. It is all superstition."

Hussein did not answer, and William said *superstition, superstition*, over and over to himself, and went to sleep, and did not dream.

142

# Chapter 16

IT was dark when William stepped shivering out of his blanket and stripped. He washed from head to foot in the stream, standing knee deep in the black rush of water. Afterward, as the light spread and mist wraiths crept out from the river, he walked through the jungle to the clearing. A heavy dew weighted the stems of grass and pearled the red sandstone robes of the idol. All the band, except the mysterious group of diggers who had appeared during the burial, stood in an untidy huddle round the neem tree. The light filtered gray and unwilling between the interstices of the jungle wall. It was cold, and William trembled. Last night in the grove everything had taken color from the fire—the jewels catching it, the faces glowing from it, the blood brightened by it. This morning the world and the people in it were gray, dusty white, dull brown.

The Jemadar greeted him solemnly, looked about as though counting, and said, "One on sentry, three buying merchandise up the road, the rest all here. Are you ready, Yasin?"

Yasin nodded and stepped out of the crowd. He spread his own and another blanket on the grass, side by side in front of the neem tree. He was carrying a brass lotah full of water in his right hand, holding it by the neck against the outside of his thigh. He set the lotah carefully down on the blankets and held out his hand imperiously. Piroo gave him a heavily filled cotton bag. Yasin held the bag upside down. A torrent of congealed lumps of coarse brown sugar poured out onto the blanket. He glanced over his shoulder. The Deceivers were separating into two groups: in one, the four or five men who William knew did not rank as stranglers; in the other, the rest—the stranglers.

William tried to edge over to the smaller group, but the Jemadar held him back, whispering, "By rank. Stay here." William saw Piroo looking at him suspiciously, and Hussein's worried eyes.

Yasin counted the smaller group, carried a part of the sugar over to them, and set it on the grass. They bowed and stood behind their portion, facing west.

Yasin returned to the blankets and placed a rupee from his scrip beside the sugar. He took the pickax from his waistband and dug a small hole in the earth just beyond the blankets. After cleaning the pick blade with his rumal, he laid the tool on the blanket beside the sugar and the rupee. He sat down at last on the forward edge of the blankets and crossed his legs.

The stranglers paced slowly forward and sat down in two tight rows on the blankets, to left and right of Yasin and behind him. All faced west. William hesitated again, but he had to go. He sat down on the left of the second row.

Yasin clasped his hands together, raised his eyes, and cried in a deep, thrilled chant, "Great goddess, as in old time thou vouchsafed one hundred and sixty-two thousand rupees to Jhora Naik and Koduk Bunwari in their need, so, we beseech thee, fulfill our desires."

The stranglers clasped their hands and bent forward from the waist, and William imitated them. They muttered together, repeating the prayer, "Great goddess, as in old time thou vouchsafed . . ." William heard the murmur of the little group on the grass behind.

All fell silent. No wind stirred the boughs of the neem. The mist had cleared, nothing blunted the hard edges of the dawn. Yasin picked up the rupee in his right hand and dropped it into the hole he had dug. He took a little sugar and crumbled it in his fingers over the hole, so that the sugar streamed down on the rupee. He took the lotah and sprinkled water into the hole. Lastly he put his rumal, folded, on his right hand, laid the pickax crosswise on the rumal, supported his right hand with his left, and raised the pickax level with his chest. He lifted his head once more.

"O Kali, greatest Kali, thy servants thank thee for the magnificence of thy gift. We have done thy will, and wrought for thy glory. We pray now for thy further guidance and blessing. Guard us and keep us, as we guard thy memory among men, now and forevermore. Amen."

144

He raised the pickax slightly on his hands, repeating the action three times. The echoes of his voice died.

A black crow descending squawking from the sky and settled on the neem tree, behind and a little to the left of the blankets. At once a shrike started out of the bushes to the right and flew like an arrow between the trees, its insect prey in its beak.

The Deceivers crooned in ecstasy. From the corner of his eye William saw the exaltation in the face of the man next to him.

Yasin Khan's organ voice boomed, "Kali, mighty Kali, we obey, we praise thy name, we are thine!"

He stood up. With a whisper of cloth all the Deceivers stood. Yasin's cupped right palm was full of the coarse sugar lumps, and his left hand supported his right. He turned and with slow steps approached the strangler who stood at the right edge of the front blanket. Yasin held out the sugar. The man took a piece, carried it to his mouth, bowed his head, and ate in silence.

Yasin murmured, "Take, eat, this is the sweetness of Kali. You are hers and she is yours."

The strangler raised his head, and Yasin moved to the next man, always keeping his feet on the blankets. He held out the sugar. "Take, eat, this is the sweetness of Kali. You are hers and she is yours."

*Take, eat, this is the sweetness of Kali . . . Take, eat . . . You are hers and she is yours . . .*

Icicles of sweat pierced William's forehead and splintered between his shoulder blades. His mouth ached. He would not be able to touch the sugar when it came to him. He wished desperately that he had something wooden, hard, to hold in his hands—a cross. Not silver, not sweet-smelling—only wood, rough bitter wood, would serve. The feel of it might help him to face what he had to, or give him strength to break away, spring off the enchanted blanket, and run. Hussein had a cross.

He saw Yasin reach Hussein, in front of him. Yasin's eyes were half closed and his prayer a litany "Take, eat, this is the sweetness of Kali." Hussein held onto something at his waist, but he had to let go. Kali required both his hands. His fingers crawled out, so slowly that he seemed to be trying to pull them back against a

145

force stronger than their own muscles. He took a piece of sugar at last, bowed, and swallowed. William closed his eyes.

When he opened them, Yasin's luminous face swam into focus a foot away. Yasin was a saint, transported now into the arms of his goddess, and love ached in his voice.

*Take, eat* . . . William put out his right hand.

*This is the sweetness of Kali* . . . William bowed his head and touched his lips to the sugar. He picked it up with his tongue. His stomach rose to meet it. He had expected it to taste of the death that tainted it, and of silver, but he swallowed it—it was just sugar. He ate it down.

*You are hers and she is yours.* Yasin moved on to the next man.

All his nausea gone, William glanced over his shoulder and saw that those on the grass were handing round their unconsecrated sugar and eating it. Yasin returned to his place, picked up the lotah, and began again, at the right of the blankets, offering each man water.

"Take, drink, this is the milk of Kali. You are hers and she is yours."

Each man held his right hand to his mouth and Yasin poured a little water onto his palm and so down his throat. William drank confidently. It was all rank superstition, and only the chill of the dawn and the remembered horrors of last night had upset his stomach.

When all had drunk, Yasin returned to his place, filled in the hole and covered it with leaves and twigs, and put the pickax back into his waistband. The Deceivers stood in silence and waited. Yasin stepped off the blankets.

The Deceivers relaxed, and moved away, and began to chatter excitedly. "Do you think the crow could see the stream from up there?" "Of course it could! Look, over those bushes. We can almost see it from down here."

The Jemadar seized William's arm. "I don't remember omens as good as that for—oh, many, many years! The crow was on a tree" —he ticked off on his fingers—"on our left, in sight of water. The omen on the right came within one second—less!" He smoothed down his mustache and beard. "Come on, let us ride to Manikwal, you and I. We've got some horses now. Yasin Khan and your friend

146

Hussein can come with us, on foot. Everyone else knows what to do."

"All right. Give me a few minutes to get packed and saddled up."

"I'll meet you in the grove."

The walled town of Manikwal lay fifteen miles to the northeast. William had heard of it as a populous little place with the provincial reputation of a Gomorrah. Its ruler he had met once in Madhya, a bawdy old reprobate who ruled his people with an open but heavy hand. In this country, on the southern marches of Bandelkhand, a tangle of tiny states overlapped and interlaced; wars and marriages had given them the most unlikely geographies—some were actually contained complete within others, and few were of any size.

William walked his horse at the Jemadar's side. The November sun warmed them. They could see the town for two hours before they reached it in the afternoon. Like Jalpura, its houses stepped up, one behind the other, on the side of a hill. It, too, had a lake, but the rajah took little care of anything except his pleasures, and the townspeople had planted water chestnut, and the lake would soon be a clogged, noisome swamp. But the town wall was in good repair, and an armed man guarded the gate. They rode past him into the town.

A press of people filled the narrow street. William looked up the hill to see what excited them, for they were all peering in that direction. He heard distant, isolated shouts and the echoing boom of a cannon fired from the rajah's fort at the crown of the slope. The Jemadar leaned down—he was so trimly correct today, the ideal of a competent tradesman—and said to a man at his stirrup, "What's happening, friend?"

"Don't know. Someone being executed, I suppose."

The Jemadar looked at William meaningfully. When on the road, the Deceivers counted it a good omen to see a man being taken to execution or a corpse on its way to the burning.

A camel lurched over the brow of the hill and walked down with short, rubbery strides between the heaving crowds. The man on its back jerked to its movement till William thought he must fall off.

147

The camel strode closer, and William saw that the rider's feet were roped together under its belly. He was a little rabbit of a man with protruding teeth and a mean, close face. His clothes were in the disarray of one already dead, torn down the front and hanging in tatters at his sides, and his head was bare. From the lonely height of the camel's hump he looked about with lackluster eyes, seeking escape but knowing there was none. The camel passed, and the horses stamped and snorted, backing away from its acrid-stale smell. The camel held its head high, its lip curled in the perpetual camel sneer.

Behind the camel an elephant paced gingerly down the steep. Two men in ragged uniform on its back shouted continually, "See the justice of our prince! A thief goes to execution! See the justice of our prince!"

The elephant passed, its ridiculously trousered backside clowning in the presence of death. The cries of the executioners passed. The people closed in across the street behind the elephant and followed. They were going to see the execution. Soon, after many ceremonies, the ragged soldiers would rope the thief to the elephant's forefoot and make it run about on the flat earth beside the lake. The elephant would try to lift its feet and not tread on the man as he dragged along under its belly; but in the end it had to trample him.

The street was deserted. The Jemadar said softly, "Just an ordinary little thief. They always get caught—and serves them right! They're so weak."

William did not know whether he agreed. Certainly the little thieves of the world led weak, ordinary lives.

The Jemadar continued, "I'm not sure that we won't get like that soon. Things aren't what they used to be in our brotherhood. Piroo's very pessimistic. Of course, he's jealous"—he smiled at William—"he threatened to quit the road. Says he's going to retire, buy some land, and take up his trade."

"What's that?" William asked idly, not really listening but waiting with painful expectancy for his inner ear to catch the elephant's bewildered trumpeting and the scream of the crowd.

The Jemadar said, "He's a carpenter."

William said, "Oh, is he?" and thought of Piroo afresh. Jealous,

148

wanting to be strong; a little weak, a little stupid. He himself was a carpenter. They were not unlike.

The Jemadar said, "Here," and turned into a lane between tall houses. The boarded lower stories facing the street showed that this was the harlots' quarter of the town. The boards would be removed at dusk. The lane smelled of filth and human urine. Behind the houses they entered a stableyard and dismounted. Hussein and Yasin stabled the horses.

An old woman stuck her head out of a glassless window opening. "Hey, what do you want?"

The Jemadar turned. "Travelers, princess. We would like to use your upper back room for a week or so."

The old woman chuckled. "Princess, my arse! How many of you, haji?"

"Four here, one more to come."

"All right. Find your own way up."

They dragged their kits up a steep, straight, very narrow flight of stairs which was walled in with bare brick. The room at the top was big and completely unfurnished. Two small square window holes in one wall, under the eaves of the house, let in light and air. Numerous stains and splotches discolored the splintered wood floor. A patch of dried mud-plaster covered the wood in one corner. A heap of gray ash, and the dark smoke smudges on the wall, and the bricks lying ready for use as pot rests, showed that that was the cooking place. Loosely joined tiles paved a second corner; there a drain hole made by removing two bricks from the outer wall denoted that it was the washing place. William did not ask where the toilet was; that, he knew, would be anywhere in the stableyard or along the alley.

The Jemadar threw his belongings down in the middle of the floor. "This'll do. Phuh, the whole place smells of women. Piroo won't like that—he's terrified of 'em. Leave room for him, by the way." He pulled a small mirror out of his saddlebag and hung it on a nail that stuck out from between the bricks. He got out a pair of tweezers and began to prune his upper lip. He said, speaking with his mouth twisted to one side, "We'll stay here a week. It's a good town to rest up and get information about who and what is moving on the roads. We'll have the feast on our last day, the Friday—

ow!—and women afterward. There's a woman waiting for you, my old friend!" He grinned at William and put away the tweezers.

There's a woman waiting . . . William thought of Mary, who waited for him in Madhya, and sewed, and got up, and sat down again, and listened to every sound inside and outside the bungalow, and waited for him to ripen in her womb. He thought of the woman who waited at the pyre beside the Seonath, and did not move, and listened, and hoped.

Yasin laid the pickax on the floor, turned it until its head pointed north, then unrolled his blanket over it and put his saddlebags over all. The Jemadar watched respectfully and, when Yasin was ready, said, "Are you coming out? I want to see about selling these nags and getting some others a little less good-looking."

"All right."

"You?" The Jemadar turned to William.

"I don't think so, Jemadar-sahib. I'll rest here a while."

"Me too," Hussein said.

The other two left the room. William listened to the Jemadar's riding slippers clack down the long stair. He watched through a window until the men had crossed the yard and gone out of view.

He turned to Hussein. "Piroo won't be here for an hour or so yet, will he?"

"No, not till after dark."

"Good. I'll get on with the first installment of my report. Tomorrow you or I can go out and bury it outside the town."

He got out the fine sheets of paper, lay down on his stomach under one of the windows, and began to write against the uneven surface of the floor, using a short pencil and forming the letters as small as he could. He had much to record, much that would help the world and his superiors to understand the Deceivers, even if he himself did not live to write another word. He licked his lip, licked the end of the pencil, and struggled on.

After half an hour Hussein, whom he had realized as a silent, vaguely unhappy presence in the room, blurted, "What do you think you're going to do with those notes?"

William put the pencil down carefully, rubbed his eyes, and looked up. "I told you. I'm going to take them outside the town

150

and bury them, and pick them up later when we've finished this—this expedition."

Hussein's face was compressed with misery. "You're never going to use any of those notes against the Deceivers."

"Of course I am," William said, growing unreasonably angry.

"You're not, because you are a Deceiver, from this dawn on forever. A strangler. Only stranglers may stand on the blanket: you stood on it. Only stranglers may take the consecrated sugar of communion: you took it. It doesn't matter what a man *thinks* he is. When he eats consecrated sugar, on the blanket, in front of the pickax, he is a strangler, because Kali enters into him. It has happened before that men with no training or aptitude have got on the blanket by mistake. Always Kali gives them the skill and the strength they need." He took his head in his hands and groaned. "Now you are a strangler. Now you will never return to your office. Now I will never be a chuprassi. We could not help it," he finished, suddenly resigned. "Kali wills it, so it is."

William said furiously, "You're talking the rankest, most idiotic superstition!" In himself he did not think so, and was frightened, and uncannily elated. He went on, "Besides, you had eaten the sugar before, when you first became a Deceiver, and you had given up your old ways."

"Had I? Had I? That's what I thought! Did you see me last night?"

Hussein came close and pushed his contorted face down into William's. William remembered a traveler across the fire last night, listening dreamily to the zither; Hussein's sharpened nose and drawn-back lips; the traveler's bolting eyes. He was silent.

Hussein continued urgently, "Gopal, do you realize that not one Deceiver's wife in a hundred knows what he is? That the Deceivers have homes and places in society? That they leave their homes, and travel as if on ordinary business, and come back? That their children never know, unless a son is initiated into his father's band? I think perhaps I have been a servant of Kali even in my treachery to her, when I preferred the woman to her, and ran away, and at last found you. Why couldn't you be a Deceiver? Why not? The Saint Nizam-ud-Din was one, the Rajah of—oh, many great men for hundreds of years past. Why not you? You travel, don't you?"

151

You meet travelers who seek the protection of your convoys. We Deceivers could find men for all your staff, all your police, clerks, bungalow servants, jailers, chuprassis."

William sprang to his feet. "You dirty murderous filth! Hold your tongue! I am not a strangler. I never will be. I am not going to kill, whatever happens. I'm not going to! Do you understand?"

Hussein said again, "You are a strangler. You cannot help yourself now."

William raised his hand to strike, but Hussein was not angry, only sad. Shivering a little, William tucked away his papers and pencil and left the room.

For a time he wandered about the streets, now sunless and gray in the hour before the lamps were lit. From the foot of the town he heard the scream of an elephant and a faint, faint human cry, caught up at once in the shrill, formless cacophony of a crowd. They had spent a long time in the lovely sunset glow beside the lake, and the ordinary little thief had given them good night.

William stood in a place where the street widened. A few small boys had foregone the execution for the equal thrill of watching a newly arrived troupe of traveling conjurors set up their pitch. The leader of the troupe led a dancing bear round and round on its chain and called shrilly to the people to come and see the wonders of his show.

"See the bear that dances like a girl! O come and see! See the cut rope that heals itself! O come and see!"

He looked straight at William as he passed and held out his bowl for alms. The bear sniffed at William's feet and whined, but the man gave no sign that he had ever seen William before. William turned and hurried back to the room above the house of the harlots.

# Chapter 17

ON the morning of the feast, a Friday six days later, William and Hussein were appointed as ceremonial assistants to Yasin. The preparations were an endless rite, hedged about with exact instructions which had come in the beginning from the mouth of the goddess herself. Generations of Deceivers had passed on the sacred words, and Yasin knew them all; that was why he was the priest of the band.

While Piroo and the Jemadar went around the town completing their purchases and gossiping with merchants and travelers, the other three worked hard. In the morning they walked into the fields and brought back covered baskets of earth and cow dung and pitchers of water; with these materials they plastered twenty square feet in the middle of the floor and let it dry. That work was a token; usually the Deceivers held their feasts on the ground level, where the whole earth floor would have to be so prepared.

At noon Yasin covered the windows with blankets, swept out the room, and stowed the baggage neatly in one far corner. Afterward he mixed turmeric and lime together and with the powder drew lines on the dried plaster of the floor, enclosing a square of one-cubit sides. Then he damped some of the same powder with water, slipped out to the landing, and rapidly painted an eye on the outside of the door, to frighten away idle visitors. Then he put rice to boil in great pots. There was not enough water, and he said briefly, intent on his sacraments of preparation, "You two, go and fetch more water. Hurry!"

William and Hussein took the pitchers and hastened down the stairs. It was hot in the midafternoon sun, and they went quickly to the wells beside the lake and drew water. The women there giggled at them because the fetching and carrying of water was women's work, but they did not laugh and the women fell silent. They stumbled back up the steep street, the sweat running down their foreheads into their eyes, and came to the stableyard.

William set down his pitcher and wiped his forehead with his hand. Flies buzzed about his ears, and dung beetles rolled away huge balls of treasure under his feet. He saw a flicker of white in the stable, and the hindquarters of a pony that had not been there before. He turned to pick up the pitcher. Here strangers could be no concern of his. This was a whorehouse, and anyone had a right to come.

Hussein stared into the stable, his eyes wide and his mouth drooping open. The stranger in there hummed to himself, muttered, "Move over, you!" in a pleasant, hoarse voice to his pony. The sun glared down on the dried filth in the yard. Under the stable roof it was black, but William looked hard, and the stranger's face came a little clearer.

William walked forward. A dreadful unease ruled in his stomach and he did not know what it was. He passed into the stable beside the horse farthest from the stranger. The stranger heard him and stopped humming and cried softly, "Greetings, Ali, my brother."

William answered over the horses' backs, "Greetings to you, O brother Ali," and slipped under the head ropes, approaching the stranger. They stood close at last, beside the pony's head in the half-darkness, and the stranger said, "Whose band?"

"Khuda Baksh's." William's voice was hoarser than the stranger's, and quavering. The light contracted as Hussein came into the stable, and spread again. The stranger's eyes were flecked brown; his shoulders wide; his forehead broad and low under the turban. He looked at William and said slowly, "Who—who in the name of Kali are you?"

William's unease concentrated in one swooping lurch of his bowels. It was himself that he saw in the expanding gray light. This face stared at him from the cracked mirror when he plucked his whiskers. This face reflected his own face, and reflected too the panic in his eyes. The stranger stepped back, stumbled over a saddlebag in the dirt, and began to fall. He fell, and the light snapped in his brown eyes, and William saw understanding there, and death. The single flash stabbed him, strangled, garroted, broke his joints, drove a stake through his belly, through all love, through

154

Mary, through all sacrifice and success, through life. The stranger was himself, and failure, and Death. He was Death. The rumal came to his hand, the rupee in the knotted corner swinging easily. He stepped forward as Gopal the weaver began to fall. He kicked at Gopal's crotch. Gopal turned away and began to say, "Ali . . ." William's rumal swung. The sound mewed like a hungry cat and choked off.

The weighted end of the rumal flew into William's left hand with a precise and simple mastery. His wrists met, he jerked them in and up against the side of Gopal's neck, under the ear. The silver rupee bit into his hand through the cloth. Gopal's head snapped sideways. His neck cracked.

William stood up. The rumal swung free in his right hand. He found his left hand streaming it through the palm to straighten out the creases, caressing the coarse woven texture. A wonderfully pure warmth flooded him. He had only seen it once, to watch closely. He had never practiced it. Now, when everything depended on it, and at his first attempt, he had killed cleanly, singlehanded.

Hussein crouched beside the body, an emanation of light from the corpse itself limning the misery in his face.

William exulted softly, "I did it! We're safe!"

Hussein looked down at the body of Gopal the weaver, then up at William. William's exultation drained away and left him trembling. He said, "I had to. Don't you see? Everything depended on it—our own lives—that the people we didn't save last night should not have died for nothing. That—that . . ."

"Yes, I saw. You had to. I told you."

"O Christ Jesus our Savior, forgive me, forgive me! I *had* to!"

"You had to. I told you. Come on, quick."

"Where?"

"On top of the wall, up there. Push him under the eaves. And his saddlebags. We'll bury him tonight, after the feast, here."

They strained and heaved and it was done. William wiped his face and leaned against the wall. "What about the pony?"

"Feed it. Leave it. We're off tomorrow."

William turned quickly and retched and retched but could not vomit. In his mouth he tasted sugar.

Hussein said curtly, "Come on."

They went out, lifted the pitchers of water, and slowly climbed the stairs.

Yasin greeted them cheerfully. "Well done, stranglers! That was quick work. I'm nearly ready here." He took the water from them and set it on the fire to boil. William stood in the middle of the room, looking at his hands, until Hussein kicked his shin in passing and said, "Salt, Gopal, and cloves! Get them out." William started, and hurried to do what he was told.

Piroo and the Jemadar came in. They mentioned the strange pony in the stable and asked if anyone knew who it belonged to. William dared not speak, but Hussein said, "Heaven knows! Nothing to do with us, anyway." The Jemadar shrugged.

Exactly at sunset the first of the band arrived for the feast. During the next hour they trickled in by twos and threes, climbing the steps like wraiths, opening the door a crack, and slipping in. At dark the last group came, carrying two black goats and two white goats smothered in blankets so that they could not bleat. These were the men of the bear troupe, by rank humble diggers of graves and therefore inferior to the rest. The Jemadar closed the door, shot the bolts, and hung up a blanket to cover the cracks so that no light would show out between door and lintel.

The band stood in a respectful, nervous huddle at one end of the room, William among them. He shivered still, and thought that Gopal the weaver must be cold by now.

Yasin bowed a minute in prayer and began the last rites of his office. He laid a white sheet on the square of turmeric and lime, completely hiding it. He brought the pots and spilled out the rice in a little white mountain on the sheet. He picked up a half-coconut shell, set it on top of the rice, and filled it with ghi. He pushed two lint wicks into the liquid, crossed them, pulled out their ends and lit them, making four small smoky flames. Last he laid down on the sheet the pickax, its blade pointing north, a twelve-inch knife, and three large jars of arrack. Then he stood to one side.

Piroo and another led forward the two black goats. The goats were young and perfectly formed at every point. The troupe leader shuffled out, a short sword swinging in his hand. The goats walked forward unprotesting and stooped down to sniff the rice. Piroo and the other let go of their halters, knelt, and held them by the hind legs. The goats faced west. Yasin suddenly emptied a pot of water over them with a wide scattering movement of his right hand. One goat bleated and reared up and tried to kick its heels loose from Piroo's grip. The other stood still for a moment, then shook itself violently to get the water out of its coat.

Instantly Yasin called, "A fit sacrifice!" He grabbed the knife from the sheet and drew the blade across the shivering goat's neck. He did not seem to press hard, but the goat's blood poured out over the floor and ran in a lake to the edge of the sheet. Simultaneously the troupe leader's sword swept, and the other black goat's head sprang off and rolled across the corner of the sheet, over the pickax, and came to rest against one of the jars of arrack. So the two black goats died, one in the Mohammedan manner, the halal, and one in the Hindu manner, its head struck off at a single blow. And so, a minute later, the two white goats died. Gopal the weaver stiffened under the eaves of the stable, and the brand of Cain burned in William's forehead.

The band cried out softly in pleasure, pressed forward, and set to work. The fire sprang up as they blew on it and put on more wood. Smoke rose, clung under the rafters, and crept down and round the blanket curtains and out of the windows. Men skinned the goats, and gralloched them, and threw the skins and the offal on a soiled sheet. They cut up the meat and thrust it into smoking pans. The smell of turmeric and spice and chili and hot butter filled the room. The Jemadar swabbed up the blood and water on the floor. Yasin blew out the wicks in the coconut shell and lit three lanterns. William watched, and helped, and saw a hurry and scurry, and in it many men working as one, without orders.

They sat down in a circle to eat. The rice was cold, the meat hot. The Jemadar passed round the arrack, and each man held up the jar with both hands and poured a thin stream down his throat, not letting the mouth of the jar touch his lips. William ate with his right hand, scooping up a fid of rice, dipping it in his gravy bowl, carrying it to his mouth, pushing it in with a flick of his thumb. He saw all that went on about him and tried to remember; but he was not sure what he was seeing and what imagining. He drank the arrack thirstily and soon forgot why he had to remember.

He was William Savage, taking ritual part in a decorous, blood-bathed fantasy. He was Gopal the weaver, eating contentedly, with respect, and carefully carrying all his bones and refuse to the soiled sheet. But Gopal the weaver lay under the eaves in the stable, and William Savage was cold.

Long before the meal ended his stomach pressed against his waistband, but he kept on, like his companions, until every last grain of rice was gone and all three arrack jars were empty. The Jemadar stood up, swaying slightly on his feet. "Our feast is over. The blessing of Kali be on us all!"

All stood. Yasin took up the pickax and returned it to its place under his bedding, the point carefully toward the north. He folded the rice sheet away to be washed and swept up the turmeric and lime and threw it on the offal. The men of the bear troupe lifted the soiled sheet, with the offal and refuse, and folded the corners over. Piroo took the blanket off the door and went out and down the stairs. He came back and nodded, and the bear leader said to the Jemadar, "In the stable?"

Hussein looked steadily at William. William heard, and to control his trembling held his hands tight to his sides.

The Jemadar answered, "Yes. Deep."

"Huzoor sahib!"

The bear men left with the offal. In twos and threes, over a period of thirty minutes, the rest left, except for the five who inhabited the room—the Jemadar, Yasin, Piroo, Hussein, and William. William listened, and listened, his ears seeming to burst with the effort. The bear men must be digging in the stables. He heard nothing; no one came back up the stairs.

After half an hour the Jemadar stuck his head out of the door and sang a snatch of the song he had sung by the Nawab's fire a week ago:

*"Moon of the north, thy hands are lotus blossoms . . ."*

He came in, closed the door, and smoothed his beard with the back of his hand.

"Now!" He rubbed his hands together, smirking. "Now, let's have a little fun."

# Chapter 18

THE Jemadar went to the corner, brought out his zither, and sat down again in the middle of the room. He began to pluck the strings. Hussein and William sat beside him, squatting forward. Piroo rummaged under his kit and brought out two hidden jars of arrack. Yasin produced a hookah, set it on the floor, and placed a glowing lump of charcoal on the bowl. In a minute he swung the mouthpiece away, coughing. "The Prophet forbids me to touch strong spirits. At a feast Kali orders me to drink. What am I to do?" He was quite drunk, and did not speak at all flippantly, but like a man worried over a conflict of spiritual loyalties.

Hussein squatted, and drank, and stared at the floor. William drank, and tried to push away the vision of the dead weaver; but when he had done that a worse memory remained: the lovely warmth of the killing. He thought suddenly of Mary, wet-lipped and hungry in the darkness. It was like that, and his knees melted as he thought of her. But it was horrible—and passionately desirable. It was the open-armed, sucking-soft body of Kali, and her embrace. He feared Kali now, and he knew why Hussein had said he must learn to fear her.

The door opened, and his legs trembled so he could not move. The Jemadar turned to him with a smile. "The girls," he said. "One each for you, and me, and Hussein here. Those two"—he pointed his chin at Yasin and Piroo—"are woman-haters, they say. Come on in!"

The three girls were young. One was sultry and heavy-lidded, and as she walked seemed to sway from the topheavy weight of her breasts. She squatted down next to the Jemadar. He grabbed her, and she leaned invitingly away from him.

The second girl had a hard, thin face and lips avaricious for things other than love. She sat down beside Hussein and began to ply him with liquor.

159

The third girl closed the door, hesitated, and came slowly toward William. She was not beautiful; she had a plain, pleasantly round face, full hips, strong legs, and brown cowlike eyes. She squatted at his side, tucked in the folds of her dress between her thighs, and reached for the hookah. She said, "What's your name?"

"Gopal."

"Gopal. Gopal? Haven't we met before?" She peered at him with an uncertain smile.

"No. Perhaps. What does it matter?"

"Nothing at all, Gopal. Give me a drink. The customers have made me very thirsty tonight." She smiled again, simply, as if she had said only that work in the fields was exhausting. She leaned against him as he picked up the jar. She opened her mouth, flashing her large teeth, and he poured a gill of arrack down her throat. He felt her warmth against him and held his breath while the glow spread through him and all the ugly visions retreated, and faded, and vanished.

The Jemadar sang, plucked the strings of the zither, and tried to keep a hand free for his woman. He was the kind of man—amoral, happy to float on the surface of life, possessed of charm and a pleasant wit—who could make a party go well in any company. The arrack jars passed round, the smoke of tobacco and charcoal cleaned the greasy after-coating of the meal off the roof of William's mouth. The girl pressed on him. She was like an English milkmaid, and he put his arm round her. She wore a loose bodice of the pattern common with harlots.

The eight of them sang together for a time, and the Jemadar became too drunk to follow his woman far up any path of desire. She saw it and began to throw liquid glances at Yasin, who smiled mournfully and shook his head.

Suddenly the Jemadar plucked a violent discord from the strings. The jangle died out in the rafters. He said, his sentences reeling together, "We're all friends here. We've known each other for a long time. What's the matter with the Deceivers?"

William glanced up cautiously as the question penetrated the fuddle in his head. The girls did not start or show surprise.

"What's the matter with us, eh? Fifty years ago, my father's time, we didn't have to bury the pickax in camp, just threw it down

160

a well, and in the morning an officer went to the well, called, the pickax jumped out into his hand."

"Have you ever seen that happen, Jemadar-sahib?" Yasin asked gloomily.

"Me? No. How should I? Those days, Deceivers kept the law strictly, didn't kill women, Sikhs, low castes, oilmen, deformed people, all the rest of the law. But we have done those things ever since I was inish—initiash—inished."

Yasin raised his head. "I do not believe the pickax ever sprang of itself out of any well. That is a superstition. It is not the ill will of Kali that causes our misfortunes but our sinfulness, and our weakness that disobeys her clear signs." He was so drunk that he spoke slowly, with unnatural clarity.

The Jemadar said belligerently, "Oh, you think so? What about getting rid of merchandise then? Isn't it true that in the beginning Kali did it for us, we didn't have to dig or anything? Didn't someone spoil it, look round against orders, see Kali throwing the bodies up in the air, catching them in her mouth, eating them? And wasn't she angry because the man had seen her naked—teats sticking out and all lovely and naked?" He suddenly remembered his harlot and thrust his hand inside her bodice and dragged out her breast. "Like this!"

The woman glanced down, then around at the men, with smoky pride. Yasin sat up straight and began to speak, his voice dropping to the organ note of his prayers, deep, slow, intoxicated now with arrack as well as religious ecstasy, but plowing majestically on, finding the words.

"Hear you, hear you the sacred story of our rights! Hear you, and know the only truth of the Deceivers, beyond which all is superstition. Hear you!"

The listeners settled back, as though to hear an oft-told tale, and watched Yasin. The woman pulled the bodice around her and hid her breast.

"In the beginning was the spirit, and of that spirit the Creator created. He gave the spirit to men, and of the spirit women gave birth, and the world began to be peopled. After the beginning came Raktabij Danava, the Demon of Blood and Seed. He killed men as the Creator created them. Kali, obeying the spirit in her, went out

161

to destroy the Demon. The Demon strode through the oceans of black water away from her, and the oceans lapped his waist, and he hurled defiance at Kali, and killed men as the Creator created them. Then Kali went over to the Demon, and waved her destroying sword about her head, and stuck out her blue-black tongue, and spat blood from her mouth, and struck at the Demon of Blood and Seed to kill him."

Yasin drew breath. The Jemadar jerked his hand in a drunken spasm and set the zither strings humming. William saw phantom shadows fighting on the wall and shut his eyes.

"The Demon's flesh was cut deep, deep! The blood and seed flowed out from his wound and poured on the earth. Where each drop touch the earth another Demon sprang up in that place, armed, and ready to kill what the Creator created. Kali swung her sword and hacked at the newborn Demons. She killed them, and from their wounds the blood and seed spurted out and fell on the earth, and where every drop fell another Demon sprang up, and ran about the world killing what the Creator created, and Kali ran about after them, and struck desperately with her sword, and the Demons bled, and from each drop of their blood and seed a new Demon sprang up.

"Kali rested, and wiped the sweat from her blue-black arms with a handkerchief, and two drops of her sweat fell on the earth. The Creator saw her distress and from her drops of sweat created two men. And Kali said to the men, 'Take my handkerchief. Kill the Demons of Blood and Seed so that no drop of their blood and seed falls to the earth.' And the men took Kali's rumal, and went out over the world, and strangled the Demons, so that no drop of their blood and seed touched the earth, but they died. And when it was done they returned to Kali and said, 'Great goddess, we have done thy will and obeyed thy orders. Here is thy rumal.' And Kali said, 'Keep my rumal. Use it to live, as you have used it that the Creator's creation of mankind may live. Mankind owes you men, and will owe you to the last reckoning, however many you kill. All mankind, *all*, is yours. Only obey me, obey my omen on the left and my omen on the right. Listen, and watch, and obey always that you may prosper always.' And the men went away and hid Kali's rumal until sixteen generations had passed from the creation. Then their children's children's children's children's children's—" He stopped

162

suddenly. "That is all the words of the sacred story of the rights of the Deceivers, and all else is superstition." He rolled over on his side and went to sleep.

The Jemadar woke up, asked why everyone was so damned quiet, and began to play on his zither. William thought the inside of his head would soon explode; he got up and stumbled to the corner to wash his face and get a drink of water. As he stood there, supporting himself in the angle of the wall, his girl came over to him and held him under the shoulders.

She said, when he had drunk, "Come to me now."

All the events of the day whirled about in his head, blown by the fumes of arrack. He was not a person but a place, cloudy with red blood and white rice, and booming to the organ surge of Yasin's voice. *Father, I have sinned and am no more worthy to be called Thy son.* He had eaten the sugar. Kali was Death. Kali was a woman. The zither urged him to spend desire. The girl's hands demanded him and crept over him. He put down the beaker, and touched her, and found her full, warm, and waiting.

She held him, and he followed his feet across the room, behind the Jemadar's back, to the door. The others did not look up. Hussein kept his eyes on the floor. The zither thrummed unsteadily.

At the head of the stair he leaned dizzily forward over the pit. The girl grabbed him, pulled him back, and held him. "Careful now, my beautiful bull." She whispered in his ear, part drunken harlot, part loving country girl, part mother, and supported him down the stairs, going a step below him so that he would not fall.

Through a narrow door they went into her room. She lit a lamp, and he saw bright cushions scattered on the floor. The walls were bare and the room was cold. The sun never shone in here. He opened his eyes wide and looked at her. She swam away from him among lust wraiths, and he did not know whether she knelt or lay or sat. This house bred fantasies, but not the known fantasies of wine and woman's silkiness; these pierced and throbbed, because the pickax pointed north in the corner of the upstairs room and Gopal the weaver lay stiff under the stable eaves.

Moving down to her, stumbling on the cushions, his feet sinking and not coming up, he became aghast and shook with fear. The pickax gave purpose and mastery to all who worshiped it, with in-

163

finite power. The power awed him. This cow-eyed girl had willing hips, but she was just pretending to be a harlot. She was unprotected by any armor of callousness. She did not know the power that Kali gave. She would whimper under the lash of his strength, and call him "lord," and on her cries he would ride in power over the whole world.

He went to her and strove with her. Suddenly she looked at him, and her eyes sprang wide open, as wide as his. The rumal was in his hands, it circled her neck. The muscles were taut in his wrists. Death and love surged up together in him, ready to flood over together, and together engulf her.

A hand clasped his neck. Cold fingers chilled his ears. Hussein stood beside him. "Come away."

The girl breathed a long, shuddering sigh and closed her eyes, and he knew that she had fainted. He looked down, inexpressibly sad for her that Kali's ultimate gift, the unknowable double ecstasy, had come so close to her and gone away. She had touched it with the tips of her senses, and now it sank away from both of them on falling, dimming waters. She lived and was not fulfilled.

She lay senseless with spread knees on the cushions. Hussein's voice trembled. "The others are all asleep. We must bury the weaver. Come."

Hussein's fingers were cold. The vision of Kali faded, and William knew who he was and what he had nearly done. He knelt and drew the girl's dress around her and whispered, half to her, half to Hussein, "I am sorry, I could not help myself."

Hussein said, "I know. That's why I came. Come." He closed the door, and William followed him out to the stable.

There, beside the quiet horses, in the dusky reflections of moonlight, they began to dig. William dug, and shook, and knew he had seen Kali's naked, appalling beauty as the Deceivers saw it. Digging, he prayed to Christ, and felt Kali struggling against his prayers. There would be more trials. Kali would embrace him again. He needed strength, and here on the road it seemed that only she could give it. Her evil lay, concealed or open, in all strength, all power. Not all—perhaps there was another strength in Hussein's little cross.

*In the drawing room of the bungalow in Madhya Mary sat on one side of the fireplace and George Angelsmith on the other.*

George sat at ease, his legs crossed at the ankle. Mary knitted, often looking up to say something, and smiling. They had been sitting here together for a couple of hours. Earlier in the evening George had come in tired and fretful from dealing with arrears of work—principally a troublesome court case William had left unfinished. For the last hour the peevishness had not been present in his voice. He spoke now with the mysteriously full timbre of a man putting himself out to attract a woman.

He smiled, crinkled up his eyes, and said with soft insolence, "No one would dream you were going to have a baby. It doesn't show at all."

Mary said matter-of-factly, "No, not yet. I don't think it will for some time." She looked down at herself, lifting her arms and smiling in self-satisfaction.

George said, "Do you think—he will ever come back?"

Mary bent her head. "I don't think so."

"But you're going to wait here?"

"Until the baby is born."

"And then?"

She looked up and met his eyes. "I don't know. I have no plans."

George did not speak for a minute. He was thinking of Mr. Wilson's future prospects. Mr. Wilson was on his way up in the service; Mr. Wilson's son-in-law could not help going up too. It was the way of the world. Any son-in-law, that is, except poor William Savage.

He said cautiously, "I wonder where he is. I feel somehow that he's not dead. I picture him troubled in his mind." His voice was sad and far away, and his lids heavy as he looked at her. "Do you feel that? Do you remember, sometimes in Sagthali—before William—we'd think of the same thing at the same time, feel it without speaking about it to each other? Do you remember?"

"Yes."

George said, "You know, everybody—I mean, the government—is very anxious to trace him." He frowned and drummed his fingers on the arm of the chair. "I can't help feeling the poor fellow has taken up the life of a wandering faqir, something like that. He might be more at home, more at ease, somehow. I can't make out why he asked you to keep quiet about his going, unless it was to give him time to get lost in a new life. We have checked his accounts, of course. It wasn't that. Didn't he give you any hint, any reason?"

Mary said, "No," her eyes suddenly hard as blue diamonds. She bent forward to pick up a stitch.

George said, "It was very—loyal—of you to let him go—get away —like that. I ought to do everything possible to find him, don't you think? If I did, you know, I believe I could. I ought to. There'll be a lot of credit for whoever does."

He spoke slowly, and the exact meaning of the words was one thing and the tiny tremble of his voice another.

Mary looked up, her needles stilled. "Do everything possible? Yes, I suppose so," and she smiled a closed smile.

George got up, seeing her face and hearing the tone of her voice. He would have liked something more definite, but of course the poor girl could not be expected to come right out until a reasonable time had elapsed for William's death or desertion to be presumed. He sat on the arm of her chair. "Come riding tomorrow. Not forbidden, is it?"

She laughed. "I don't know. I haven't seen any surgeon, and don't intend to. But I'll come riding. It'll be fun. I've sat cooped up long enough in here."

George put his hand on her arm in a natural, beautifully executed gesture. She rose quickly, without haste. "Good night, Mr. Angelsmith." She went out of the room. George rose lazily to his feet and bowed. "Good night, Mary."

In the passage she bumped against Sher Dil, who was standing outside the drawing-room door. She closed the door carefully and whispered, "Sher Dil! What are you doing here? I told you an hour ago that you could go."

She could feel the hurt where something metal-hard on Sher Dil's hip had grazed her. Looking down in the dim-lit passage, she saw the dagger's point under his short coat.

Sher Dil said stonily, "I thought I saw a light in the study. I often come around to see that no one is getting at Savage-sahib's property."

Mary left him and walked slowly into her bedroom, her eyes full of tears.

166

# Chapter 19

IN the morning, when the band set out again, William asked for the role of inveigler, and received it, and rode half a stage ahead of the rest. Hussein accompanied him on foot as his servant and groom. On the fourth day, long before the sun was high, the Jemadar rode up in a dust cloud and slowed to a walk beside him. Here the trail was a broad earth ribbon climbing northward in gradual inclines to another of Bandelkhand's innumerable small escarpments.

William greeted the Jemadar with the mixture of respect and affection which was the tone of their relationship. The Jemadar said, "When are you going to get us some merchandise? Two or three parties have come back past us, but you hadn't sent any sign, so we let them go. What was wrong with them?"

William said, "Bad omens, every time."

It was not true, and he flushed as he said it. The omens had been good—uncannily good, magically well timed. But his memories of the stable chained him. The blisters on his hands would hurt suddenly as travelers passed and the birds or beasts of good omen flashed across the path. There had been much digging that night after the feast, in the back of the stable, beside the patient horses. Now on the trail the girl of the harlots' house walked at his left hand, her eyes widening as the final paroxysm of lust and death approached her. The woman at the pyre by Kahari walked on his right, begging for release.

The Jemadar said, "Oh, well, it can't be helped then. But Piroo's nagging me."

William grunted contemptuously, "Oh, him!" He did not feel contemptuous; the little man with the bat ears was shrewd and sharp-eyed. The Jemadar continued, "Piroo's jealous. He points

167

out that we've had no luck—for nearly four days, isn't it?—with you out in front as inveigler. He whispers that it's your fault. He even hints—"

"Does he want us to defy the omens?" Hussein interrupted sourly from William's stirrup. "What sort of a Deceiver is it who questions Kali's orders?"

The Jemadar shrugged. "Oh, he obeys them, all right. What Deceiver does not? By the Creation, does not our goddess show us her hand every minute of every day? But he's jealous. Let's trot. Everyone's getting impatient, and we spent most of our cash in Manikwal."

"When are we converting the rest, the jewels?" William asked innocently.

The Jemadar looked up with sudden suspicion. "Why do you ask? You'd know—"

"We weren't present when your band formed for the season's work, Jemadar-sahib," Hussein said with his deferential firmness. He loped easily, holding William's stirrup, and did not grunt from shortness of breath as he spoke. "You know, too, that we have been off the road for some years."

"Of course, of course, I forgot, silly of me. Well, we're disposing of the jewels at the end of the season, in March. The sale's going to be in the usual place, Parsola. All the usual crowd will come, that is, any band based in the Kaimur and Mahadeo Territories or southern Bandelkhand." He laughed happily and slapped his thigh as he turned to William. "It's a wonderful system we have now. And all new since you last used a rumal. Do you remember how we had to sell our jewels ourselves? And the difficulty of getting a fair price for stuff that was so obviously stolen? And the way stinking little rajahs would catch our people in the markets and sew them up in pigskin and have them trampled by elephants just because they were found in possession of some diamond that was unluckily recognized? Well, Chandra Sen changed all that. There's a man for you! The best brain this brotherhood ever had, like yours promised to be the best pair of hands."

William started, then fidgeted about as though it was discomfort in the saddle that had made him jump. He said, "Chandra Sen? The patel of Padwa and Kahari?"

The Jemadar chuckled. "Yes. I forgot your home's there. He's a very discreet gentleman."

William looked down and saw in Hussein's eye that this about Chandra Sen was no news to him.

The Jemadar shook his head reminiscently. "It's quite different from the old days. Chandra Sen brings a crowd of jewel brokers down to our sale. They buy up everything, wholesale, at very fair prices. They're happy, we're happy, everybody's happy—except the beetoos!"

William thought first of Mary. He must get the information to her that Chandra Sen was a Deceiver. Otherwise she might confide something to him in her loneliness, and then . . . He had to put that aside; just now it was impossible to reach Mary. He wondered bitterly whether he would ever be able to arrest Chandra Sen, in face of the fuss that followed the temporary detainment of much less important people. Nothing would do but to catch the patel redhanded, preferably in the presence of Mr. Wilson.

Hussein had known. What did that mean? Why hadn't he mentioned it? He glanced fiercely under his brows at the running man, and Hussein looked coldly back up at him. Chandra Sen might have found out where William Savage, Collector of Madhya, had gone. He might have known all the time. Hussein might have told him. Hussein might have planned it all with him. Why?

William twisted the reins in his fingers. A few days back Death was a man with his own face, met in the shadows of a stable. He had killed that Death, but still Death was everywhere. Perhaps Death had already reached the gang behind, and was a man, an emissary from Chandra Sen, talking earnestly with Piroo. He looked sideways at the Jemadar, and the palms of his hands tingled. His blisters had healed and no longer smarted.

They reached the brow of the escarpment, and the Jemadar said sharply, excitement in his voice, "Stop! Pull in here. What's that?"

William turned his horse out of the middle of the road and glanced down, following the direction of the Jemadar's upflung hand. A rolling plain, not wide but fertile and patched with dark green jungle and light green grass, spread out before them. A haze of dust hung over the center of it. Staring under his hand, William thought he saw splashes of red in the dust.

169

He said, "Women—taking the cattle home."

"Have you gone blind, Gopal? And since when have the women of Bandelkhand brought the cattle in from the fields at ten o'clock in the morning? They're redcoats, sepoys"—he peered keenly down —"*with* their women. Going the same way as us. I wonder . . ." He sat musing unhurriedly in the saddle, like a man who debates with himself some little question of convenience, such as whether to stop now or later for a morning pipe.

Away to the left and far down on the plain a lonely jack donkey set up an agonized braying. The Jemadar tensed and waited, his head turned to the right. Faintly the bray rebounded in hiccuping echoes from the face of the escarpment. The Jemadar lifted his eyes and clasped his hands. "O Kali, greatest Kali, we hear and obey. I had almost begun to *think*. Folly, folly! Faith is all."

He turned to them, the authority of a general in his face and voice. "How many would you say there are?"

William hesitated. Without a glass he could see only the dust and a blur of little red dots and neutral-colored spots. Hussein answered at once, catching up the question so that the Jemadar did not have time to notice William's delay in answering, "Eight sepoys I can see. There are probably one or two more ahead as scouts. Five women, four or five small children. I can't see whether one of the women is carrying a baby or a bundle."

"That's what I make it. Hussein, you go ahead, catch them up. Beg their protection. Put out the signs if they change direction, move faster—you know. Gopal, get out to the east, four miles. There's a trail along the ridges. Our buriers are moving by it with the bear, giving shows in the villages. Bring them in to this road at the ford below Padampur—that's two days ahead—early in the morning. Lie up close. That'll be the bhil, so prepare the grave. I'm going back now. I've got to warn the party on the other flank. Let's see, there are eight over that side, and—oh, we'll have plenty for the job. All clear? Kali is with us! Remember, the ford below Padampur, and we will come about midday."

He jerked his reins, waved his hand, and cantered back down the road, riding on the grassy verge where his horse raised no dust as it flew along under the boughs.

William sat motionless, his horse drooping its head in the shade.

170

Hussein said brusquely, "I knew about Chandra Sen. And he knows about me. He's one of the few men in this part of India who does. That's why I had to get out of your jail. He got the news that I'd been taken that day, all right. Haven't you worked out that he left his village the same evening?"

"But why didn't you tell me?"

"Would you have believed me, before the murder of the thakur's party made you see how big the Deceivers are? Before you caught Chandra Sen? Even then you didn't realize! I told you I had to lift the curtain slowly, or you'd be blinded. Besides, it was no good just knowing about Chandra Sen. You'd have had to get evidence. Don't worry. He doesn't know where I've gone or that you're with me."

William sat silent. At last he said, "I still have to get evidence against him."

Hussein said, "You? You're a strangler."

"Hold your tongue! Are we going to kill those sepoys?"

"Of course."

"Some of them might be armed."

"They might," Hussein said dryly. "They are sometimes allowed to take muskets on leave as protection against dacoits on the road. And once, I know, they were warned against Deceivers, but that was fifteen years ago and everyone's forgotten. Several times some English official or other has got hold of information about us. Then he has chased us out of his district, and reported, I suppose. But they've never worked together, and it always blew over. They'll never destroy us until one of them finds out everything, and forces the Lat Sahib to believe everything, and plans a campaign to cover all India. And that one who finds out must fear Kali, or he will not understand her. But he must not love her." His voice was sad. It roughened suddenly. "The sepoys are our merchandise. You are the beloved of Kali. And a strangler. Behave like one, or die."

Two days later William and the eight men of the bear troupe sat in a wood three hundred yards from the point where the trail came out of thin jungle and crossed the Padampur stream. The town and fortress of Padampur lay out of sight three miles to the north, across the stream and behind undulating hills.

William's horse stood under a tree and swished its tail. The bear sat up on its hunkers inside the wooden-slatted cage built for it on the frame of a bullock cart. The bullocks were lying down, securely tethered. The bear looked toward William, and slavered, and beat its forepaws together. It had taken a liking to him, and William hated it and its obscene gestures of affection.

The men of the troupe looked like—men of a troupe with a dancing bear. At this season scores of such parties moved about the roads of India. Some of the villagers might have wondered why they had no women with them, as was customary. But who cared? They sat quietly, grouped around William, and waited. These men, who were mere buriers by rank, treated him with respect because of his reputation as a strangler, and because of the high regard which they knew their Jemadar held for him.

The grave was dug, under the bank of a dry backwater nearby, and concealed in thick brush. The men had dug without making noise, pressing their picks and hoes into the earth rather than striking with them. The sharpened stakes, the log, the rough club lay neatly stacked beside the pit. No stranger who came in by accident to the troupe's resting place would see anything suspicious. Besides, there would be ample warning. One of the diggers, a man who could whistle like a parakeet, lay hidden in the trees across the stream where he could see in both directions. Another crouched in concealment a mile back up the trail, ready to talk with the Jemadar or receive a sign from him.

William waited, fingered his rumal, and tried not to look at the bear. By logic, it was no more evil to murder the sepoys than to murder the Nawab and his wives and their innocent followers: if anything, less evil, because the sepoys were at least well-armed men in the vigor of life and capable of defending themselves. But William had been an officer of sepoys, and in his mind this coming affair had grown until it was the giant embodiment of evil. He was sick at heart. He had meant only to do good. In trying to help his people, he had caught himself in these chains of evil. But if he had not followed the Deceivers, and become one of them, the evil would never have been uncovered. In the time since he set out with Hussein, no circumstances had changed. What had been true then was true now. If he fled now, and acted on what he already

172

knew, he could make only a little cut in the Deceivers' organization, which would quickly heal, and all would soon again be as it was before. "A campaign to cover all India," Hussein had said; and it was true. Where was God, the true Christian God? Had God arranged it, so loathing Kali, that even to know her was to know Death, become Death?

The oppression of the goddess's widespreading sins bore down on him. He had said he would not kill. He had been a Christian, believing in the value of the life that God lent to mankind and sanctified by the lending. He could stand no more. He had become two men, a Christian and a Deceiver, and was being torn apart by remorse. His notes had enough in them to bring the evil fully out into the open. Then, surely, no one could deny that there was need of a great unified campaign. Thinking further, he swore to himself, and knew that men could deny, and would, and still not be wicked, only complacent. The weight of death began to pile up on his head. He had failed Mary, and God.

The chief of the buriers muttered, "Gopal-ji, one comes, running. It is the sentry from the road." The men rose to their feet, hitched up their loincloths, hefted their hoes in their hands, and stood unobtrusively ready. The bear raised its head and stopped whining. The bullocks champed on their cud.

The sentry ran through the trees and came to them. "A traveler, southbound, cries that the Padampur rajah's cavalry is getting ready in the city for some job down this way. I managed to tell the Jemadar. He's going to do our affair just the same. The omens are good." The sentry leaned forward, panting and holding his sides. "Quick, to the ford! Hide there. The signal, 'The water is deep,' from the Jemadar. Hurry!" He was gone.

One man stayed with the bear; William and the rest scurried crouching through the tall grass beside the river until they saw the road ahead. They lay down, in cover beside the ford, on the right of the road.

As they dropped, breathing hard, to the earth, the leading sepoys came down the incline to the ford. They looked uneasily alert and their muskets were ready in their hands. Some of the Deceivers walked behind them, mingling with women and other sepoys. William did not know what had put the sepoys on their guard, but it was clear that they did not trust their newfound companions of the road. Yet they could do nothing. Relying on their arms, ignorant of the octopus power of the organization that sought to kill them, they came on.

At the water those in front waited for the others to catch up. The main party came down the road in a close-knit group, surrounding a bullock cart. A heavily pregnant woman rode in the cart on top of a pile of baggage; a sepoy sat on the bar, driving it; his musket was slung across his shoulders. Two children, of about six and nine years old, played tag immediately behind the cart. The other women swung lightly along together with no loads on their heads, their saris drawn half across their faces. One carried a baby on her hip. The Jemadar and two or three more Deceivers walked among the soldiers and women, and seemed to be talking, and kept glancing over their shoulders at the remainder of the band coming along close behind.

William crumbled the earth between his fingers where he lay. He saw that the Jemadar had gained the confidence of the sepoys. They had come to trust his large friendliness and engaging personality. It was probably he who had planted in them their suspicions of the rest of the band, so, naturally, they drew closer to him. That was it. He saw another five Deceivers hurry up from the rear, to be received into the party about the bullock cart.

Now all of them glanced suspiciously, almost warningly, at the other travelers in the caravan. The Jemadar whispered with Hussein and a sepoy. William could not hear the words but he could guess at them: "This ford is a dangerous place. If these fellows are indeed bad men, as I suspect, let us close up for protection." The more the sepoys closed up, the less effective would their firearms be.

He could hear nothing to the north, and wondered whether the rajah of Padampur's cavalry would come, and what their errand was. That situation was far from clear. He would have to find out about it as soon as he could. Had the rajah known the band was coming? If so, how? How much else did he know? And why didn't the Jemadar postpone this attack until the cavalry were past?

But he himself did not have to wait. This was his moment of release, offered to him in perfect circumstances. The success of the ambush depended as much on him and the men of the bear troupe

174

as on anything. A force of law—the rajah's cavalry—was at hand. How far were they? Cautiously he eyed the men lying around him. None carried the rumal which, seen in another's hand or imagined in another's loincloth, now made William sweat and tremble; but they were all armed with their digging implements and hidden knives.

Yet this was the moment. He must shout his warning now, run out, and take his chance among the sepoys.

No, not now; in a second or two, when he would have a better chance of surviving. The risk of death did not frighten him; but if he was killed all the evidence would be lost forever, all the dead dead in vain. Hussein alone knew where he had buried the notes. Hussein could go back and dig them up, but he wouldn't. Hussein seemed to be struggling still against Kali, but William knew he would lose his fight and his soul.

William waited, his mouth open, and watched the Jemadar, and listened for the hoof beats of cavalry. The Jemadar stood in his stirrups to peer down at the shallow stream. He said with owlish surprise, "The water is deep," and leaped off his horse onto the back of a sepoy who was already in the shallows and beginning to cross the ford, and bore him down into the water. On the bank Piroo's cloth whirled in a semicircle, pulled out by the weight of the wrapped rupee. The sepoys and women broke out in a wild confusion of shouts and screams. The men of the bear troupe crouched like sprinters about to begin a race and looked at William. William sprang to his feet and opened his mouth wide to shout a warning.

The moment had passed. Already men and women and children had died.

A sepoy with a fear-crazed face, running to find shelter from the inexplicable horror, burst into William's hiding place. The man was on him, and had a musket in his hands. He saw William, his pupils contracted, his arms jerked down, and he thrust the muzzle of the musket against William's breast. William yelled, "Look out!" and flung himself sideways. He heard his own hysterical laugh. Whom was he warning now?

His sideways movement ended in a pivot off the left foot, the rumal jumped into his hands and whirled through the air. Both ends were in his hands. He looked down and saw nothing but his tight, white knuckles. He felt the powerful jerk from his thighs and waist and shoulders. His wrists cracked in and up against the sepoy's neck. Another crack burst over it. A slow warmth crept up his spine and mingled in his brain with the falling, fading scarlet coat.

At last he heard his own choking sobs. He stumbled forward out of the sheltering bushes. The Jemadar lay on his face in the water at the edge of the river. Blood trickled from his head, reddening the placid water downstream where it ran over submerged green and brown stones. The tang of gunpowder burned sharp in William's nostrils, but he had heard nothing. His arm hurt; he saw black powder marks on it near the elbow. The sepoy must have fired his musket before he died.

Another shot boomed as he stood panting by the ford, gaping to understand the panoramic struggle about him. A last sepoy, cornered, his back against a tree, swung his empty musket as five Deceivers ran at him. They pressed him back against the trunk; a man behind him swung the rumal. Another Deceiver moved quickly, caught the screaming children, and in two quick motions they lay sprawled in the road. The other children were dead. The women were dead in their dull reds and blacks. The sepoys were dead in their scarlet coats; their white drawers, blue edged, were soiled with the dust and mud of the road.

Piroo's sharp face pressed into his own. "You, Jemadar-sahib! Yes, you are our Jemadar now. *He* said so, didn't he?" He motioned to the corpse in the water. "What now? Quick. The cavalry are on us."

"Why?" William faltered.

"We didn't pay the rajah his cut last time we were through here. He heard we were coming somehow. What now? Quick!"

William thought quickly, his stupor gone and self-hatred ruling in its place. Everyone who had deserved to live was dead. Should he now let the band be caught by the cavalry? Why? The rajah of Padampur was just another murderer, from what Piroo said. Like the Deceivers, he picked up money by every means in his power. He knew about them, and their bands paid him "protection" to be left alone while in his territories. He might punish one band, as now, but he would do nothing to help destroy the system. He would have William put away, quietly.

William knew that, whatever he did later, now he must somehow lead the band to safety. It was no use telling them to disperse and slip away in small groups. In this country, cavalry would catch most of them. The valley was wide open except near the river, where trees and scrub and rank grass made riding difficult. Besides, there was a better way. He remembered Chandra Sen's tactics on the Betul road.

The Deceivers pressed round him. He said urgently, "Get the muskets and ammunition. Reload. Drag the bodies out of sight, no farther. Horsemen, mount! Ride up the road, meet the cavalry, pretend to fight them. When they're engaged, break and flee, *that* way, into that edge of grass there. Make sure they follow at split gallop. The rest of you, get in there in the grass. Trip the horses, bring them down, then use all your weapons. Don't let anyone escape!"

Piroo raised his hand in acknowledgment, and a gleam of admiration shone unwillingly in his face. The band ran to carry out William's orders, moving silently, with speed and practiced certainty. They hurled the children's bodies over the thorns into the darkness of the bush. They dragged the sepoys out of sight. A minute more and the dead women with the dusty skirts were gone. The five horsemen, Yasin leading them, splashed fast through the ford and galloped north and out of sight.

Piroo took charge of the rest and ran with them across the stream into the tall grass on the far bank. William hurried after, struggling to keep his feet in the knee-deep water. A clangor and mingled shouts sounded down the road from the north. Only a minute had passed since Yasin's mounted band had rattled round that corner a quarter of a mile away.

In the grass the bear troupe and the other men on foot worked with the speed and energy of ants. Some quickly, surely, loaded the muskets, lying on their sides so that the muzzles and the stabbing ramrods would not show above the grass. Others cut swathes of grass, then worked in pairs, twisting in opposite directions, plaiting short loose ropes. Knives flickered under the river bank where

177

three men cut stakes and with short, desperate strokes sharpened them.

William remembered his horse, and the bullocks, and the bear across the river, and the man in charge of them. None of those were doing any work. How many stranglings and garrotings and burials had that horribly human bear seen? Surely it too could choke a man to death, or dig, or cut sharp stakes? He turned and stared north.

Yasin's horsemen flashed into sight, bending low, as if in terror, over their horses' withers. At the corner they left the road and galloped across country directly toward the band hidden in the grass. One of them, waving a musket, turned and fired clumsily at unseen pursuers.

The Padampur cavalry galloped into view, brilliant in pink cloaks and tight green silk trousers and chain-mail jerkins and round steel helmets. The wild shouting grew to a roar. William counted anxiously and made it seventeen. A man more gorgeously dressed than the rest, wearing a fan of egret plumes on his helmet, rode at their head. He heard Piroo's voice in his ear. "The rajah-sahib himself. He must be very angry."

William's lips twisted in a derisive smile. He had another person to despise now, to place in the long gallery with himself and the rest of the human race. The rajah of Padampur had an unctuous record in his dealings with the English. He kept a brilliant court and entertained with a lavish, unexpectedly civilized charm. William sneered because so many Residents and Political Agents had been deceived; because so much power for good, so much wealth, nourished itself on banditry and was expended for the benefit of murder. What terrors did the ordinary people of India not have to live with?

The horsemen under Yasin played their role perfectly. The pursuing cavalry could not see their contorted faces, but they had written panic into the stoop of their backs. They reached the grass and did not look down as they galloped past. Yasin's horse swerved wildly but could not avoid stamping on a Deceiver's back. The man writhed like a wounded snake, his face greeny-brown and his back broken, but he made no sound.

The rajah's long, aristocrat's face was contorted like a wolf's as he screamed, "Come back, swine! Sons of whores! Come back! Pigs! Cowards!"

His cavalry screamed behind him. Yasin's men urged their horses over the bank forty yards ahead and plunged into the water. The cavalry, riding in a loose crescent, the rajah in the middle and the points back, pounded into the long grass.

The hidden men jerked the plaited ropes which lay between them, leaned back, and held the ropes two feet off the ground. Men propped the butts of the sharp stakes against the unyielding soil and inclined the points forward so that they slid into muscle and flesh as the horses galloped onto them. The grass rose up, and weapons reached out of it. Yasin's horsemen turned round and galloped back into the battle. Muskets exploded in a sudden fusillade. The black puffs of powder smoke drifted through the grass. Daggers flashed in the bright sun, the triumphant yells of the cavalry died in hiccuped cries of panic, from across the river the bear roared in his cage. The Deceivers rose up screaming. William stood with them, and his heart pounded, and his fingers kneaded the rumal in his waistband.

The rajah's horse stumbled beside him. The rajah's black mustache and blazing-black eyes hurtled down on him. He saw them near, and as personal enemies, against the background of heaving grass and embossed round shields and colored clothes and whirling swords. The rajah fell forward at his feet and struggled to free a short dagger from his sash.

All the brightness outside, and the movement, were reflected in black mirrors behind William's eyes, and the rumal was in his hand. A wolf snarled at his feet. It was the evil of Kali, as the harlot girl had been the lust of Kali, and he could strangle it in one motion. It was the evil thing that God made and, having made, strove to destroy. His knuckles sprang up white . . . he heard the double crack.

He bowed his head and slowly, luxuriously, let his wrists turn down. The rumal unloosed. There was never such power as this in all the world, or such fulfillment.

Piroo was beside him. The fight was finished. William said, "All done?"

"All, Jemadar-sahib. Some of their horses have run away, some are dead, some we have."

Piroo's voice was pure respect, and in his face the awe of a man who meets Death walking in at his gate or comes suddenly upon Dedication praying in the streets. The awe was in Hussein's eyes too, mixed there with a panic fear, as of the supernatural.

The chief burier lifted up his voice. "Oh, Jemadar-sahib-bahadur, now we know why our leader who is dead said you might be the greatest that the Deceivers have ever known."

Here was the second of the strong emotions that exalted him— the admiration of a smaller for a greater in the same craft. A village carpenter had praised a chair he'd made once, and it had felt like this.

"What now, Jemadar-sahib?" Piroo asked humbly. "There will be trouble over this. From Padampur they will send the rest of the army after us."

William shrugged. "I think not. There will be a new rajah. After this, he will be advised to make peace with us."

It was true. The Deceivers were a monster, shapeless but universal, headless but possessed of many brains. Anything wielding less than the full power of the English government would have to come to terms with them. William knew now that nearly every rajah, nearly every important squire and landowner in the country, must know something of the Deceivers. Some helped them overtly, some did not, all kept silent. Together they strengthened and executed the law of nature, which always weakens the weak, robs the poor, and murders the defenseless.

He raised his head quickly. "What's that?"

Piroo sniffed. "A fire! Quick, someone, run and put it out, over there!"

Flames, almost without color in the sunlight, leaped up where a musket blast had set fire to tinder-dry grass. Blue smoke rose denser and denser, carrying with it black shreds of burned grass.

"No!" William's voice was imperative. "Take everything of value off the cavalrymen, leave the bodies. Bring the sepoys and the women and children out of the bushes. Scatter them about in the grass. Leave them all to the fire. The flames will mar them, half hiding, half revealing. Leave their muskets by the sepoys, their swords and shields by the cavalry. Hurry!"

180

Already his men were dragging up the hastily hidden victims of the massacre at the ford.

He went on steadily, talking to Piroo. "It is well known that the cavalrymen of these petty rajahs are robbers each and every one— the rajahs too. Here is the story of a robbery, and a brave defense. The new rajah will be quiet, or he will have to explain to the English Company what happened to ten of their sepoys."

He was the leader. There was no dispute among his men or within himself. His heart was hard, and he could watch without emotion as the foolish women and the stupid soldiers were thrown into the flames. The woman at Kahari should be here, in this pyre, with her dreams. The acrid smoke smarted in his eyes. He was the leader. He had to be. Only so could he cover the thin sheets of paper and record forever the beautiful honeycomb detail of the Deceivers' world. It would be the work not of months but of years, years on the wonderful road where a man could find power and fulfillment. At the end, after he was dead perhaps, that outside world of Governors and Governors General could read, and admire, and be staggered with their own pettiness.

He said, "Bury our dead in the pit we dug for the others. Thanksgiving tomorrow morning. We'll move now. East first, until we're out of Padampur."

Hussein trotted up, the two dead children under his arms flopping like bundles of cloth. He threw them down. William's eyes hurt as the flames roared up, and Hussein backed away, shading his face and holding his hands across his mouth.

# Chapter 20

A DRY wind of March blew steadily out of the south and scorched his face. Since November he had led his band in a great circle: north to the Jumna and beyond, east through Rohilkand, Tirhut, and the foothills of the Oudh Terai; south through the villages that skirt the city of Allahabad; thence south by west. Sagthali lay six stages ahead on this road, but the band would turn off tomorrow or the next day.

Yesterday Mr. Wilson had passed, riding in the same direction among many police and servants, his head sunk on his chest. William noted the pistols in the saddle holsters and the armed men behind him, and wondered again that the Deceivers never attacked Europeans. His band had on occasion murdered travelers better armed than that. But the English never carried cash or valuables on them, and the ensuing commotion would be dangerous. Kali knew best.

He had thought then, and many times since the affair at Padampur, whether he should get a message to Mr. Wilson—and to Madhya perhaps—telling him of the Deceivers' rendezvous at Parsola, and asking him to bring up cavalry. He had not done it before, and he did not do it now, when Mr. Wilson's passing gave him an opportunity. For one thing, he did not think he would be believed; then the rumors would go out, the Deceivers would hear, the rendezvous would be altered, the sale canceled. Further, though it would be a big step forward to catch all the Deceivers who came to the Parsola sale, he knew that, however many came, they would still be only a small fraction of the whole network. He had decided that if circumstances permitted he would bide his time, complete this phase of his investigations at Parsola, and spend the summer persuading the government that large-scale operations must begin with the following Dussehra.

182

He hitched his weight forward to sit more easily in the rough saddle of the Cutch mare he now rode. The horse that Yasin had bought for him in Manikwal had long since been sold. They had captured and disposed of forty horses since then. Hussein had bought this mare in the Kuraon bazaar a few days back. No one would find it easy to trace the movements of the band through its horses. And now the end of the journey was in sight. Soon they would reach Parsola by the Mala marsh. The village and the marsh were in his district, not twenty-five miles from his headquarters at Madhya. *His* district? *His* headquarters? The phrases sounded ridiculous.

At Parsola they would meet many other bands and dispose of their jewels to the brokers assembled by Chandra Sen. But, according to report, Chandra Sen himself never came to the annual sales. He stayed at his home or chose that time to visit in Madhya. His object was to keep in touch with the authorities and be ready to distract them if for any reason they showed signs of investigating the area of the sale.

It was lucky that Chandra Sen would not be at Parsola, because he had already seen William in the guise of Gopal the weaver, and he knew that the Collector of Madhya had disappeared. If he saw "Gopal" again, he would certainly connect the two things.

William thought of Mary. Their child would be born next month. He would like to be with her then. With luck, it should be possible.

His face was set in the grim and thoughtful mask that the grass fire had scorched onto it the day of the massacre at the Padampur ford. Behind the mask he feared for himself, because he had learned the power of Kali, and his own weakness, and had learned in the spasms of his three murders to love the evil of the goddess. Since Padampur he had not killed with his own hands; he was the great Jemadar, the planner. But the terrible beauty lingered, a warmth at his wrists and heart, and he was afraid of the moment when he must meet Mary's eyes. He clung grimly to his purpose, but even there he was afraid. His notes lay concealed in twenty clever places along the miles of road he had traversed since first meeting with the band at Jalpura. To men of good intent the notes would be above any assessment of value. He had met hundreds of other Deceivers, and the notes were a complete tale of all he had seen and heard and done; of all the Deceivers who had engaged in any action, with their descriptions, habits, and homes; of each murder, and how it had gone, and how it might have been prevented—or improved upon. The words could be read for either purpose, according to the spirit of the reader. The spirit of the writer was ambiguous. This long season of murder would in the end save lives; but William remembered that sometimes he had written his notes in professional pride and critical admiration, and therefore he was afraid.

As he rode he exchanged easy words with his companions. It was not difficult now for him to think and make conversation at the same time. This particular group of travelers was like a circus, and he did not have to listen with great concentration to what was said. It would have been all but impossible; the beetoos numbered over eighty—eighty-four at his last count—with whom were eleven Deceivers, counting himself. The whole straggled like a racecourse crowd down the road, in high spirits for the most part. There were several horses; palanquins for the trio of rich old ladies who formed the kernel of the party; two Hindustani cavaliers riding south to seek employment with a Deccan rajah; six harlots and their servants, moving house from Allahabad to Sagthali; a few merchants; a few tradesmen; a farmer or two; children, goats, bullock carts—cows.

William stared at the four stunted cows ahead of him. They were a serious matter. The laws of Kali expressly forbade Deceivers to kill any traveler accompanied by a cow; Yasin didn't agree, but that was the general interpretation of Kali's rules. A cow had to be got out of the traveler's possession. One common method was to buy it. All the laws of Kali had reason behind them, though sometimes her servants were too foolish to see it. They had to have faith.

The Deceivers, after centuries of prosperity, were beginning to lose faith and disobey. How many women had William seen strangled?—and *that* was forbidden. Every Deceiver, his own band included, believed that Kali was only biding her time to punish them, and yet they disobeyed. William looked with hard, sad eyes at his companions. It was impossible to know Kali without fearing her, to fear her without serving her. He had become her servant.

184

Even when the time came to act, when his hand and voice sent Deceivers by hundreds to the scaffold, he would be the servant of her anger against them. He had eaten the sugar.

His band was much bigger now. Success had crowded him on the long journey. As he traveled, other bands had joined him in a loose confederation. The jemadars willingly submitted their authority to his in the conduct of affairs, while keeping in their own hands the detailed religious and disciplinary control of their men. That was because of his success. If they had been English they would have called him "Lucky" Savage. As it was, behind his back they called him "Gopal Kali-Pyara," Gopal the Beloved of Kali. The bear troupe had four bullock carts now, and, beside the dancing bear, a hyena, a baby deer, and two mangy wild red dogs. All the cart floors were false, and jewels and specie and gold bars filled the drawers below.

On the road he had made contact with perhaps a twentieth part of the Deceiver network. In addition, he had heard gossip around the campfires, and the words he had heard threw light far beyond the power of the blazing logs, far beyond the limits of his voyaging. One little anecdote revealed the existence of Deceivers who worked in boats in the Sunderbunds to the east, beyond Calcutta. A bright pearl, and its story, told of Deceivers in the steaming, forested hills that overlook Adam's Bridge in the far south and the narrow channel to Ceylon. Round the fires he had heard of Deceivers who were the body-servants of British officers; of rajahs who had eaten Kali's sugar and now guided the operations of Deceiver bands from their palaces; of moneylenders in Bombay, roving gentlemen-at-arms in the west. He had heard . . . too much. Kali's hand lay over India.

The sun was low, and the three old ladies shouted to the coolies to carry their palanquins off the road into an extensive mango grove. Yasin always rode beside them. He had captivated them with his quiet charm and confessional manner. He was just like a rosy English vicar among valued parishioners. Whatever he suggested to the old ladies became the law of the party.

William left the road in his turn and found a spot in the grove to tie up his horse and unpack his meager belongings. This was the ultimate stage for eighty-four human beings, this coming night their last, and the moon, when it rose, their final moon. Tomorrow the

185

band would kill them all. It would not be the biggest job Deceivers had ever undertaken, but it was big enough. William tried to wish he could draw back, cancel it all, but he could not find that wish. The old, now familiar excitement grew in him. He had to go on because his reputation as a great Jemadar depended on it, and on that his life, and on his life his notes and the final destruction of Kali. But his hands were warm, and he was afraid. He began to collect sticks, wandering always farther from the mango grove and its brackish well.

The others came one by one to the appointed place, and no word was said. Yasin spread the sheet and laid the pickax on it. William stood behind, and expectation and unwilling reverence swept down from the quiet sky upon him.

"O Kali, thy servants are waiting," Yasin cried in passion and wonder. "Grant them thy approval, they pray."

They waited with heads bowed in silence. No animal moved, no bird called. The tops of the trees stirred in the evening breeze, bending toward the north. The silence pressed down on them. They stood for fifteen minutes. The darkness spread from the jungle to cover them.

To the right an owl called, the hollow pulse of sound moaning away under the boughs. To the left a second owl answered. For a minute the birds called to each other.

The Deceivers backed away. Yasin snatched up the pickax and sheet and stammered, "We must cancel it—everything."

Kali rose up in the twilight, a definite shape before William's eyes, black-browed and serpent-haired. Always before, she had answered him at once, and answered "Yes." Now his torn spirit, and his fear of her, cried out to him to heed her warning. But the spirit under the spirit spoke, and that was deep based, and Christian, and English. That would not bow to heathen superstition. He turned furiously on his men and flung out his arms in the gloom.

"We will go on!" he cried harshly. "We cannot go back. A hundred and forty of our comrades are on their way to the killing ground. We cannot stop them or communicate with them. We will go on!"

Piroo said slowly, "Kali—"

"Kali gave me a private sign, in the night when I first planned this adventure," William answered desperately. "It is all right. It is on my head."

The deep-planted obstinacy brushed Kali aside. Only an hour ago he had looked for a way to abandon this horrible enterprise. Now the way opened clear in front of him, and he could not, would not, take it.

The stranglers slipped away. Yasin tucked the pickax into his waistband and said heavily, "So be it. It is on your head. Have the buriers dug yet? It is an enormous task to dig for so many."

"We rely on Hussein. He said there were big pits in the jungle, where men used to dig up the ironstone."

Yasin said again, "So be it," and William followed him back to the encampment.

He lay down at last and began to review his plans for the next day. About two miles on from this grove the road entered a rock defile, where it climbed over a low saddle among thick forest. On either side small hills swept down to the saddle. He had never seen the place, but others had, and their descriptions had been detailed and enthusiastic. A little skill was necessary to telescope the party so that all the travelers would be in the defile at the same time. Yasin was to do that by contriving to get the old ladies in front to stop at the far end. The column would pile up behind them. As for strengths, beside the eleven Deceivers here a hundred and forty others, all under William's orders, had been moving for days in twos and threes and larger groups on parallel roads, and ahead, and behind. Those men were on the move now, hurrying by footpaths and byways to the defile. They should be in position by dawn. The travelers would get there about an hour later.

As in all good plans, the rest was simple. William would ride in the middle of the column and, when the best moment came, stand in his stirrups and shout, "O Kali, hear us!" Five Deceivers of his band were to be alongside the two young cavaliers, the other five with the old ladies and their escort of even older retainers. When William shouted, the mass in hiding would rush out and finish the affair. It was simple. But *would* Kali hear him?

He turned over on his face and prayed, and in his prayer English words stumbled among the words of the Deceivers' language. It all depended on Hussein. It was Hussein who had remembered the

187

old iron workings half a mile into the wood near the defile. It was Hussein who had been William's link of communication with the supporting bands; Hussein who had ridden off on a fast horse to tell them of the rendezvous and the details of the operation. Tomorrow morning, all that done, Hussein was to pass down the road in the opposite direction, to meet the party just before it reached the defile. As he passed he would say a word to William to confirm that all was ready.

William turned over on his back. Usually, when he had thought over his arrangements, he went to sleep. Tonight he could not sleep. All night he could not sleep, and his face was gray when he got up. He began to collect his kit and load it on his horse. He saw the misery in his men's eyes and forced himself to smile encouragingly at them. The bustle of preparation for the move was far off and unreal today; unreal the figures who stretched their arms in the last warm darkness; far off the cries of the children who raced about the grove and played tag among the mango trees. The black mirrors enclosed him within himself, and there he grimaced at himself and was afraid, because Kali held him so that he could not find pity.

He mounted painfully and, among a group on foot, moved out onto the dusty road. It was very early. He rode with his head up but noticed nothing. On the dark glass a reflected figure moved, coming up from the south, a small and lonely horseman, unfocused in the pale vastness of the morning, lonelier by the bulk of the crowd traveling against him. The horseman carried his head slightly on one side. He increased in size, coming closer, fumbling through the crowd, filling at last William's horizon. His horse bumped against William's thigh. William saw Hussein's eyes level with his own.

"Maharaj, your pardon. You are all right? All is well." With downcast eyes the lopsided horseman shook his reins and went on his way. William turned to glance after him. He knew him now, and knew he was different from what he had been. Today Kali had indeed hidden her light from them, so that there was no warmth, only the cold dawn in men's eyes.

He was in the middle of the defile. Ahead he saw that the three palanquins had stopped. Yasin leaned down from his horse to point out something in the far distance. Already men and women on foot

188

began to edge past the palanquins where they blocked the middle of the road.

William stood in his stirrups and, hearing his own voice as a stranger's, shouted, "Kali, O Kali, hear us!"

The travelers around him looked up in fear, for passion cracked his voice. He reined in his horse. He heard screams from the front as Yasin and a mounted servant slid to the ground, locked together by a rumal. He heard a flurry and clash behind, and saw his Deceivers drag the young cavaliers from their saddles. Close at hand a traveler shouted, "Robbers, robbers, close up!" The travelers began to run together into tight little circles, like sheep at the coming of a wolf. The men among them brandished sticks and shouted defiance at—nothing.

For two full minutes the separate struggles continued, one at the front around the old ladies, one at the back around the cavaliers. Between, nothing, and William astride his horse. Still nothing.

Hesitatingly men broke away from the protective circles and ran toward the fights. From the front a voice screamed again in desperation, "O Kali, hear us!" It was Yasin. William saw the flash of steel. The pickax circled through the air and landed in the edge of the trees. And daggers stabbed and swords swung.

The flanking forests were silent.

The Deceivers broke away from the fighting, front and rear, and ran into the woods. William counted: four, six, seven. That was all. Three taken or dead, Yasin among them. The consecrated pickax lay in the dust. Piroo had escaped. The forests were silent.

The voices of the travelers rose to a scream as they realized that the robbers had failed. They surged forward in pursuit to the edge of the wood. One of the old ladies lay in the path and fought for breath as a heart attack gripped her.

Already men were moving toward William, connecting his cry with the cry of Yasin, who had proved himself a murderer. He found his voice and yelled, "Get back! It may be a trap. I will see."

He clapped his heels into the mare's flanks and bounded forward. Opposite the palanquins he slowed, leaned far down from the saddle, and snatched up the pickax. Then he turned and plunged into the woods.

After galloping for a space, spread forward on the withers, he stopped. He heard the crackle of leaves and the far, confused anger of the crowd. He would have to go to the pits and wait for his men —the seven survivors. They would move slowly and fearfully. They had no horses or had lost them. The jungle was empty; there should have been seven score men lying ready back here with club and knife and rumal.

He found the overgrown trace of a bullock-cart track and followed it. The pits were desolate hummocks and holes, the wounds of earth healed and bandaged with grass and scrub. The silver-white trunks of kulpa trees stood about between the pits, and in every bark an unknown hand had cut the sacred names *Ram* and *Sita*: the hand of God, men believed.

Hussein was there, dismounted, waiting for him. William swung slowly to the ground and tethered the mare. Not ten minutes ago Hussein had given the words: *All is well*.

His fear of Kali vanished; he forgot her and was a furiously angry Englishman. His eyes snapped and his teeth ground together. He grated, "You, explain!"

Hussein rose to his feet and stood closer, an ordinary little man, summoning dignity and not finding it. "I gave them all the wrong orders."

William's anger choked him so that the words fought together in his throat. His hand took hold of the rumal at his waist.

"You! On purpose? Have you gone mad? Yasin was killed. I had to rescue the pickax."

Hussein's jaw trembled and his voice shook. "Sahib, I took my own omens three nights ago, when you first suggested this plan. They were bad, but I held your wife's cross and was not frightened. I knew, holding your God's charm, that all I needed was courage. I had to try once more against Kali, because you had eaten her sugar and sold yourself to her. I had no hope unless I *fought* Kali for you—and for my red coat. Sahib, do not deceive yourself. If this had gone well today, you would never have returned to your place. It's true!"

William swung the rumal but did not jerk his wrists. He held it tight, shaking Hussein wildly to and fro, shouting, "Dog, pig, traitor! I'm getting information! That's all, all, all!"

"Never—gone—back—never!"

Hussein jerked the words out one by one between his rattling teeth. He did not struggle to get away but leaned with William's fury so that his neck would not be broken.

William tasted sugar in the back of his mouth. Through the fury that drove him out of all reason he heard Hussein's choked sobbing. "I thought—of my red coat—and strength came. It is made—by the best tailor of—my town. It is in a locked box—under my bed—at my home—waiting."

William loosed the rumal slowly. A red coat, with a badge of office. He used to have the power to bestow that. Bestow happiness. He could have given Hussein a badge double the regulation size. Double happiness, full pressed, running over. It was so ridiculous an ambition for a man to have, set against these voluptuous dreams of wealth and death. Almost the banality of it made Kali herself tawdry, for all her blood-wet mouth and lascivious tongue.

Silvery cracks splintered the black mirrors. There was light, but contorted. Kali's hold was slackening, but he could not stand another trial. Whatever the cost, this passion—half fear, half love—must be ended. He said to Hussein, "Go to Madhya. Tell her. See the new Collector. Tell him to bring the cavalry at once, from Khapa, from Sagthali. I can't stand any more or—or I don't know what I'll do.

Hussein had mounted his horse. Tears streamed down his face. He said, "The others are coming. Do not try and tell them what happened in the affair. They'll know Kali did it. You had bad omens? I was not there, but I knew."

He turned the horse's head, and William, not looking up, said "Go! And on the way back, tell the woman at Kahari that her husband is dead."

"Sahib, I cannot. That you must do yourself. You know it."

Hussein waved his free hand, and Mary's cross was in it. Triumph filled the little lopsided man's face. Then he was gone.

One by one, Deceivers crept out of the woods. William stood up and, with effort, piece by piece, broke up the black mirror so that he could see more clearly. He was William Savage, and no servant of Kali. She had touched him and held him for a time. Hussein had today broken some of the chains; but some silver links still shone on William's wrists, and he did not know whether they were a brand or an ornament.

The mirror was breaking, but— Kali's omens last night had been bad; so she had meant the affair today to fail; and it had. Was Hussein therefore the servant of Christ, or of Kali? . . . It was Christ who, in the last resort, had forced him, William, to ignore the superstition of omens; so it was Christ who had wanted him to kill the travelers? All travelers?

A week ago such thoughts as these would run like silver deer, horned and beautiful, across the jet mirror as he lay awake or, unseeing, rode his horse. Now he saw the madness in them and prayed for a little more strength until the time should come to stand free, himself once more, not fearing Kali's eyes, not loving her liquid mouth, but having understanding and compassion.

The Deceivers waited for their Jemadar to speak, and did not interrupt, because they saw that he prayed.

# Chapter 21

WILLIAM knew that the desiccated jungles north and west of Parsola and the Mala marsh must be full of Deceivers, but when he reached there at the head of his band, late at night on March 20, 1826, he could see no trace of them or of anyone else. He settled his men in camp in a secluded valley, and when they were all asleep sat for a time over the fire with Piroo.

Piroo said, "Jemadar-sahib, who are you going to send to the corn-chandler's? I don't suppose you've ever been there?"

Piroo's voice was still respectful in spite of the fiasco near the iron workings. William had expected furious recriminations from all of them, but they had only been sympathetic and solicitous. They seemed to think that Kali had deliberately misled him, as any proud woman will sometimes harry a lover to prove her independence. They seemed to have guessed, too, that Hussein had failed him, and never mentioned the little man's name. Probably they thought William had strangled his friend, and that his moroseness sprang from that.

William said, "Yes, I know Parsola."

There was a corn-chandler's store at the head of the only street in the village. On arrival in the forests, every band was to send a man there to receive instructions about the sale.

William knew Parsola. The Mala marsh nearby was a favorite of flighting wildfowl; he had shot over it two or three times every cold weather since his coming to Madhya. He knew several people in Parsola by sight, including the corn-chandler whose store seemed to be the local headquarters of the Deceivers. In his memories Parsola was a small, dirty, friendly little place, typical of all that he had liked best about his work in this district—shy peasant farmers, sturdy women, a marshy lake, jungles and fields. He wondered for a minute how such a gathering as this—there must be eight hun-

193

dred Deceivers collecting in the forests—could come together, and deliberate, and send envoys in and out of the village, without the inhabitants becoming aware of it.

He thought of Chandra Sen, while Piroo whittled a stick and waited patiently. Chandra Sen must have returned from his expedition to the south; William remembered now that in past years the patel had been away from his village only between Dussehra and the New Year. Chandra Sen was said never to attend these sales in person; nevertheless it was a risk. But he himself would have to go if he was to round out these five months' work. Hussein would reach Madhya tonight or tomorrow. The new Collector couldn't get the cavalry in time to catch the Deceivers at the sale, but he could round them up before they had dispersed afterward. Many would stay a day or two to make preparations for the road.

He said, "I'll go to Parsola myself, first thing in the morning."

"Very good, Jemadar-sahib."

A moment longer William stared into the embers. Then he said, "I'm going to sleep now. Good night."

"Good night, Jemadar-sahib."

In the morning William set out early, walking fast through the jungle but without the appearance of hurrying. He saw no one until the trail came out of the woods and skirted the Mala marsh. There three peasants jumped up nervously from a bullock cart they were mending and whined, "Ram ram, maharaj. Have you lost your way? This track leads nowhere."

"I'm going to Parsola, and I know this is the way there," he answered curtly. They were owlish, open-mouthed yokels, and he was in a hurry. They came closer round him. One of them jumped back, shrieking, "Aiiih! A snake!"

William leaped aside, exclaiming automatically, "Brother of Ali! A snake!"

The rumal choked him, the silver rupee in it bit against the bone under his left ear. The rumal dropped away. There was no snake. Two of the yokels had their hands on him, one at each side. He had jumped into the noose.

The man with the rumal put it away, grumbling, "Why the hell

194

can't you answer a greeting properly in the first place? It's careless fools like you that get us into trouble."

"I am Gopal Jemadar," William said shakily, feeling his neck. The three walked back, muttering, and bent over their cart. William saw that its axle was broken. It would not get mended for several days; during that time no stranger who passed by chance through this unfrequented jungle would reach Parsola with a tale of many men seen in the woods. On the other paths there would be other carts, other watchers.

Long-horned white cattle grazed in the hummocky grass at the farther side of the marsh. Half a dozen buffaloes wallowed in a mud hole where a stream trickled out of the reeds. Three brown boys lay on their backs under a tree there. The blazing scarlet blossoms of the flame-of-the-forest hung over the stream and were reflected in it. It was a hot, still morning. A group of women stood round the village well and chattered amiably. He wondered what they would think if they knew that eight hundred men, murderers by religion, lay hidden in the woods across the marsh. He braced himself to pass them and enter the village. Kahari was not far away. There might be people here who knew Gopal the weaver. Then the word would reach the woman at the pyre, and hold her there, waiting forever. Not forever. Sooner or later he had to go to her.

At the corn-chandler's shop there was a man squatting on the beaten-earth platform that jutted a little into the street. The place smelled pleasantly of jute sacking, bajri, and rice. There was no sign of the merchant himself, and William squatted down to wait.

The other man rose to his feet and walked away. William looked suspiciously after him; the man had glanced at him carelessly, showing no sign of recognition; but it was too late now. The man had gone.

He waited, remembering that he had sat more than once on this platform, his gun beside him, while paying off the guides and coolies who had helped to give him a good day's sport. No one would recognize him as that shuffly, shy old fool Captain Savage.

The chandler came out of his house behind the store, and William said, "Greetings, brother Ali. I want some flour for a long journey."

195

"How many men in your band?" the chandler said testily. People were moving up and down the street in front of the store; a woman had entered and stood on the platform awaiting her turn. William thought quickly what answer he could give that would not cause suspicion.

The chandler glanced at the pickax at William's waist and said, "Speak up. What's the size of your band—ten, twenty, what?"

William said, "Twenty-one," in a low voice, adding half hysterically, "and a bear." The chandler looked at him in astonishment, peering into his face as though he were mad. His eyes contracted as he stared, and he said slowly, "Isn't it Gopal the weaver from Kahari?"

The woman turned suddenly and came close to William, walking with the hipswinging gait of those used to heavy loads. She cried, "It is!" Her face was bare in the manner of the low-caste poor. She added gently, "Don't worry. We all knew here that you'd gone back to Kali. We haven't told the one of your house. She waits by her pyre for you." A couple of passers-by had stopped to listen; they nodded, and smiled at William, and went on their way. The woman took a bag of rice, paid for it, and swung down into the street.

William looked after her and could not speak. She knew what the Deceivers were and what they did. Everyone in Parsola knew; they were the servants of Kali—all of them, everyone in the village. None of them cared what happened to the woman at the pyre.

He turned to the chandler and said bitterly, "I am Gopal the Jemadar, not Gopal the weaver. What orders?"

The chandler washed his hands. "Yes indeed, sir, I quite realize. The jewel buying will be in the barn here, two hours after sunset the day after tomorrow, the twenty-third. The order is that only two men from each band are to come, Jemadar-sahib."

William nodded, stooped, twisted the sack onto his shoulder, and walked out. Trudging down the street, he glanced covertly at the villagers as they passed by or sat in their yards. Great was Kali and uncountable her servants. These people looked no different now from when he had seen them all those incarnations back, as a white sahib with a gun. Did they kill strangers here at all seasons, or only during the annual sale? Perhaps the point didn't arise. Parsola

196

was well chosen; the track through it led nowhere; it was a dead end and might see only two or three visitors in a year.

He reached his camp again without being challenged, although the cart stood abandoned in the same place, and a tingling in his neck warned him that the sentries watched from the trees. He told Piroo of the arrangements for the sale and added, "You come with me. Assuredly our Deceivers have a great and wonderful organization here. That whole village is of us."

Piroo smiled. "Yes. The women can't actually be Deceivers of course, but Parsola is one of the places where even they know all about us. They have to. There are several like it in India, where everybody has taken the oath to Kali. Some towns too, in rajahs' country. We keep the peace while we are in them and take no merchandise. A few of the men travel with Deceiver bands, but not many. It's better not to arouse suspicion about places which are so useful as refuges and gathering points."

Six months ago William could not have believed it. Now it all seemed plain enough. At some moment, centuries past perhaps, the Deceivers had descended on the village in strength and given it the choice: be destroyed, or provide refuge, hold silence, and receive an annual payment from the spoils. Embraced in the choice were immense difficulties, both moral and physical, for the people of the village. The Deceivers' worship of Kali was genuinely religious. Indians of an older generation might have felt it impiety in them not to help these seekers after salvation, even if the Deceivers' way to grace was not their own. Then, the payments would raise the community an inch or two above starvation; the danger of starvation, actual and ever present, does not breed respect for law. On the other hand, if the village refused and spoke up against the Deceivers, the local powers of order, which had sometimes been weak and always venal, could not have saved them from torture and annihilation. Probably the old rulers had received their percentage of the spoils too, in return for keeping their troops away and their eyes and ears shut. The close interlocking of so many self-interests formed a conspiracy of silence as effective as the conspiracy of murder.

In the nine years of the English Company's rule nothing had been done against the Deceivers. But William realized now that most Indians knew at least of the existence of the Deceivers; and, knowing, they could not believe the English did not also know; therefore the English officials too were sharing in the spoils; so what was the use of informing? He had found Kali on the road, and followed her, and found her in palaces, and now in hovels. Kali's hand truly lay over all India.

He fell to wondering again about the man who had seen him at the corn-chandler's and gone away so quickly.

Mary stood in the carpenter's shop behind the bungalow, absently stroking the edge of the bench where William's hands used to rest. For five months, once every week, she had come here in secret to oil his tools. She had finished; it was dark outside, and in a minute she would pick up the lamp and carry it to the bungalow. She was heavy now, and swollen out in the last month of her pregnancy. For five months she had bound herself in, and her young muscles had almost to the last contained and preserved her virginal beauty. Today, March 22, she had let it go and put on loose clothes, and all day worn pride instead of a cloak about her.

She picked up the lamp, closed and latched the door, and walked slowly to the bungalow. At the drawing room she stopped in surprise and put the lamp down on a table. Chandra Sen, the patel of Padwa and Kahari, stood respectfully erect near the windows. George turned as she came in, and she saw the mixed anger and relief on his face. He said, "Oh, come in, Mary. Chandra Sen has some news. I don't know whether it's good or bad."

"I think I know where Savage-sahib is. Indeed, I am sure that I do," the patel said quietly. "I have just told Mr. Angelsmith."

"He's wandering round in native clothes, alone, begging his way. He's in the district, came recently. A friend of Chandra Sen's recognized him. I'm afraid he's insane, Mary. I'll have to go and get him."

He looked at her as he spoke. Her happiness that William was alive warmed her heart and shone in her face. This was the first news she had had of him for five months. George's lips tightened.

Chandra Sen said, "I do not think that would be safe, sahib. Your honor cannot travel without being remarked. People pass the

198

word of your coming ahead of you. Everyone wants to know when the Collector is near, so that they can bring petitions to him."

"What of it? I've got to get hold of Captain Savage."

"Let me go, sahib. He is on the move, beyond Parsola. I can find out where he will be and come upon him suddenly. Unless we are very careful, he will disappear again. As it is, I fear he will do himself a mischief when we try to hold him. His mind is upside down. I have some experience in these matters. But I will do my best to bring him back safe."

"He won't hurt himself," Mary burst out, "he's—" She bit off the sentence. William had agreed, at Hussein's insistence, that no one must know why he had left Madhya. Chandra Sen looked at her thoughtfully. When she did not finish George said, "There's always the risk with people whose minds are—upset. I think Chandra Sen is right. Will you do that, then, patel-ji?"

"Very well." Chandra Sen bowed slowly to each of them in turn and left the room. They heard a mutter of talk between the patel and his servant on the veranda, then the creak of saddlery, the quickening, dying beat of hoofs.

The sounds faded at last, and George said with sudden spite, "You knew all the time what William was doing. I saw it in your face just now. You lied to your father."

"I did not lie to anyone." She put a perceptible emphasis on the "anyone." George was not thinking of her father but of his own misty hopes and of her subtle encouragement. It had never been much; it could not be, with William's child growing in her; with another man it would have been nothing; but it had been enough. She had done her part, and by a look, a shrug, an implied promise, deceived George so that he had not used his power to track William down.

George shrugged petulantly, "Oh, well, it's all the same now. I'm afraid he'll be put into an asylum."

She felt tears coming and shook her head furiously. She would not cry in front of George. The baby stirred inside her, and all the loneliness of the months came to overwhelm her.

Words fell tiny and all but soundless into her ear. "Memsahib, it is I, Hussein. Let me in quickly."

Astonishment held her without fear, and yet for weeks past she had expected to hear that faraway voice. She opened the windows through which Chandra Sen had five minutes ago left the bungalow. The moon shone bright on the drive and the wall and the road beyond. Hussein slipped into the room and stood beside the windows, where he could not be seen from the road.

George started up. "Who in hell are you? Mary, who is—"

Hussein ignored him and spoke to Mary in slow, clear Hindustani. "Your sahib needs help. He is at Parsola, with many Deceivers. He has found out all that is wanted. Tell this sahib now what he was doing. Make him send for all the cavalry, and come at once with them, or it will be too late. Your sahib is in danger."

She understood from Hussein's strained face and haunted eyes that it was not mere physical danger which threatened William. "Fear of the gods"—she remembered that, and looked out at the cold moonlight, and turned to George.

George said, "My good man, I can understand Hindustani better than the memsahib. What's all this about Deceivers? And"—he moved forward to get between Hussein and the windows—"you stay there! I've heard of you. You're the man with his head on one side who was implicated in the Chikhli murders and the Bhadora affair. You're under arrest. Sher Dil!" He raised his voice to a shout.

Hussein's right hand trembled at his waistband. Then he gritted his teeth and stood motionless in George's grip. He said, "Sahib, send for the cavalry! From Sagthali or Khapa, or both. They'll take a day and a half to come, and meanwhile I will explain everything. Do not hold me. I do not want to run away, because if I go outside now I think I will die. But if I stay here, and you do nothing, Savage-sahib will die."

"Why will you die?" George snarled. "Not that it matters. I've turned out the military before, on your account, you lying little swine! It's on the scaffold that you'll die! We happen to know where Savage-sahib really is—and he's not with or after any Deceivers. Chandra Sen, Patel of Padwa and Kahari, has gone to get him.

Hussein hung his head. His expression of misery deepened, but his eyes gleamed and he looked sideways at Mary. Mary heard Sher Dil shuffling across the compound from the servants' quarters.

Sher Dil never hurried to obey George's commands. Hussein seemed to shrink, and Mary, watching him, called out, "George!" so that George turned to look at her. Hussein drove his bony left elbow into George's stomach. Dumb amazement gaped in George's open mouth. The windows rattled and Hussein was gone.

Sher Dil padded in. "Your honor called?"

George gripped his stomach and groaned. Mary's mind raced but her feet were lead and she could not move. At last George said, "Man . . . Hussein . . . lopsided head . . . attacked me. Send for the police." Sher Dil ambled out of the room.

Mary ran to George and grabbed his arm. "Hussein is telling the truth! I promised not to tell you before, but William went off with him in the beginning, to track down the Deceivers."

George sat limply in a chair and looked up at her. "I don't believe it! And who are the Deceivers?"

"Do you accuse me of lying?" she whispered with a tense, sick fury.

He hesitated, quailing before the lightning in her eyes. "No, not you. But you're accusing Chandra Sen of lying. I'd rather take his word than Hussein's, damn it. The little swine's a murderer. From what Chandra Sen said, we'd be as good as killing William if we descended on him with squadrons of cavalry. Is that what you want?" He was cornered and bitter.

She said, "Are you going to send for the cavalry?"

"No."

Her hands itched to claw his handsome face, pull out his golden curls in tufts and strew them on the floor. She gathered herself up, leaning over him in wordless rage. Then she rushed out of the room.

The morning of the sale William walked apart and alone in the jungles. Hussein might come any time with news. Then he could put Kali behind him, but not before, because there were moments at night when she was still beautiful in his dreams. As the sun moved across the sky and the hour of the sale approached, he felt physical fear. Chandra Sen might be there. And yet it was not Chandra Sen, or death, that he feared. Kali would stand at the patel's right hand and reproach him with her burning eyes, and his fear was of her.

The sun bent down, and before the night's full moon set the sale would be over. A day or so more, and eight hundred Deceivers would be on the way to wives and homes and children. And he among them. But he dared not face Mary and embrace her because he had embraced the brutalities of Kali. Mary would know at once, while he would remember the harlot girl at Manikwal. He walked slowly through the woods, his head bent, and Hussein did not come to him.

At sunset, as the moon rose, his men took the jewels out of the bullock carts and loaded them in saddlebags on two packhorses. The hyena set up its maniacal call; the bear shuffled and slavered in farewell. Piroo led the horses in tandem, and William walked behind. Three times on the path through the jungles a voice challenged them from the moon-splashed darkness. Three times Piroo prefaced his answering greeting with the words, "Ali, my brother." William never saw any of the challengers.

Lights blazed in Parsola, and the moving, eddying people lent the little place the excitement of a great city. Men and pack animals—horses, donkeys, bullocks—crowded the street. Piroo turned his head to say, "We're the only band that needs two horses."

They came to the barn. It was a large low building, made of earth and cow dung, a relic of times past when the local landowner had built it to hold his tributes of produce. William knew it; officially it had been in disuse for some years. The thatched roof had decayed and drooped down like an old drunken woman's bonnet over the outsides of the walls. Four unglazed windows peered out on the side facing away from the street, and there was a great door in that wall.

Piroo led the horses inside, and William looked about him. Reeds and marsh rushes covered the earth floor. A few small lamps gave a feeble light; he could not see Chandra Sen anywhere. He found an empty space near the door, took the bridles, and said to Piroo, "Unload here."

Piroo spread two blankets and quietly emptied the first saddlebags. All over the barn these blankets covered the rushes, at least thirty of them, each afire with rings, bangles, and necklaces. By each blanket two men sat. Another score of men, marked plainly with the stamp of "bannia," did not sit beside any blanket but wandered around, talking with one another and with the men on the floor.

Piroo went out to tether the animals. William again searched the yellow, sparkling gloom. He squatted slowly down on his haunches and closed his eyes. Suddenly he thought of the catacombs of Rome as he had imagined them when he was a boy. In those daydreams he had seen a place like this, where men brought their gifts to Holy Church, and sentries held guard against the Roman law, which was cold and did not know the Word.

Men closed the door behind him. He wanted to get up and run away, but could not. It was too late now. The hum of talk in the barn quieted, giving place to light and smell. Ten thousand gems threw up a spectral brilliance. The Deceivers were angels bathed in light. The roof of the barn, all grimed and smoky black, became a barred mosaic, a cathedral under the earth, a sacred arch held up by the worship of men's hearts. Kali stepped down, and the smells of mold and damp, as from a grave, pierced his nostrils.

An unseen man raised his voice at the far end of the barn. "I ask silence, my friends and fellow Deceivers . . ."

William recognized Chandra Sen's voice and tried to keep his hands steady. The men behind him blocked the door. He strained to see the patel, but could pick out only a white robe above the heads of the gathering. A trick of shadow concealed the face.

The high, familiar voice went on, "Before we start with the sale of these jewels, which are Kali's gifts to us, there is something you must know. We have found a man who, having eaten Kali's sugar, would deny her."

The men in the barn groaned low, not angry but shocked and outraged. Still William could not see Chandra Sen's head.

"That man is here," the high voice cried. "On earth, we are the hands of Kali, and act for her. What does she wish us to do?"

William rose slowly to his feet. Here at the side of the barn he had no hope of escaping. He must get forward, speak to Chandra Sen, warn him that the cavalry were coming, tell him that no violence, only submission, might save him.

Chandra Sen moved, and a lamp shone up into his face. William locked eyes with him, and tucked the forefinger of his right hand into his waistband.

"Yes, yes, Jemadar-sahib, the rumal, Kali's rumal!" the men in the barn murmured. "The rumal for the apostate!" They had seen William when he came into the barn. They had whispered of him as the great jemadar whose band had killed more and won more than any

203

other. Now they saw him get up and walk forward, touching the place where his rumal lay, and they murmured in agreement.

The warm waves of their approval lapped William's back. He relaxed his shoulders. These men were his, not Chandra Sen's, because he was a killer while Chandra Sen was a thinker. He could do with them what he willed. He walked on, much more slowly, looking into Chandra Sen's eyes.

Suddenly from the darkness Chandra Sen dragged out a man whose hands were bound behind his back and thrust him into the light. It was Hussein, dusty, head hanging on one side, eyes downcast.

Chandra Sen spoke only to William, but with a piercing softness that all in the barn could hear. "This is the man, great Jemadar."

William did not look at Hussein. He stood close against Chandra Sen, and stared into his face, and sought the meaning of the riddle. Chandra Sen said, "Ask him, great Jemadar, can the sweetness of Kali's sugar ever leave the mouth of man?"

William said, not turning his head, "Hussein, can the sweetness of Kali's sugar ever leave the mouth of man?"

"Of some men, yes," Hussein said and lifted his head.

"No, no, never!" Chandra Sen cried, and the Deceivers echoed, "Never, never!"

Chandra Sen said to William, "Great Jemadar, Prince of Stranglers, Beloved of Kali, give this traitor his disproof. Strangle him."

William gazed at the thin, ascetic face and knit his brows. An inner radiance transfigured Chandra Sen and glowed behind the wide eyes, wider now in a wonder of adoration. Chandra Sen knew him but had not come here to kill him. This was not Chandra Sen the patel, or Chandra Sen the jagirdar. This was a priest of Kali, at whose right hand Kali now stood. No vengeance or anger troubled the soul behind the eyes, only a burning glory of salvation—William's salvation. William might have to be killed, but first the priest must save his soul and fix him forever in Kali's breast.

Chandra Sen said again, "This is the man, great Jemadar. How can he escape, in life, when he has eaten the sugar, taken the silver, used the rumal? Only Kali can give him back his wife, his unborn child. Strangle him!"

The large eyes were warming William's own, and his wrists itched,

204

and the goddess touched the small of his back with her lips. Hussein had no wife, and no child, born or unborn. It was Mary, and his old life, that Kali offered him through Chandra Sen's two-edged words. To recover them he must give up his soul to Kali. For them he must take the oath in the death throes of this lopsided little man who was looking at him and who wanted a red coat. The Deceivers in the barn waited for him to kill. They were his servants only while he loved Kali. To keep them he had to kill—someone, Hussein. He could make up a story afterward, but now he had to kill. Here was the crisis of his spirit, for death was Kali's love.

He stood, blinded by the white clarity of his mind, his hands at his waist. Why should he not kill Hussein, and so save his own life, and Mary's? And afterward, when they were safe, tell all? Hussein was a murderer many times over and worthy of death.

He saw in Chandra Sen's eyes that he would be let free if he killed. And he saw that Chandra Sen knew that the oath, so taken, would not be broken. There was nothing to stop him—except himself.

Chandra Sen was right, Kali was right. To kill, in this mind and in these circumstances, would break him loose forever from the love he had believed in and sought now so desperately to find again. Once he had been an ordinary man, one among a thousand million undistinguished others of every race and color and creed, who lived, strongly or weakly, by love. This killing that tingled in his hands would rank him forever where he now stood, among the select who lived by scorn, without love. Nor was he just a man, or only of this place and time; he was a part of eternity. If he failed, how many others, following, would fail? Kali's road wound up high hills, and from their summits she had shown him the spreading cities of the plain which could be his kingdom. He felt the press of the future, the pushing feet of men unborn who would dedicate whole peoples to the rule of Kali, and take possession of countries in her name, and still call themselves Christian, and their feet would follow only where his had led.

He thought of Mary and his child. They were the actual flesh of love. He would not see his wife or his baby unless he whirled the rumal. For the fourth time. A murderer, a soldier, a robber-baron . . . another murderer. What was the difference?

Hussein was an ordinary man who wanted a red coat. All the simple world, and love, were there. William smiled suddenly at him and swung round, the rumal in his hand. Hussein jumped at Chandra Sen, throwing himself bodily on top of him. A thickset man lunged at William from the shadows. It was Bhimoo the watchman. William began to swing the rumal, but it burned in his hand and he punched the watchman in the throat, then hurled the rumal down the barn. It flew through the air, its tail curling out behind the weight of the rupee in its head, and landed on a blanket of jewels. The Deceivers came struggling to their feet, gasped, and began to shout.

Hussein fought to his knees, his hands still locked behind his back. Mary's oak cross fell from his waist among the rushes. He shouted to William, "They haven't taken her yet! Go, go, for your God's sake, go!" and threw his body forward onto the nearest lamp. It smashed, spilling oil over the floor, and the rushes took fire. William struck out with his fists and reached a window. The pickax hanging at his waist caught on the sill and he tugged it fiercely through. Until then he had forgotten it—but he would not let them have it back now.

Hands grabbed at his feet. He kicked out. Under his arm he saw Hussein's face and the flames that ran up Hussein's hair and clothes and sent Chandra Sen and the Deceivers reeling away from him to grab at the corners of the jewel-laden blankets. As he fell to the ground outside he heard the little lopsided man's last cry: "*Ane wala hun!—I am coming!*" the standard, million-times-heard answer of a chuprassi to his master's call.

# Chapter 22

THE uproar in the barn had not permeated to the street. A knot of men near the corn-chandler's store rose in astonishment as William ran out of the yard. They started to run because he was running. He flung up his arm and shouted, "Traitors! Thieves!"

They all ran together, shouting. William burst through among them, untethered the nearest horse, leaped into the saddle, and jabbed his heels into its sides. The animal broke into an ungainly seesawing gallow and lumbered west down the street. The tumult behind increased. At the limit of the village William looked over his shoulder and saw men tumbling out of the barn and running for their horses. Their shouts clashed out in anger against the night. His horse had a mouth of iron; he tugged savagely at the right rein and turned into the fields.

For an hour the pursuit hovered behind him. Under the full moon his horse ran strong and surefooted, but not fast. Sometimes the pursuers would guess that the lay of the land would force him to turn; then he heard them moving out on a flank and calling to one another across the fields. Sometimes, in the woodland stretches, he heard nothing. He rode straight on, as near northwest as possible, through thicket and bush and field and marsh.

A jungle wall sprang back and a river opened up in front of him. The horse shied, backed away, and screamed. He pounded the pickax helve on its quarters until it jumped off the bank, splashed thunderously into the water, and began to swim. This must be the Seonath; the Bhadora ferry was a mile or two to his left. On the other side of the river he galloped through a narrow strip of jungle and saw a rise of land, and on it the ghostly ramparts and shadows of a moonlit village—Chandra Sen's domain of Padwa. He galloped up the street, watching the silent houses, wondering whether here too Deceivers flanked his path. The gray dogs ran out from the big house to snarl at his horse's heels, until it bucked and lashed out and broke one's head, and the other fell back.

William galloped on, always northwest. Under the moon the country began to whisper in his ear. By this lonely shrine he had talked with Chandra Sen one cold-weather morning. Under that hill he had sat beside the little stream and waited for the gudgeon in the pools to bite. His horse was stumbling now and would not jump. He forced it through the stream and rode on.

Near midnight he came to his bungalow in Madhya and slid down at the steps. He held a pillar for support and cried, "Hey! William Savage here! Let me in!" Then, toward the distant servants' quarters, "Sher Dil! *Koi hai! A-jao, jaldi!*"

The horse hung its head, and shuddered, and breathed in roaring gasps. Someone moved about inside the bungalow. A tremulous voice behind the door said, "Who—who's there?"

"William Savage. Is my wife there? Let me in. Quick, man!"

Footsteps came to him, running across the compound, and he turned with his fists doubled, but it was only Sher Dil, disbelieving wonder in his face and tears in his eyes. He seized William's knees and hugged them and sobbed loudly. The bungalow door opened an inch, and George Angelsmith looked out. He came forward, a pistol in one hand, a candle in the other. The candlelight dimmed under the brilliant moon. George's face was dead white, the pistol jumping in his fist. William stared at him, confused for the moment, wondering whether he had come to the wrong place. He did not know whom he had expected to see in Madhya, but certainly it was not George Angelsmith.

George said, "William—?"

"Where's Mary?"

"Gone to Sagthali this afternoon."

"Christ's mercy! When, what route, what escort? Sher Dil, take this horse away, get food, load my pistols, tell the groom to saddle Jerry, send a man running to bring all the police here."

Sher Dil grabbed the horse's bridle and ran off without a word. William pushed past George into the bungalow. George put the candle down on top of the escritoire in the drawing room but kept the pistol in his hand, half concealed behind his back.

William snapped, "Why did you let her go?"

208

George began to talk slowly, carefully examining William and his clothes as he spoke. "She wanted to go. I tried to stop her. I did delay her. She wanted to go in the middle of last night. Where have you been?"

"Following the Deceivers. Didn't a man come here with a message —Hussein, the fellow with his head twisted on one side? Didn't he come? Didn't he say something?"

"He came," George said slowly. "He had some story about Deceivers at Parsola."

"Yes, yes, what have you done?"

"I was to get the cavalry out from Khapa or Sagthali—again! But Chandra Sen had just told me you were alone in Parsola, begging, mad. I did nothing."

"*What?*" William sprang up, shouting.

George whipped up the pistol and pointed it at the pit of William's stomach. He said unsteadily, "Keep off, Savage! Keep your distance!"

William found his hand fumbling in the loincloth for the rumal, but it was not there, and even in his white passion of anger he thanked God it was not. Holding himself in, he said carefully, "Do you think I am mad?"

After these months on the road he knew men. George Angelsmith was relieved that he had come back, and frightened at the expression on his face, and—something else. Angry. He relaxed as George suddenly began to talk. The police were on their way, so no time was being wasted.

George said, "I don't know if you are mad, but I do know you are under departmental arrest. Orders. And what do you mean by running away from all the important things here? For the first four months I had to double up, do my work at Khapa as well as yours here. It's too much. Everything's gone wrong. Complaints. Troubles. The people are swine—keep coming in, complaining, writing to Mr. Wilson. I had no time."

William laughed suddenly. "D'you mean to say you've got a black mark in the record, George? That's calamitous!" He began to speak with insistent force. He could not be angry with George any more. "Listen, please. The biggest criminal conspiracy in history is on your doorstep, in Parsola, ready to be unmasked. There's glory for you in Parsola—far more than in finding me. Act fast and boldly now, and your name will be greater in the department than anyone's has ever been. More than that: you will be world famous. I don't want any credit, honestly I don't."

For this man he had no better bait to offer, and he watched narrowly as George swam up like a golden fish out of the weeds of indecision to inspect the lure. But George wasn't a fish, just a shiny, shallow man. William saw the old gentleman with the purple ribbon land on George's shoulders, and saw George's mouth curl unhappily. His own muscles flexed of themselves for action. The pickax at his waist came under his hand.

"Here is food for my sahib. He is hungry." Sher Dil's low voice was behind him.

George nodded. "All right, put it down. I don't believe you, William. You want to ruin me for—for—I don't know. Jealousy. You're out of your mind. I'm going to lock you up in the bathroom here. Didn't I hear you send for the police? That's all they'll do tonight—guard you. I'm the Collector."

"Here, sahib," Sher Dil said, bowing respectfully, a plate of cold curried vegetables on his palm. As he bowed he scooped back his hand and hurled the plate into George Angelsmith's face. George shrieked as the mess stung his eyes, raised the pistol and jerked the trigger. The ball thumped through the ceiling cloth into the rafters. William knocked the pistol from his hand and turned and ran, shouting over his shoulder, "For God's sake, believe me, and send to Khapa for the cavalry! I'm going to Sagthali."

He jumped into Jerry's saddle and found Sher Dil beside him on George Angelsmith's Arab. "It's no good waiting for the police, sahib," the butler muttered. "They will only arrest you. The memsahib was going to take the Jabera road." William nodded, gripped with his thighs, and began to ride. On the Arab, Sher Dil flopped and jolted along in the unaccustomed English saddle.

"Who's with her?" William asked.

"The tirewoman, a groom, and the bearer. And the palanquin coolies, of course. She's in that. The groom rides, the others walk."

"How is she?"

"She is well. Sahib, I came to know her in these months, and I am her servant. For a time I did not understand. She will tell you.

210

Then I understood, for she is skillful and brave. She heaped fire on my head, and I knew I was only a foolish, jealous, black man."

*Kala admi*—black man. How often had William heard Indians use the words in self-depreciation? Was it the conquering British who had led them to exaggerate and despise the color of their skins? Or was it other conquerors of long ago, Alexander's olive-skinned phalanx? He said, "You are a good man, Sher Dil; better than I. Ride faster. Sit down, let the horse move beneath you. Did you see the lopsided man Hussein?"

"No. He struck Angelsmith-sahib, but I could not catch him. The memsahib left at noon today—yesterday. We could not get a palanquin earlier. She was not going to stop anywhere. They will be about at Jabera by the time we catch them up."

"If!"

"We will. Your pistols are in the holsters on the saddle."

"Good. Listen, Sher Dil, you've got to know what's happened. I'm going to send you straight on to Mr. Wilson in Sagthali."

They rode southeast as fast as the fresh horses would carry them, and William jerked out the present situation of the Deceivers. Another part of his mind ran racing ahead among the gathering dangers. He could only guess what the Deceivers had done, where they had gone. They might have thought it would be safer to scatter; but it was not likely because eight hundred of them had been there in the jungles round Parsola. He thought that few would yet be west of the Seonath. Under Chandra Sen's leadership they would be spreading across country and along the roads beyond the Bhadora ferry—if they had not yet taken Mary. If they had, they would be there to tell him so.

Certainly he dare not cross the Bhadora ferry now. He knew from remembered inflections that the ferrymen there were all Deceivers. "We'll have to cut off the road soon," he cried across to Sher Dil, and the butler replied, "Yes. Which way, north or south?"

The trail pointed vaguely forward. The three o'clock moon shone over their right shoulders and gave them enough light to hold the horses at a hand gallop. Parsola lay north, left, of the Jabera road. The Deceivers had not had much time to gather and move out in strength. Most of them would still be on that side.

William cried, "South, here!" and turned off on a jungle track.

The track soon died, and they trotted among the ghostly army of trees, finding their way as best they could, haltingly, much more slowly. The river shone among the trees ahead. They walked the horses down the shelving bank, urging them on with heel and voice until the huge muscles of back and haunch gathered and released, and the horses struck out to swim. William looked to the right and could not see what he had hoped to see, the shadowy outlines of the village of Deori. They had gone too far to the left and were crossing now less than a mile from the ferry—less than a quarter of a mile from the place where the widow of Gopal the weaver waited by her fire. He glanced downstream but could make out no human shape in the moonlight and turned again to the front. The horses stretched out their necks, and gnashed their teeth, and plowed up the water into silver foam, and their tails streamed out behind.

A convulsive scramble, and they stood for a moment on top of the steep eastern bank and smiled at each other. They crossed the Tendukheda road and galloped on, southeast, keeping two miles to the right of the Jabera road. They left the country William knew well and entered areas where he had been only once or twice. The light grew in the east ahead, the moon sank low behind, and sometimes he would recognize the loom of a far hill, the gray hulk of a village as they skirted it. Their pace slowed. Splashes and stripes of foam streaked the horses' flanks; sweat lathered them, and they stumbled more often and put their hoofs into holes and rapped them against the roots of trees. William felt the strength draining from his own muscles and knew that only an urgent energy of the spirit held him in the saddle. He thought of food, even the food spread on George's face, and saliva came painfully into his mouth.

They plunged on, swaying, turning back at the mouths of blind valleys, swinging away from the hidden hamlets that sprang up before them. The sun rose, and on the instant the land awoke and the air grew hot in their faces.

They came suddenly upon six men on foot, moving fast from north to south across their path. William recognized Piroo in the same moment that Piroo recognized him. He rode his horse furiously at him. The six ran apart. Piroo shouted, "That's him, catch him!" but his men broke before the scarlet-eyed horses, and

William and Sher Dil rode through between them. William looked back and saw Piroo gesticulating; then all six turned and ran north.

How far away were other Deceivers, and in which direction were they going? He had to reach Mary before they did, and get away again, get into hiding at least, before the scattered, searching bands could concentrate. There was some reason to hope: Chandra Sen had had to send out from Parsola to collect the bands and give them orders; the majority of the Deceivers were on foot; they must be expecting cavalry and police to be at hand, enforcing caution on them; there would be confusion.

An hour later William said, "We must get on the road now, at any cost, or we'll miss them."

"*Achchi bat!*"

They turned left, plunged through a jumble of thorny brakes and muddled water courses, and, without warning, reached the Jabera road. They swung right, and William knew that Jabera lay five miles ahead. Far on, dust clouded the road. With hands and knees and voice he urged Jerry forward.

The road ran down the rim of a low plateau. Flat valley country, the floor of an old lake, spread out on the left, and there the sun picked out the white clothes of three horsemen. Other men on foot ran at their stirrups, and they came on at a diagonal toward the road. On that course they would intercept the moving dust ahead two miles or more before it could reach Jabera—and Jabera held no sanctuary. They were coming now, these that he saw, and Piroo's six, and countless others, using many trails and running forward like a far-searching pack of red dogs.

In a few minutes he saw that the dust in front rose from the feet of four coolies hurrying along with a palanquin. Four more trotted beside it. The groom rode a little ahead on Mary's bay hack. The tirewoman and the bearer walked behind the palanquin.

The bearer turned, saw the two of them galloping up the road, turned again, and shouted and waved his arm. The coolies dropped the palanquin heavily and ran into the bush, followed by the spare coolies. The bearer fled a second later. The tirewoman fell on her knees beside the palanquin. The groom edged in on his horse, raised the fowling piece he held across his saddle, and aimed it.

Then he recognized Sher Dil and lowered the gun. Sher Dil's

213

companion he did not know, and stared in astonishment as William pulled Jerry back on his haunches, jumped down, and knelt in the dust.

William thrust his head through the palanquin curtain and looked down the muzzle of a pistol. Over it, Mary's bright blue eyes, unfrightened and angry, glared at him. She knew him at once, seeming to expect that the road would have turned her husband into just this brown-skinned, decisive, half-naked adventurer. She sighed slowly, lowering the pistol.

He bent forward and gathered her gently in his arms.

"Is it all over?" she asked quietly. "Are we going to die?"

"No. Get out." He caught her wrists and pulled. She rose slowly and stood up in the road. The harsh sun glared on her ungainliness, made deep the rings under her eyes, patched her skin with blotches. She was not beautiful now, and she could not ride a mile. His love flooded up so that he forgot their present danger and for a second stood relaxed before her, rejoicing in the affection they had for each other.

He glanced up and down the road. No one was in sight. A line of trees hid the fields to the north, where the three horsemen and their followers ran in the valley. He rapped out orders. "Tire-woman, give the memsahib your sari, take her cloak. Cover your face. Take a cushion from the palanquin for your stomach. There! Get up on my horse. All right now. Groom, are you ready? All three of you, ride round Jabera, then straight on to Sagthali, as fast as you can go, for your lives. Sher Dil, you know what to say, what to do. Give me one of those horse pistols. Go!"

While he spoke Mary took off her long dust cloak and wrapped the tirewoman's sari loosely over her dress. The tirewoman struggled into the cloak, pushed a cushion under it, drew the thick white veil across her face, and was hurled up into Jerry's saddle. Sher Dil shouted, the horses reared, and the three plunged away toward Sagthali.

William took his wife's hand and led her quickly into the brush on the south side of the road. From its shelter he looked back at the palanquin overturned in the dust. The sun was up, the shadows shortening. The breathless heat of day closed in under the trees. On the road he saw movement to the northwest and crouched lower. The Deceivers were coming.

Help too would come—in time; but it was him they sought, the apostate, the traitor whose memory alone recorded the graves of the notes, whose mind alone knew all the ways of Kali, whose spirit alone held the will to root out her and her Deceivers from the roads of India and from the memory of man. Only William Savage had the power, the knowledge, and the desire to make the Deceivers, the Thugs, an evil word and nothing more.

They were coming. How many he did not know. But they were coming, with Kali in their hearts and the taste of sugar in their mouths.

# Chapter 23

HE crept back, and turned, and led Mary south into the jungle. Among the trees he saw on his left the hills of Jarod shimmering under the sun. He remembered passing under them with Mary, on their bridal journey so many months and lives ago. Jarod's cliffs and caves offered refuge, and he considered heading for it now, but while Mary could move it was better to cut south and east, cross the Bhanrer hills near Selwara, and reach the comparative safety of the peopled plains.

Mindful of Mary, he moved at a snail's pace. After a minute she touched his shoulder and said in a businesslike tone, "William, I've got about three weeks to go yet. I've told you before that you don't have to treat me like a china doll. I'll tell you when I can't go on."

"You must, Mary," he said and tried to smile at her. She carried the heavy pistol in her hand. Already it weighted her down, but she would not give it up. His own he tucked into his waistband, where the rumal had been, and brought out the little pickax; with that he held the boughs aside for her.

They walked faster than before, but still slowly, over the shelving rock ledges of the hills. They rested many times, and in the afternoon found a brown pool and drank from it. He felt shy with her in spite of their danger and spoke little. The sun sank, and they stumbled on. When it was full dark and they could not see at all, they stopped and lay down together on the ground and waited for the moon to rise.

Mary reached for his hand, and took it, and held it to her breast with both her own. He whispered suddenly, "I didn't know George had come to Madhya. He ought to have guessed what I was doing. He knew how I felt about these murders. I should have thought he could have found me if he'd tried."

216

Her hands stiffened over his. "William dearest, I had something —a little—to do with that. But really it was he himself. He was a —a muddled man." She did not speak for a minute, then whispered, "Do you love me?"

"Yes."

"He wanted to marry me if you didn't come back. Rather, he wanted to marry Mr. Wilson's daughter. Darling"—he thought she was looking at him—"George was important only because he is the man you thought you wanted to be, once, didn't you?"

He said, "Yes. What did Hussein say?"

"He told me you were in all sorts of danger. His face was dreadful, terrified but somehow exalted too. I saw it just as he ran out. The hangman might have been waiting outside for him."

"He was."

"Oh, darling! I think he died happy, though." Her voice was hoarse from thirst, but calm and steady. "You must tell me more about him later. I don't want to know everything."

"He wanted to be a chuprassi and was faithful."

"That's it. William, have you got anything we can eat? My insides are rumbling."

He said, "Nothing. There was some curry. Sher Dil threw it in George's face."

She giggled suddenly and moved his hand. "Put your hand—here. Feel? That's your baby." Her voice was fond and warm. William felt the baby's sudden kick lift her skin under his hand.

"*She!*" he said and kissed her ear. She wriggled her head in a tiny spurt of voluptuous abandon, and for him the sky roofed over and the hard stone became their bed in Madhya. He kissed her longingly. She broke away. "Oh, William! There's a Peeping Tom." The moon climbed out of the hills and peered at them between the trees.

They walked on slowly and haltingly. They crossed jungle clearings washed by mysterious light, slipped down the banks of a small stream, drank, scrambled up the other side, and wound on in Indian file between the trunks of trees where the jungle grew thick. Twice every hour they lay down to rest.

After many hours, as they lay, he heard that Mary's breath came in shallow gasps, and he did not get up to move on when the ten

217

minutes were over. Half an hour later, breathing more easily, she fell into a doze. The first daylight began to etch a black horizon ahead. The contrasting gray pallor spread up and reached fingers round the eastern sky. He looked across a grassy upland, a mile and more wide between these trees and others on the farther side. He did not properly remember this country; he had traversed it only once; he did not know exactly where they were, but he knew that the far trees must crown a slope that led down to the Hiran River. Katangi Beacon reared up black to his left. The dawn came over the ridge and the blackness on the hill retreated downward, leaving the trees green behind it. Away to his right, low blue smoke from Selwara tinted the air over the plateau. He saw five or six of the hamlet's outlying houses, but no movement.

He touched Mary's shoulder. "Wake up. Look." Her eyes fluttered, and her face in the cold light was like sweat-streaked marble. He said, "We've got to get across this plateau. Then we can rest." She gathered herself and was ready. For the last time he swept his field of view, from Katangi Beacon on the left to Selwara on the right, shading his eyes against the sunrays now flat in his face.

A brown animal moved out from a clump of trees in the center of the plateau. He stared at it and frowned because he could not make out what it was. It was not a cow, or a fox, or a leopard, or a deer, or a pig.

It did not matter what it was. One animal could not hurt them. He rose up, still staring. The animal moved in an awkward swinging shamble, head down on the grass. It stopped slowly, then raised its head, higher and higher, and sat up on its haunches. A light wind blew from west to east. The animal moved on a pace, stopped short with a jerk, and shambled back into the copse.

It was a bear on a long chain. Someone out of sight had pulled the chain. The sap ran out of William's knees and he sank down. After a minute, when he had mastered the trembling in his legs, he took Mary's hand and led her back into the jungle.

He would have to go to Jarod and hide there with her—and hope. Mr. Wilson with the cavalry regiment from Sagthali might reach the area late tonight, by furious riding, but he could do nothing till the morning. He might not come at all. Like George Angelsmith, he might refuse to believe the whole fantastic story.

218

At all events, this day and this coming night belonged to the Deceivers, and to the sharp-nostriled, lascivious, loving bear.

After an hour's hurried scramble Mary groaned, and they sat down. She lay back against a tree. He said, "Can you go on? We can fight here. We have two pistols."

"I can go on, in a minute," she said. "Where are we going?"

"Jarod."

The heat of day increased. Mary weaved between the trees and tripped over every twig and stone. They passed across the lower slopes of Katangi Beacon and came late in the afternoon to a shallow stream. The sticky phlegm clogged their mouths so that at first they could not drink. Then Mary lay down in the water, but he said, "Come on, come on." They walked in the stream bed, scrambling up the transverse rock faults which made little falls, and stooping to pass under the overhanging bushes. When they stepped out of the stream they heard a call on the hill behind them, not faint, not far, and it was answered from the right.

They crossed a rock slope where the sun poured down and the sparse trees made lonely islands of shadow. Beyond, the land rose steadily. Now Mary moved one foot at a time and moaned at every step. Just before dark a straight line, straighter than any in nature, loomed horizontally among the trees ahead. They climbed a short, steep, evenly sloped bank. The top of it was twenty feet wide and level. Brown grass grew plentifully, and the trees were spaced even more thinly. They stood on the outer glacis of Jarod.

The glacis dropped twelve feet, a cliff made of stone blocks, to a wide dry ditch. Across the ditch rose a vertical face of earth and stone—the inner rampart. The whole—the outer glacis, the inner rampart, the ditch enclosed like a roofless corridor between them—ran up hill and down dale to right and left through the jungle, curving irregularly back on itself to form a complete circle of two miles' circumference. They could see little enough of it, for the triple barrier soon disappeared among the trees and folds of land. But through her pain Mary gasped in admiration.

This he had spoken of on the bridal journey, and she remembered. This was the forgotten fortress of Jarod, built by the Gond aborigines in a time when they had had the power, against enemies not possessing firearms, to hold this pass through the hills. The glacis and ditch and rampart enclosed a section of the side of the mountain. There were no buildings, and never had been; nor had the Gonds leveled the ground. Inside the rampart, as outside, trees grew and spiny bushes ran across the earth, and there were small cliffs, a stream, clearings, flat ground, rock slides. Here the Gond tribes had once encamped against the Aryan invaders who pressed them back into their own jungles and made them savages. In this dusk of a later century William felt still the presence of the small black sentries, and saw them hurry together with their bows and poisoned arrows to the point of danger.

Many parts of glacis and rampart had fallen down, pushed out by the roots of the trees that had grown on them. William and Mary scrambled down the glacis over a cascade of tumbled stones. They walked along the ditch and after a hundred yards found a breach in the inner rampart and climbed up onto it. Again William paused and looked about him.

Jarod was a good place for a last stand. Others had stood here before him, others who, like him, had wives and children beside them and death all round. This had been the majesty and the mighty work of a forgotten people, and lent him now a little of the hope that had gone to the making of it.

Abruptly he led the way into the fortress. Voices called again on the hillsides. He did not know where sanctuary lay, but he knew he could not turn back. Forward, the ground fell away. Here, near its source, a stream ran in a steep small gorge. It had once given the Gonds of Jarod their water. He dragged Mary up the stream bed and hurried on, scanning the low cliffs on either hand. To the right he saw a dense luxuriance of stinging nettles. He left Mary and carefully pushed the nettles aside with his hand. There was no cave, but the stream had cut in under the basalt cliff and made an overhang.

He led Mary in, pulled the nettles over, and lay down. The stings burned his hands and legs, but hunger overcame all pain and he groaned softly, holding his stomach in both hands.

In the very last light he looked out between the nettles. They stung his face. He saw nothing and, listening, heard only the faint hum of bees. He saw their nests under the cliff across the gorge and thought of their honey.

A voice called on the left and was answered at once on the right. It was not honey, but sugar, that he seemed to taste.

Night came, and the darkness whispered up the hill. When the moon rose the night became alive. The murmuring took form and pattern; from an indistinguishable something it became men, known by the paces of several feet, walking, scrambling quickly. Mary began to cry softly, then stopped and squeezed his hand. Sticks snapped, water splashed, stones stirred. They fell asleep.

Down in the valley a trumpet called the *Halt*. Other trumpets answered it. The silver echoes broke on the hillside and ran splintered among the trees. William awoke, and heard, and shook so that his teeth rattled. The trumpet was so near, so far. Close at hand he heard a soft, choked wheezing, like a man with asthma; a pleased whine and a snuffle. The links of a chain were pulled taut, so that they clinked.

The bearleader's voice said, "Here."

Chandra Sen answered from up the hill. "Stand away. Dawn is coming."

The light came. The bear snuffled and moaned somewhere to the left. They listened and soon could not distinguish the sounds of their enemies from the undertones of day—the shaking of leaves, the hum of insects, the tinkle of the stream, the sighs as the earth breathed. William looked at his wife. She was pasty gray, and her skin flaccid. Dirt festered in her scratches and cuts, and never-ceasing pain cut deep lines into her young face.

Before they died, he had to tell her what he had been. He muttered in the way he had learned with the Deceivers. "I told you I could not kill. I promised. I broke my promise."

She said gently, "I know. But you redeemed it somewhere, somehow, or you wouldn't be here."

What she said was true. He had redeemed his promise, and his soul, with the rumal and the sacred silver swinging in his hand and Hussein's neck the token of self-sacrifice or self-destruction.

Chandra Sen's voice called out quietly, echoing hollowly under the overhang. "Collector-sahib, come out."

They did not answer. William pushed his pistol forward, and with his hand held back the nettles so that he could see a little,

221

ready to shoot. Chandra Sen was standing out of sight, under the cliff to the right. The bees hummed, making a low sawing noise, as if there were many of them.

William said, and found his voice uncertain, "It is no use, Chandra Sen. I know you are a murderer. So does Mr. Wilson by now. You will have to come in and fetch us."

"About Mr. Wilson—I know, sahib. My life here is finished. There are other places, other bands. But the Deceivers will still be able to worship Kali in their appointed manner—if you die. It is not for myself that I am here to kill you, but for all Deceivers everywhere, for Kali. Come out."

William did not answer. After a minute Chandra Sen said, "Come out quickly, sahib, or we will hurt you both very much."

"What if we do?"

"The rumal, sahib. For you at once. For her, after she is delivered. The child will live, and will be a boy, and we will look after him, and he will become the greatest that ever tasted the sweetness of Kali." He spoke in halting English. He wanted Mary to understand what he was saying.

Mary caught her breath. William half crouched, ready to run out and fight. But he knew that Mary's heart ached to shriek, "Yes, yes! Do anything, but let me bear my baby, let me see him!" She did not fear death, but voices louder than fear, older than the first death of the first woman, shouted that she was the bearer of life, his and hers. If that life survived they would not die, but live on together in it.

He would surrender. Mary should live a few days more, and their child should live, even in Kali. In those few days anything might happen. He said in a firm voice, "We will come, Deceivers," and reached out his hand and pushed aside the nettles.

Again they stung his swollen hand. He remembered raiding old Farmer Taylor's beehives when he was a boy. Those bees had stung like this, but worse. In the gorge the bees hummed, the bees that ruled the Bhanrer and the Kaimur and the Mahadeo hills. The gorge sides were black with their gigantic hanging nests. Even the sounds of men talking or the faint aroma of tobacco smoke offended their delicate senses and sometimes drove them to action. Their

222

buzzing had increased and dropped in tone since Chandra Sen began to speak. They ruled the central hills of India, and were more feared than tigers or cobras, because they wanted peace to work and because they did not fear death. And because there were a quarter of a million of them in each place where they built their clustered nests.

He drew back, aimed his pistol carefully at the center of a nest across the gorge, fired, and threw the smoking pistol over the nettles into the stream. Without hurrying, he took the other pistol from Mary's hand, aimed, fired, and threw it after the first.

The heavy lead balls smashed into the nests and spattered against the rock face. Splinters of stone and lead droned along the cliff. He whispered, "Wrap up!" and pulled in the nettles to block the overhang. They lay down together and Mary covered him with her sari.

A drone like the rising ocean drowned all other sounds. The bees came out. Their buzzing grew to the bellow of a giant organ, rising and falling in rhythmical waves. One bee came into the darkness under the cliff with them. William felt the tiny sting on his lip and welcomed the pain, measuring it, and did not stir a muscle.

His mind ventured out of this refuge and saw the gorge and the hillside above. Out there the bees of Jarod swarmed in hundreds of thousands on their enemies, and died, and in dying killed—and saved. Out there it was black as midnight under them. Their drumming thunder swallowed the shrieks and scrambles and clattering of stones.

He closed his eyes and in that darkness saw the strong men outside, who now dragged themselves away step by slower faltering step, loaded down with the weight of bees. They would be found a hundred, two hundred yards from this place, no farther, black, contorted, swollen to twice their size, dead under dead armies of bees, their skins spotted gray-white where the bees' entrails still clung to the embedded stings. It was not the Deceivers' killing of men, but their despisal of man, that gave this punishment the majesty of justice.

The sound of the shots carried far, and the trumpets sounded from the valley. Mr. Wilson would come, and Sher Dil, and the cavalry, who wore uniforms and were ordinary men. There would be much to do. But Kali the Destroyer had been defeated, here and now, by the smallest servants of the Creator and Preserver. Pressed against Mary, he did not move, but lay still, and waited.

# Chapter 24

TWICE during the day the cavalry came up the hill. They came prepared to fight, the trumpets screaming orders, the horses scrambling and slipping on the rocks; but when they saw the bees the trumpets said *Retire*, and they went away again. The bees had been quiet; as the cavalry approached, their noise dropped again to the organ note, and the trumpets shrieked *Gallop!*

But William knew they must have seen the dead men lying on the sides of the gorge and on the hillside above. He felt no hunger, only the lassitude of utter exhaustion, like a man at the end of a long race, who has won.

After dark the horsemen came again, twenty or thirty of them. On the hill Mr. Wilson said, "Dismount here, please. We will go on foot and search for their bodies." The familiar voice was firm, but slow and heavy.

Men moving with naked torches threw light into the gorge. The bees slept in their nests. William crawled out through the nettles, trying to shield his face, and wincing under the pain of the stings which had before been so unimportant.

He called feebly, "Here, in the gorge."

A cavalryman on the top of the cliff cried out and ran round and down. Mr. Wilson shouted and scrambled after him. The soldier held up his torch, and Mr. Wilson dropped to his knees where William lay on his face in the stream, sucking up water. He helped William up, staring at his ragged loincloth and brown skin, and William said, "She's all right. In there."

They stumbled down the hill. A soldier held each of William's arms. Mr. Wilson and a captain of cavalry—William remembered his broad, grinning face from the wedding—helped Mary. The horses slithered down behind. Noises reverberated in the darkness and echoed distantly from the road and the hills—horses trotting,

225

vague crashes among far-off trees, a sudden shot, a fusillade from the open country to the west.

Mr. Wilson said, "I have ordered the arrest and search of every traveler found within fifty miles of here. Several seemingly innocent parties have already become desperate and resisted arrest. A few men are dead, including some of ours. The amount of jewelry found is staggering. Most of the regiment is out at work."

William nodded. Mr. Wilson said energetically, "Now, young lady, we must take you back to Sagthali. A palanquin is waiting, and the cavalry surgeon."

They reached the road at the foot of Jarod. Hand lanterns on the grass showed men lying anyhow, fully accoutered, asleep beside their horses, and fires twinkling, and mounted sentries with swords drawn, and huddles of prisoners. A flag bearing the Honourable East India Company's crest hung from a short staff stuck into the earth beside the stream, and near it was the cavalry's regimental guidon.

The surgeon ran up, and Mary slipped down on blankets spread beside a fire. Sher Dil brought chicken broth to her. William shook his servant's hand and smiled wearily. Mary sipped the broth. The surgeon knelt at her side and cleared his throat impatiently.

She said, "I'm not going to Sagthali, Daddy. My son is going to be born in Madhya."

On the hillside Mr. Wilson had been pale, wet-eyed. Now he swelled up, turned red, and stuttered incoherently.

She laughed and held out her hand to him. "Careful, Daddy, or you'll break a blood vessel. Madhya is no farther from here than Sagthali. What better place is there for me than my own room in my own bungalow?"

"That's true, ma'am," the surgeon said. "But I think—"

"I'm going back to Madhya. William has to go there, anyway."

"Yes," William said abruptly, "I have to go to Madhya. I must have control of these operations. No one else really knows what to do. Now is the time, not next week. We have to seize every Deceiver we can, try some, get others to turn informer, then move again, keep on moving. We have to act now, hard, and show we are in earnest. Later it will be like a snowball. It will get bigger and easier every year."

226

He fell silent. Mary's proposal was best. He too wanted his daughter to be born in Madhya. And he had to see the woman of Kahari. There could be no absolution, no rest, until he had faced her.

Mr. Wilson recovered himself and said sternly, "Very well, sir, have it your own way. But if it were my wife, I would—"

"No, you wouldn't, Daddy." Mary squeezed his hand, and he coughed and did not finish his sentence. She went on, "I want to start at once, now. I don't think I have much time."

Mr. Wilson swelled up again, but the surgeon sent them all away and hung blankets from swords stuck in the ground, and began to examine Mary. When he came over to them he said, "We'd better move, sir. She's in good shape, and should have no trouble, but I don't think there's much time." Mr. Wilson spoke to the cavalry colonel and in a minute the trumpeter blew *Boots and Saddles*.

The stars flared in a clear sky, the moon was rising. The cavalcade moved down the road northwestward and wound under the black loom of Jarod, a hundred and twenty horsemen with drawn swords resting on their shoulders. The leading men carried lanterns in their hands. Twelve Deceiver prisoners bore Mary's litter in turns. Behind it rode Mr. Wilson, all in black, with a wide-brimmed hat and a handkerchief to protect the back of his neck from the daytime sun. William gnawed meat off a chicken bone as he rode.

William threw the bone into the darkness and said, "We've got to form a new organization to deal with the Deceivers, sir. No one can do it and administer a district too. The Deceivers extend all over India. I'll have to have jurisdiction over them—wherever they are found—regardless of where they have done their murders."

Mr. Wilson thought before replying. "That will involve legislation in Council and a large appropriation of funds. For how long, do you think?"

"Ten, fifteen years."

"Hmm. I have not heard all the details yet, but I assure you that you will have my full support in obtaining all that you need. I *must*—" He swallowed and struggled to get the words out.

William knew what he was going to say, and knew that probably he had never used the words before, except to his wife.

"I apologize, both personally and on behalf of—"

William cut in, "There's no need to apologize, sir. None of us has acted quite sensibly. The biggest danger now is that these people from Parsola will scatter—we'll never catch them all, of course—and take the cult to places it's never been before, if there are any such places. It's the story of the Demon of Blood and Seed. It's happened before. The Deceivers were not altogether unknown. I've found out that our people would get an inkling about them, at different times, in different parts of India. Then perhaps they'd write a report, perhaps go out after the Deceivers. Always the same result: the report pigeonholed, the band chased away to flourish in new localities. There has not been enough coordination, of information or of action. We've got to get that first, all over India."

Mr. Wilson said, "It will be difficult to persuade the Presidencies to believe it, Savage, and agree to surrender some of their powers to a central organization such as you propose."

"They've got to!" William said forcefully. "The rajahs too! The Governor General's got to do it. I'll tell him. He'll see."

Mr. Wilson looked sideways at him thoughtfully and said nothing.

William glanced up and saw the cavalry's device of a running black horse on a background of woven silver thread. The guidon fluttered in the dawn breeze on top of its staff, and the first light touched it. Ahead, all the swords twinkled and like a river of silver fire poured on into the northwest. In the palanquin Mary called out, and the surgeon jumped down from his horse. The column halted, and the chargers champed and tossed their heads.

The surgeon looked up. "Better hurry, sir. We won't get to Madhya, but I'd like to reach water at any rate."

"Bhadora, about half a mile," William said shortly. Here, at the top of this shallow rise, they had waited for George to catch up on that honeymoon journey. Here the man on the bullock cart had passed, and the child absorbed in watching the dust. The flame-of-the-forest again sparkled about him.

Mr. Wilson, who had been about to speak, closed his mouth and looked almost nervously at William. The colonel nodded, and the column moved on.

At the river the ferrymen had vanished. The barge lay moored at the near bank, and several early travelers waited there in a frightened huddle beside it. From downstream the breeze brought the faint clash of arms and distant shouting. Mary insisted on crossing, and at the colonel's order some of the escorting cavalrymen dismounted and with laughing, childlike excitement clambered into the barge and poled it erratically across the river. Once on the far bank, the surgeon hung up blankets and Sher Dil boiled water. William talked with the cavalry colonel and tried to concentrate on what he was saying, but he could not because of Mary's low, regular moans. He sat down and pulled to pieces a cheroot the colonel gave him.

The surgeon said, "Captain Savage, go away, please. Come back in an hour."

"I'll stay here."

"Go away, sir."

William got up, rubbing his hands together, for they were cold. He had with these hands made a noose that lay around the neck of the Deceivers of India, and would in the end hang them. With these hands, too, with the mind that guided them, with the heart that should have stayed them, he had done great wrong that could not be mended. With these hands—he looked at them, and they were strong and sure, though cold, and he had been proud of the skill in them—he had strangled three men: Gopal the weaver, the sepoy at the ford, the Rajah of Padampur.

Gopal had been a Deceiver and a murderer; if William had not killed him, he would have killed William. The sepoy at the ford had done William no harm, but he had been going to; surely, Forgiver above, that was self-defense—when the man sprang at me through the bushes there, his musket in his hand and crazed panic in his eyes? The Rajah of Padampur—a robber bandit, a deceiver linked with Deceivers; did not he deserve death?

Perhaps he could forgive himself for those. But he had stood aside and directed the murder of—how many? He could not remember. All those were innocent. He had allowed them to die that, in the end, other innocents might live. For them he could not forgive himself.

There were too many of them to be remembered distinctly and carried as separate crosses. From the beginning all the wrong he had done—that right should result—had gathered to increase the wrongs of the woman of Kahari, the wife of Gopal the weaver. He had deceived her, so that she thought her husband lived. But he did

229

not live. William had killed him. Whatever punishment God inflicted would come to him through the woman at the pyre.

William stood awhile, expressionless, preparing himself to face what he had to face. He started to walk away up the river bank.

Mr. Wilson called, "Come over here and keep me company, Savage."

William looked at him. "I have to see the woman of Kahari, the wife of Gopal the weaver."

Mr. Wilson made to speak, but after three attempts, with William's burning deep-sunk eyes fixed on his, he said only, "God rest her soul."

William walked slowly. Mr. Wilson had said, "God rest her soul," but he had meant, "God rest your soul." Mr. Wilson understood at last.

William came to the pyre. A leaf shelter stood beside it. The woman sat in the open, not squatting but sitting on the grass. Her white dress, the same one, was still torn. It was ragged now, and grimed, and showed her skin through great holes. She sat with head bowed, and her hair hung in matted filth about her face and neck. The witch locks reached her waist and hid her nakedness.

Hearing him, she looked up. She had become an old woman in the year of waiting—almost toothless, with cracked lips, ringed haggard eyes, dirt-scored skin. She saw him where he came on, and could not move, but her eyes widened. He stopped three paces from her, and she lifted her arms to him.

"My darling, my darling, my lover, you have come!"

He said, "I am not Gopal. I am William Savage. It was I who came last time, to deceive you."

She looked at his head, into his eyes, at the line of his jaw. Her arms sank and her fingers lay crumpled on the grass. She bent her head and tears ran down in the dirt on her face. She had no strength to sob. Her tears flowed silently, like little rivers.

He said, "Gopal is dead. I killed him."

After a minute she said, not asking a question, "Another woman was there." She continued, "Was she—his? That, my dream did not tell me, and tormented me with not knowing."

"Another woman?" The stableyard in Manikwal had been here, and Hussein there, and the wall there, and there the stable roof

230

and the horses in a row. The harlot girls had not come out. No woman had stood beside him to watch Gopal die.

It was a vivid memory. Now almost he felt the heat of Kali's desire as it had pulsed through him that day. So he said slowly, "There was a woman. She was mine, not his. Her, too, I have mortally wounded."

All the strength she needed came to her in a flood. She rose to her feet and hurried close to him. She said, "You are my darling, and I your lover, because you have been Gopal." She smiled at him with a luminous, secret brilliance and whispered, "No man dies by the hand of man. I am going to my husband." She kissed his fingers and stroked them against her cheek.

William's fingers were warm where they had touched her skin. He had been crouching before God, awaiting the lash, and received instead a kiss.

The girl hastened to the pyre, singing softly a cradle song, and walked three times around it. In the east the sun cast up a fan of golden bars from below the hills, and the Seonath became a river of dull gold.

She said, "You have flint and tinder? Light it."

He stepped forward and struck steel to flint, touched the tinder, held the tiny bundle in his hand, and waved it about in the warm air. The little flames snapped. On his left the river whispered, flowing north to the Ken, and the Ken to the Jumna, and the Jumna to the Ganges, where the ashes must at last rest. The woman emptied jars of ghi onto the pyre, and still sang.

The flames in the tinder bunch touched his fingers, and did not hurt. He pushed the tinder into the pyre. The butter streams crackled, thick smoke curled out, the fire caught hold and sprang high, twenty feet into the air, jumped through between the logs laid longwise and crosswise, reached out from side to side of the pyre, and made a shouting noise.

The woman knelt, facing the east. She cried out with lyrical passion, her voice strong and sure, "I see you in your place beside the sun, my darling and my lover. They have kept me from you where you sit in majesty and honor. I love you, my lord, I worship you with my body and spirit. I am your wife and your servant. I come to our bridal bed, to lie with you in the sun."

The sun sprang over the eastern rim of the world, and the woman stepped into the flames and lay down and held out her open arms. In a flash the fire ripped her clothes off her, and the marks of age, and her long hair, and for a blinding second she lay naked, golden, again young, on the cushion of flames, her arms out to William, her eyes on him and the sun in him and Gopal in him. The fire roared up and the yellow and red spires leaned back against the trees, and he could not see her.

After thirty minutes the priest came running from Kahari. He stopped short when he saw William standing motionless at the fire. William turned, and walked a pace away, and turned again, and took out the pickax from his waistband, and threw it into the flames.

At the ferry Mr. Wilson ran toward him. "William, William, you are a father! A fine boy, half an hour ago!" He pumphandled William's arm. His strong face was alight, as the woman's had been, from a lamp behind the skin which softened his strength and made it love. William did not speak, and Mr. Wilson said, "Mary is well. She wants you now. Come."

Still William did not move. Mr. Wilson glanced upriver to the smoke drifting over the trees. He said, suddenly firm and gentle, "God give that love to him, your son."

William said, "God *is* love," and went to Mary and the baby.

# Postscript

IN a story of this sort the reader has a right to know how much was fact, how much fiction. My purpose in this book, as in *Nightrunners of Bengal*, was to re-create the "feel" of a historical episode rather than write a minutely accurate report. To do this I had to use the novelist's freedom to imagine people and create places for them to live in; but the times and circumstances of those people are fixed by history, and I believe this book gives a true picture of them.

In general, therefore, the facts about the Deceivers (the *Thugs*) and all the details of their cult and their operations (called collectively *Thuggee*) are accurate. They did flourish for many centuries, they did believe in their religious call, they did live by the omens and ceremonies described, they did kill travelers in the manner and the numbers suggested. It is thought that, first and last, *Thuggee* must have murdered well over a million people. Ironically enough, after existing hundreds of years, it was uncovered and uprooted shortly before the coming of railroads and telegraphs to India would in any case have destroyed it. Nonetheless, William Savage's remark that it constituted the greatest criminal conspiracy of history was justified at the time he made it.

The setting of the story in time is correct within a year or two. The physical shape of the land we have traveled in (the area bounded by a line Jubbulpore–Nagpur–Jhansi–Allahabad–Jubbulpore) is correct, and it was in this area that *Thuggee* was first comprehensively discovered and attacked. Incidentally, the bees there are numerous and dangerous. Many a bather, hunter, and traveler has met the death which my Deceivers met.

All the incidents are imagined. All the characters are imagined, except a few bystanders. Please note particularly that if any one man can be credited with the real-life destruction of *Thuggee*, that man was William Henry Sleeman of the Indian Political Service. Sleeman did not use the methods I have ascribed to William Savage —at least he has not said he did. William Savage is in no sense a portrait of William Sleeman.

All places should be treated as imaginary, though in fact most of the rivers and hills and a few small villages are real. My reason for this is that it is not now feasible for me to find out what, say, Damoh looked like in 1825, and I do not think it is proper to invent "facts" about real places; I must invent the whole town—and call it Madhya.

The glossary contains notes on the few real people mentioned in the story and translations of Indian words to amplify the meanings that I have always tried to make clear in the context.

There are not many source books about *Thuggee*. One of them is a novel, first published in 1839, by an officer who had taken part in operations against *Thugs: Confessions of a Thug* by Meadows Taylor. If my story of this terrible byway of man's religious faith has interested you, you will find more details in three books by Sleeman himself: *Ramaseeana, or a Vocabulary of the peculiar language used by Thugs; Report on the depredations committed by the Thug gangs of upper and central India; The Thugs or Phansigars of India;* and in one by Sleeman's grandson, Colonel James L. Sleeman—*Thug, or A Million Murders.*

# GLOSSARY

This glossary contains notes only on Hindustani words and on people who really lived. The meanings given for Hindustani words apply only to this story; other meanings and shades of meaning are not given. Pronunciations are given in parentheses. If an average American from the Middle-Eastern states says the word exactly as he sees it here, his pronunciation will be a close enough approximation of standard Anglo-Indian—not necessarily correct Indian.

**achchi bat** (utchy bat), very good!

**a-jao, jaldi** (ah-jow, juldy), come quickly!

**Amherst,** William Pitt Amherst, Earl Amherst of Arakan, 1773–1857; a nephew of Lord Jeffrey Amherst; Governor General of India 1823–1828.

**ane wala hun** (ahny wolla hoo), coming! (literally, "I am the coming one").

**arrack** (urrack), palm toddy, or, among poorer people, spirit made from flowers of mahua tree.

**bahut** (bote), very, much.

**bajri** (budjri), pearl millet (*annisetum glaucum*).

**baksheesh** (bucksheesh), tip, gratuity.

**bannia** (bun-ya), merchant.

**bara-sahib** (burra-sahb), the chief, the boss.

**beetoo** (beetoo), anyone not a Thug (Thug argot).

**bhil** (bheel), place selected for killing (Thug argot).

**Bhonsla** (Bhonsla), family name of Mahratta rulers of Nagpur.

**bijasal** (beeja-sahl), kino tree (*ptero-carpus marsupium*).

**bulbul** (bull-bull), a bird, a species of nightingale (*daulias philomela africana*).

**chaudhri** (chowdry), agent, contractor; also, a caste title confined to several upper castes.

**chhota hazri** (choe-ta hahzry), early morning meal (literally, "little breakfast").

**chupatti** (ch'patty), flat disk of unleavened wheat bread.

**chuprassi** (ch'prassy), doorkeeper, messenger.

**dacoit** (d'koyt), armed bandit.

**daffadar** (duffa-dah), sergeant of horse.

**dal** (dahl), a thick lentil stew.

**Dewali** (D'wahly), festival of light, marking the beginning of the year for traders and businessmen in India; always falls twenty lunar days after Dussehra, *q.v.*

**Dussehra** (D'sarah), ten-day festival at close of rainy season, in September or October, hence at opening of season for war and travel.

**Elphinstone,** Mountstuart Elphinstone, 1779–1859; served in Bengal and (later) Bombay Civil Service; Resident at Court of Mahratta Peshwa, 1810–1819.

**flame-of-the-forest,** moderate-sized deciduous tree (*butea frondosa*).

235

**ghi** (ghee), clarified butter.

**hai** (hay), is.

**haji** (hudgey), title of respect applied to Mohammedans who have made the pilgrimage to Mecca.

**halal** (h'lahl), method of killing an animal by letting it bleed to death, required by Mohammedan religious law—comparable to the kosher method.

**Hastings,** Francis Rawdon, 1st Marquess of Hastings and 2nd Earl of Moira, 1754–1826; Governor General and Commander-in-Chief in India, 1812–23.

**huzoor** (h'zoor), honorific term of address (literally, "presence").

**jagirdar** (juggeerdahr), man holding land in a type of feudal tenure.

**jemadar** (jemma-dah), junior officer.

**Jenkins,** Sir Richard Jenkins, 1785–1853; served in Bombay Civil Service; Resident at Court of Bhonslas, Nagpur, 1810–27.

**Jhora Naik** (Jhora Nike), a leader of Multan Thugs. He and his servant Koduk Bunwari are supposed to have killed a man who had 162,000 rupees on a mule. As Jhora Naik made an equitable distribution of this enormous spoil, even among members of his band who were not with him at the time, the Thugs canonized him, his servant, and his wife (Thug legend).

**kala admi** (kahla ahdmy), black man.

**Kali** (Kahlee), "Dark Mother"; cult title of Durga, wife of Shiva. In true Hinduism Kali represents the active aspect of Reality, and her image is a symbol of Reality's creative and destructive principles. The Thugs prostituted the destructive aspect—which is in nature—to their own evil purpose.

**Kali-Pyara** (Kahlee-Peeyahra), the beloved of Kali.

**kirpan** (kirrpahn), short dagger carried for religious reasons by Sikhs.

**Koduk Bunwari** (Koe-d'k Boonwahry), see Jhora Naik, above.

**koi hai** (kwa hi), a call for service (literally, "is anyone there?"); used instead of "Boy!" etc.

**Krishna,** regarded by Hindus as an incarnation of God—specifically, of Vishnu. Krishna is a very important character in the Mahabharata, *q.v.*

**kulla** (koolla), pointed or domed brimless hat worn under the turban by Mohammedans.

**Lat Sahib** (Laht Sahb), the Governor General of India (Indian corruption of the Lord Sahib; because the Governor General was often the only peer in Indian service).

**lotah** (loe-ta), metal pot used for carrying water.

**Mahabharata** (Ma-ha-bherta), one of the two epic poems of ancient India (the other is the Ramayana).

**maharaj** (ma-h'rahj), lord, master (honorific sense).

**mahua** (ma-hwa), large deciduous tree (*bassia latifolia*).

**mahngga** (mengga), expensive.

**maul** (mowl), creeper (*bauminia vahlii*).

**maulvi** (mowlvy), Mohammedan scholar or teacher, often of religion.

**memsahib** (memsahb), English lady.

**mohur** (mohoor), gold coin of Moguls.

**mynah** (mine-ah), bird of starling family (*acridotheres tristis*).

**neem,** fairly large evergreen tree (*azadirachta indicus*), considered sacred by Thugs.

**Nizam-ud-din** (Nizzahm-oodeen), 1236–1325; considered a saint by Sunni sect of Mohammedans; also rumored to have been a Thug.

**patel** (p'tail), chief official of village in certain parts of India.

**Pindaris** (Pindahrys), bands of marauding plunderers; originally only the members of a tribe who lived in Central India along the Nerbudda River.

**ram ram** (rahm rahm), a form of greeting.

**rumal** (roomahl), handkerchief, cloth.

**sahib** (sahb), honorific title used alone or as suffix to other titles.

**saj** (sahj), large deciduous tree, with long clear bole (*terminalia tomentosa*).

**Saugor Pandits** (Sawga Pundits), rulers of the Saugor area under the Mahratta power.

**shikar** (sh'kahr), hunting, game.

**shikari** (sh'kahry), professional hunter, hence, sportsman.

**sirdar** (sir-dahr), title of honor, used of and to all Sikhs.

**suttee** (suttee), a woman who immolates herself on her husband's funeral pyre, or the custom of so doing.

**thakur** (tah-koor), in Rajputana, or of Rajputs, a landholder or minor nobleman; in other parts of India, a sort of caste title.

**Thug,** member of a religious association devoted to highway murder and robbery; **Thuggee,** the association and its acts. (The Thugs are the Deceivers of this book; the words should properly be pronounced "Toog," "Tooggee," and were so pronounced before they became popular in their present English sense of "gangster.")

**woh** (wvoh), it, that.

**zemindar** (z'meendah), landowner.